THE HUNTED SOUL

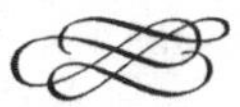

MIRANDA BROCK

REBECCA HAMILTON

COPYRIGHT

CHAPTER 1

Sweat rolled down my temple and stung at the corner of my eye. I squared up my stance and threw my arm forward. My fist impacted the heavy punching bag with a force that reverberated up my bones.

"Is that all you got, Perez?"

I wiped damp hair from my face and turned to look at the bear of a man behind me.

When I said bear of a man, I meant that literally. Aidan was a bear shifter, and head honcho at the gym owned and operated by the Paranormal Intelligence and Tracking Organization. He was tall and broad and wrapped in thick muscle that made him look like a UFC heavyweight champion.

I shook my arms in an attempt to ease the burning in my own muscles and stared up at Aidan. "What? You want me to try it on your face and see how I'm doing?"

Disapproving murmurs hummed through the room, but a wide smile cracked the bear shifter's face. "You've got spirit, I'll give you that."

"Spirit won't necessarily keep her alive," a voice grumbled behind my left shoulder.

Kael Rivera strode up from where he had been lifting weights on the other side of the gym. My mouth went a little dry at the sight of the man who had partnered with me to chase a dark mage across the world.

He didn't have the physique of the bear shifter, but his broad shoulders and hard, lean, almost cat-like muscles were just as impressive. Appropriate for a jaguar shifter.

Sweat trickled down his chest, and it wasn't until I was staring at his abs that I realized what I was doing and pulled my gaze from him.

What was wrong with me? We'd spent time laying together in the wilderness for God's sake—I'd seen him naked on more than one account when he'd had to shift to his jaguar form. Over the past month, though, I'd found myself staring at him more.

"I've managed to keep myself alive well enough so far," I pointed out.

He stood beside me with a disapproving frown, as if he hadn't noticed my ogling. "For one thing, you shouldn't speak to Aidan like that, especially in front of the others."

Mortifying. The last person on earth I wanted a lecture from was Kael.

Most of the other occupants in the room had gone back to their workout routines and sparring. Some still stared at me with obvious distaste. So as much as I hated to admit it, Kael was right.

Every single person in the gym was a shifter. I had been unsure about training here, especially given the unfortunate encounter with the rogue wolf shifters in England, but Kael had assured me it was safe. Aidan had been the only one that had welcomed me openly. If any of the other shifters had a problem with it, they'd yet to voice it. Perhaps they were afraid of a reprimand by Aidan.

I crossed my arms and turned my attention to Kael,

keeping my gaze firmly on his face. "Aidan doesn't care what I say to him."

"And secondly," Kael said firmly, "you're standing wrong." He grabbed my hips and twisted me so my body wasn't completely facing the heavy bag. Instead, I was slightly angled away from it. He kicked my heels. "Get on the balls of your feet. How do you expect to make a good hit if you're glued to the floor? A powerful hit always starts with your feet."

I lifted my wrapped hands and took a breath. I twisted from my feet, up through my body, and snapped my right fist in a crossing strike. My fist struck the bag in a powerful hit that I could feel was much improved.

Aidan let out a low whistle. "She learns fast. I'd hate to be on the other end of that." He winked at me.

"She's still sloppy."

I dropped my arms and turned to scowl at Kael. Would a compliment kill him?

"Why are you making me train so hard here, anyway?" I asked. "I can use magic, remember?"

True, I hadn't really been practicing with that supernatural part of me. For the past month, since leaving my home to come with Kael to his headquarters in Charleston, South Carolina, I'd only tapped into the magic humming beneath my skin a handful of times. Part of it was the fear of losing control. The other was lack of proper space. I couldn't exactly use it in the city around others, and the hotel room I was staying at already had a burn mark on the wall from an incident where I'd misjudged my own strength.

Kael stepped around me and fixed me with an intense gaze. I hated when he stared at me like that, if only because it made me want something more. Images flashed through my mind of tangling my fingers in his dark hair, breathing in his unusual citrus and petrichor scent, lifting myself up to press my lips to his.

No, I reprimanded myself. He was my friend. Nothing more. Heck, maybe even something less. There were times I felt we were friends, but most of the time, I still felt more like I was his responsibility and his mission. Once all of this was over, would he ever even talk to me again?

"You won't always be able to rely on magic," Kael said. "You can run out of energy, or face someone more powerful than yourself. Physical strength is necessary. So you need to work on improving your strikes."

He was right, but I still ground my teeth. "Fine."

Kael nodded, then glanced at a clock on the right wall. "It's nearly six. I have a meeting with the boss."

I started unwrapping my hands. "I'm going to head back to the hotel. It's your turn to buy."

This had quickly become an everyday thing for us after arriving in Charleston. I stayed at a hotel merely a block away from the massive building that held the PITO headquarters. Kael came over every evening, and we ate supper together, taking turns buying the food. I was thankful for the company, but I also knew the reason he ate with me, and sometimes fell asleep in the big red chair, was because he was keeping an eye on me.

I wiped sweat from my face and chest, careful to keep the two keys hanging around my neck tucked into my sports bra. One of the keys seemed to be carved out of bone. I had found it in Scotland in the hands of druids. The other key was an aged gold color and had been plucked from an ancient ruin in the Amazon rainforest.

It was also bound to my soul by an unfortunate magical mishap on my part.

If that key got into the wrong hands, the person possessing it would be able to control me...and my power along with it.

That had been the main reason Kael had brought me to Charleston, and why he insisted on this training. The dark mage, Vehrin, was still on the loose and still searching for something more important than myself and the keys I possessed. A daunting prospect. What could be more important to him than the keys, so much so that he didn't care who found me?

I pulled on a T-shirt and jacket, then grabbed my bag from a nearby bench and lifted the strap over my shoulder. "I'll see you later, Kael."

He smiled and gave me a nod before he headed toward the locker room.

"Want me to walk you home?" Aidan offered.

I fought against rolling my eyes. It was nice of him to offer, I knew, especially coming from someone with such a high ranking in his organization, but I didn't need a babysitter.

"No, thank you, Aidan." I gave him a smile. "I can manage."

Aidan crossed his arms across his massive chest. "He cares for you, you know."

"Kael's a good friend."

The bear shifter smirked. "Yeah, a good friend." The smirk faltered. "Seriously, you need to be careful."

"I will be. See you tomorrow."

"Later, Perez."

I gave him a wave and walked away.

What the hell had that smirk been about? No doubt he'd caught me ogling Kael. I needed to get a better control on my irrational hormones.

The gym was large, and the exit was all the way on the other side of the room. I ignored the stares and murmurs, along with the occasional person naked from head to toe. That had taken some getting used to. The gym was always full of shifters who trained in not only their human form, but animal form, as well. I had seen bears, wolves, lions, eagles. All but that one horse shifter Kael had once told me he'd seen. Nudity was a common occurrence here as they shifted from one form to another, and it was not something any of them were shy about.

The nearly hostile muttering I caught on occasion was also something that had taken some getting used to in this place. I was an outsider here, though it was hard to pass myself off as a mere human when I had the abilities of a mage. The shifters here were very closely guarded about not only themselves, but their training as well. I was let in on certain battle tactics and intelligence passed to me from Kael with permission of his superiors.

At least they seemed to trust me, even if the other shifters were wary. What did they think I was going to do? Run to the mage despite the fact that I had fought against him? Hadn't I proven myself enough already?

I let the gym doors slam closed behind me with a loud, metallic thud. Fresh air hit me that smelled like salt from the Atlantic only a few blocks away, and I pulled in a deep breath. I'd always enjoyed the ocean. Every morning I jogged along the beach, usually with Kael, though my heart still yearned for dense, humid jungles and adventures in dangerous, but rewarding locations.

A few cars passed quickly as I made my way down the sidewalk. Most people were heading home after work, or going out to eat. Kael told me that, in the summer, the place was packed with tourists and vacationers, but in late November, there weren't too many about.

I pulled a ten-dollar bill from my bag and headed into a small shop that sold smoothies halfway between PITO headquarters and the hotel. I grabbed my favorite green machine smoothie and stepped back onto the sidewalk, taking a big gulp.

As a chill tingled up my spine, I glanced behind me.

I could have sworn I felt someone watching me.

At first, I thought perhaps Aidan had decided to accompany me regardless of being told it wasn't unnecessary. When I looked, though, I saw no one except a couple pushing a stroller with a sleeping toddler inside. I shrugged it off and continued, though the itch never truly left.

It wasn't often that I felt the need to tap into my magic, but I did as I neared the hotel and the unnerving sensation of being followed persisted. I didn't fully draw on the magic. It was more like touching it, ensuring myself that it was there and within reach. The power inside me was warm, for the most part, but there was also an alien sensation that hadn't been there until after I had confronted the mage and bound my soul to the golden relic.

That was the part of my magic that made me afraid to use it—that wild, ancient power that didn't truly feel like myself.

I pushed through the rotating doors of the hotel and nodded to the small woman behind the glossy front desk.

"Evening, Alice," I told her.

"Hey." She sighed. The woman didn't bother to look up from her phone, a bored expression on her face.

"Long day?"

She pursed her lips and nodded. I gave up on cordial conversation and headed to the elevator. I glanced back toward the doors before I stepped in, but no one followed me into the hotel. I was probably just being paranoid. Kael's worry was rubbing off on me.

Overprotective male.

I rolled my sore shoulders on the way up to the fourth floor and promised myself a nice soak in the bathtub before Kael came over. The elevator stopped, and I nodded politely at an older gentleman who stood aside to let me out. After passing several doors, I reached my room, dug the key card out of my bag, slid it into the lock beneath the handle, and, giving one more glance around, went into my room.

I dropped my bag onto the desk that was scattered with papers both Kael and I had pored over numerous times.

Reports on the mage's whereabouts, mostly, but also some information on mage magic in general.

I walked to the dresser that held my meager amount of clothing and pulled out a fresh outfit for after my bath. But when I turned around, my heart jumped.

There was a stranger in my room.

CHAPTER 2

THE MAN STOOD in front of my closed door, wearing a dark blue hoodie that obscured his face. Had Kael sent him to be extra protection for me?

No, that's not right. He had never sent other people here, and if he had, he would have sent Aidan.

Whoever this man was, he was definitely no friend. There was something incredibly off about him. His presence gave me a chill, as if leeching the warmth out of the room.

The stranger moved forward, and his steps *rustled*, like a snake slithering through leaves.

I retreated a step, and my back hit the dresser. The dark opening of his hood followed my movement, and finally, I got a glimpse of his eyes as my dresser lamp illuminated his face. His pupils were dark and narrow like a serpent. He pulled in a deep breath through wide nostrils and grinned, revealing a mouth full of sharp teeth.

What the hell was this guy?

Fae, perhaps? Renathe, my new fae friend who owned a ritzy club back in my hometown, had been filling me in on his kind over our chats on the phone. I knew that some had wings, or horns, or scales. Of course, there were those like Ren who looked just as human as myself. Whether this man was a fae or not, I could see the intentions in his stare, and they were anything but friendly.

My gaze flicked to my bag where I'd dropped it on my desk. By instinct, I wanted to get to my knife, only to remember I no longer had the weapon. During the altercation in England, the blade had been disintegrated when I stabbed a giant panther with it.

It was too soon for Kael to be arriving any second, so I would have to fight the strange man alone. I had no weapons…except myself.

Magic hummed and swirled beneath my skin, ready and eager to be released. The man took another step forward, and I shifted to the side. I could probably take him on, but there were others in the hotel, and they were innocent people. I didn't want to risk anyone getting hurt.

The man charged at me. I grabbed the office chair to my left and wheeled it in front of me. He stumbled as it collided with him, and I took the chance to go for my bag. If I could get to my cell inside of it, I could call Kael for backup.

Before I could reach it, the man leaped back to his feet and jumped onto the bed. He crouched there and leaned forward slightly. His eyes glowing with greed and excitement.

"Give me the key."

His voice was shockingly normal. Given his appearance, I had expected something akin to rasping or hissing.

"What key?" Yep, I was going for the play dumb tactic to buy myself some time.

I inched another step toward my bag on the desk, but he lunged forward, and I stopped in my tracks.

He inhaled another deep breath. "I can smell the power within you. I can smell your magic-touched soul, and I want it." His eyes dropped to my shirt, as if he was drawn to the keys beneath. More specifically, the one tethered to my soul.

I had no choice.

Energy swirled above my palms and caressed my fingers. It was still unusual to me, bringing forth the ancient magic that had been unlocked inside myself with a cursed key. Even more disconcerting were the flashes of a past life, *my past life*, it had brought with it. Sacrifice and blood and death, mostly. True, the dark mage Vehrin had been there, wreaking havoc on humanity, but the sacrifices still twisted my gut whenever the memory came to mind.

The man in front of me had stilled at the sight of the magic licking across my skin. It didn't seem to be fear that had him holding his ground, though. His slow smile told me he was seeing a glimpse of the prize he thought he was about to win.

I dashed toward him, but he lurched to the side. I wheeled around to find him skidding across the wall, his sharp nails ripping through the flower-patterned wallpaper.

Gritting my teeth, I let loose a sphere of swirling energy at the intruder as his feet hit the floor. The magic collided with him, and he stumbled. He recovered quickly, much faster than was humanly possible. He yelled, and as he took a step toward me, I hit him with my magic again, forcing him to retreat into a corner.

I've got him, I thought. I squared my shoulders and settled my gaze on him. I could hold him here long enough for—

My door burst open. A brief flash of relief washed through me. *Kael.*

But when I looked over my shoulder, I found another stranger dashing into my room. A man with Herculean muscles that would put Aidan to shame. He had a pair of small, black horns on his head and a peculiar greenish tint to his skin.

A horrible odor preceded him, like rot and sour mud. I wrinkled my nose, and a grin cracked his wide face, revealing spittle hanging from his yellow teeth.

Gross.

I peeked quickly at the first assailant still crouched against the corner. He was peering at the giant man with narrowed eyes and a tight jaw. Obviously, these two weren't working together.

"Give me the key." The second man, or thing rather since he was obviously not human, had a deep and guttural voice.

"I was here first," the other man argued. "She's mine."

"Excuse me," I cut in. "No one is getting me or the key."

They seemed unaware of the fact that I possessed *two* keys, or perhaps they were only interested in the one that was tied to my soul. If they managed to get the golden relic, I would have no choice but to do their bidding.

I couldn't let that happen. No one was going to control me.

The horned man laughed. "You're going to beg for mercy when I get my hands on you."

He started for me on heavy footsteps, and then a loud and vicious snarling broke through the room.

A large jaguar leaped up and the man yelped, reaching back and trying to get a hold of the cat that was sinking his claws through clothes and flesh.

Kael.

For real this time.

And a few other jaguar shifters that worked for PITO accompanied him. I'd seen them several times, but I would know Kael anywhere. Over our time spent chasing the mage and staying here, I had come to easily recognize the pattern of spots that splashed across his golden-brown fur. Plus, he was easily the largest jaguar shifter I had seen so far.

I turned from Kael's attack to the first man, but he was already getting to his feet. *Idiot.* I shouldn't have let myself get distracted.

He reached for me so fast, his sharp nails eager to take a hold of me, that I didn't even think of releasing another attack of magic on him. Instead, my fist shot forward and smashed into his face.

He yelled as he brought his hands up to his nose that had crunched beneath my knuckles. His strange, slit eyes narrowed as he lowered his hands. He bared his teeth, blood running down over his stretched lips.

Intent burned in his gaze. He was going to take me.

My hand seemed to burst into fire as something uncontrollable rose to the surface. The man's eyes widened with greed. I smirked, then my hand shot forward…right into his chest. My magic-coated fingers tore right through skin, and muscle, and bone. He fixed me with a gaze that grew cold with confusion and fear. He let out a ragged gasp, and then his body collapsed heavily to the floor.

The yearning for death and destruction burned through my veins and tugged at my muscles. I would kill them all to keep my power, to keep myself from being taken. I would crack the bones and spill the blood of everyone. I would hear their screams and—

No.

I squeezed my eyes shut and pulled in deep breaths through my nose.

No, that isn't me.

I fought down the magic that felt foreign and delightful at the same time. I had to get control of it.

I opened my eyes, and my throat burned with bile. Blood smeared up my hand and over my wrist. The man on the floor had blood soaking the front of his shirt and puddling beneath him. I swallowed, certain a few moments ago I had felt the erratic, pumping muscle of his heart in my fingers. My ears rang.

What was I becoming?

A warm nudge on the back of my leg made me jump, and I glanced down. It was Kael. He peered up at me with intense, amber eyes. Blood flecked his jaw, and his thick tail twitched impatiently. His sides heaved, but he didn't appear to be injured. Behind him, the other intruder lay dead with his throat torn out.

I pushed past Kael and went straight to the bathroom, closing and locking the door behind me. I wrenched on the handle of the sink, grabbed a washcloth and a bar of soap, and started scrubbing. Steam rose quickly, but I didn't care if the water was near scalding. I just wanted the blood off my skin.

It wasn't as if it were the first time I had blood from another on me. Reality told me it wouldn't likely be the last, either. It was the way the blood was there, and the fact that I had shoved my fist into another being's chest. Killing with a weapon was one thing, but doing it with nothing more than my hand seemed barbaric. It wasn't like me.

I turned the water off, my skin pink from the hot water but thoroughly clean, and peered at myself in the mirror. A part of me was afraid I would see someone else staring back, someone ancient and dark.

The worst part was not knowing myself. When I had first found myself with magic after my trip to the Amazon, I had been scared, but the magic had grown to be a part of me. After the fight with the mage, and binding my soul to the key, it was as if something else had tied itself to me. A different magic—more powerful, dangerous, and wild. Was it part of Vehrin's power, leeched to me from wounding him, or had something else been unlocked from within?

I wasn't certain how long I stared at myself in the mirror, searching for any hint that something had changed, that someone else was hiding within, but a soft knock eventually broke me from my trance.

"Livvie?" Kael's voice was quiet and strained.

Livvie. I hadn't been certain what to think of his sudden nickname for me. Everyone else called me Olivia, but I had grown accustomed to, and even liked, Kael's pet name for me.

"Are you all right? Are you hurt?"

I pulled in a deep breath and opened the door. He stepped back, gaze running up and down me in what I knew was a wound-check.

"I said I'm fine." My words were heavy with exhaustion. That unnerving attack of mine had left my energy drained.

Kael didn't say anything, but his brows were pinched with worry. More often than not when Kael was around me, his face was either creased with worry or irritation. He had a really great smile, when I could squeeze one out of him.

Wanting the attention off of me, I jerked my head toward the bodies soaking the carpet with blood. "Who were they?"

"Demons."

My mouth dropped open. *Demons*? I was barely used to the knowledge that shifters, witches, and fae existed, but now there were *demons*? I was tempted to ask if dragons and unicorns existed, but Kael continued.

"Vehrin is growing more powerful. Dark beings are starting to wriggle up through the cracks."

Fantastic.

"How can he be growing more powerful without the keys?"

Kael shrugged. "He still has magic. I would assume it is waking, growing more powerful, just like yours."

I glanced at the demon I had killed. Growing more powerful seemed like a daunting prospect to me, both for Vehrin and myself.

"Maybe your strikes aren't as sloppy as I thought." Kael pulled his gaze from the demon with a hole in his chest that my fist had put there. There was a rare grin on his face.

I couldn't bring myself to smile. "You're back early."

"We have a location for the mage. I came to tell you to get your things packed. We need to go."

Packing was a short affair, since I didn't have much. Kael had dropped his bag in the hallway, and he scooped it up and slung it onto his shoulder as we headed down the hallway. He had made a quick phone call, telling the person on the other end about the mess we'd left behind. Thank goodness we wouldn't be required to clean up. I couldn't stomach the thought of being around all that blood for a second longer.

As we stepped onto the elevator, an eagerness settled into my bones. I was uncertain if it was my own, or the ancient magic within me that was looking forward to once again hunting the mage.

Soon, excitement was replaced by a crawling fear that, eventually, I was going to lose myself. And if I did, what sort of dark, dangerous power would be unleashed then?

CHAPTER 3

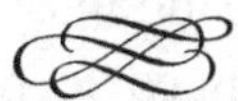

"WHAT ARE YOU DOING?" Kael asked. He sat beside me as we waited to board our flight. His foot was propped on his knee and he was leaning back, though his eyes were zeroed in on the phone in my hands.

I pulled it back so he couldn't see what I was doing. "Nosy much?"

The shifter huffed and shook his head, instead turning his attention to the large windows on the right.

"I'm texting Ren." Not that it was any of his business, really, but Kael seemed annoyed and taking a long flight with a cantankerous shifter was not something I wanted to endure.

Kael scowled. "This is classified business." His voice was low so the others in the airport couldn't hear, but his tone was hard.

I rolled my eyes. "I didn't tell him where we were going, just that I was going to be traveling and he may not be able to get a hold of me."

My partner went back to the window, muttering something about "ridiculous fae." Perhaps Ren was a bit ridiculous, but I enjoyed our chats. He was witty and mysterious, the total opposite of the blunt and emotional man beside me.

On the other hand, Ren never failed to remind me that I still owed him a date, a debt on my part for his help. I didn't mind, but as I glanced at Kael, I couldn't help but wonder if he were jealous.

Surely not. I was under no illusion that Kael felt anything toward me other than a need to protect me. Friendship, at best.

I quickly tapped out a goodbye to Ren, more out of the desire to soothe whatever was riling up Kael, and stuck my phone in my bag. I stretched out my legs in front of me and turned my attention to a T.V. ahead. I was only watching it for a few seconds when I straightened, catching sight of someone familiar.

It was Sarah. She was a member of my team. According to the anchor speaking on the news, there was some high-profile dig going on in India.

I'd always wanted to go to India and now there was a dig there, with *my team*, that I was missing.

That should have been my dig. My story. Now that opportunity had been stolen from me, and I'd likely never see an opportunity like that again in this lifetime

My employer hadn't been very happy when I'd told her I had to go on an extended leave. Aside from a couple of reports, I hadn't had any new material to send in. But the PITO. wouldn't allow me to go on digs, especially with who knew what after me and the keys.

Still, for her to send my team to a place I'd always wanted to go, and for no one to tell me about it, well, I was surprised and hurt. I couldn't blame them for taking the opportunity, but it still made me yearn to be there with them.

Before I could fully process the unexpected news, it was time for us to board. I was thankful Kael let me have a window seat, and for a long while, I stared out of it silently.

Eventually, Kael put his arm across my shoulders, and his warm hand cupped the side of my neck. The gesture was so surprising, it briefly took my breath away.

"Livvie…"

"What?" It took everything in me not to lean farther into his touch. What the hell was wrong with me?

"Is something bothering you?"

Other than your uncharacteristic touching? "No. Why do you say that?"

Kael's mouth lifted in a slight grin. "Liar. You've been so quiet. You're never this quiet."

He took his hand from me, and I found myself regretting his withdrawal. Kael still held me with his expectant gaze.

I crossed my arms. "I saw a news report of a dig in India. My team was there. It's a high-profile dig, meaning they will likely find something priceless and spectacular, and I'm not there with them." I looked down at my knees. "I guess I didn't realize how much I missed it."

It seemed childish, perhaps, but I couldn't help it. Until I had unearthed a cursed key, woken some ancient part of my past life, and found myself tangled in a battle with a dark mage, archaeology had been everything to me. The discovery, the risk, and the adventure of it all was what drove me. Now, it was scarcely a part of me.

"It's okay for you to miss it," Kael said.

I nodded, but kept my face tilted down because, to my horror, my eyes were starting to sting. I would not cry about this, especially not in front of Kael.

The shifter wouldn't leave it alone, though, and he took my chin and pulled it toward him. His eyes widened, but thankfully he didn't say anything about my watery gaze.

"You will get back to what you love, Olivia. It may take time, but you will get there."

I gave him a smile. "Thanks, Kael."

It was a small pep talk, but it did make me feel a bit better.

The rest of our flight was filled with chit chat and sleep. By the time we got off the plane at the airport in Denver, thoughts of the India dig were pushed back.

For now, it was time to find the mage.

"So, what now?" I asked, hefting my bag farther up onto my shoulder.

Kael pulled out his cell and opened up a map on a locked file. He squinted at it and zoomed in on the image. He was blocking the exit and didn't notice a few people waiting to get out. I grabbed his arm and shuffled him to the side. He scarcely looked up.

I leaned against the wall and waited. "How were you guys even able to pinpoint the mage? Last time we had to use the key to find him."

It was a shame it wasn't working this time. I had tried. The second key had been more of a way to find the first key, not specifically the mage.

Kael put the phone back in his pocket. "Beings such as Vehrin give off a certain kind of dark energy. It's faint, and often hard to pinpoint, but as he grows stronger, his trail is easier to track."

I was almost afraid to ask, but… "Do I give off a dark energy?"

The pair of us hadn't talked about the brutal way I had killed the demon attacker in the hotel room. I had been grateful, too afraid to learn I may have something twisted and evil living inside of me, but curiosity finally got the better of me.

At that moment, our rental car pulled up to the curb out front, and Kael brushed off my question to usher me outside. My breath hissed in at the sharp, biting wind I hadn't been expecting. Colorado was definitely colder than South Carolina. I glanced at Kael as I hugged my jacket closer. He was completely at ease in his hoodie.

Well, colder for *some* people.

The vehicle Kael had rented for us turned out to be a black Jeep with big, knobby tires that looked like they could climb straight up a cliff.

I slid into the passenger seat, though I was itching to drive this beast. "Where exactly are we going?"

"The mountains," he replied. He pointed to the chain of mountains rising up against the western sky. We were off to seek out the mage in the cold mountains underneath dark gray clouds that looked ready to dump a load of snow on us any moment.

Just perfect.

I twisted the knobs between us, cranking the heat. Kael complained, swerving slightly on the highway leading out of the city as he pulled off his hoodie.

"Well, I'm sorry, but not everyone is blessed with perpetual warmth, you know."

Kael shoved his hoodie at me. "Here, take this, just quit trying to roast me." He turned the heat back down to what was probably a more reasonable degree.

I didn't complain and instead pulled my arms in and folded the hoodie over me like a blanket. It was still warm and Kael's scent of rain and citrus clung to it.

"You don't give off a dark energy."

"Huh?" It took me a moment to recall the question I had asked Kael before our rental arrived. I blinked. "Oh."

He didn't take his eyes from the road. "I know you've been worried about what happened in the hotel. You aren't dark, Livvie, just…powerful."

And dangerous. I could almost hear him bite back the words.

"I don't want to be powerful."

"That's good," Kael said. He turned off the main highway and onto what seemed to be some sort of county road. "That means you won't abuse it. Power doesn't make you evil, and it doesn't make you good. It gives you strength, certainly, but how you exercise that strength is what really matters."

I smiled at him. "You know, you're pretty wise when you want to be."

The man actually cracked a big grin, and it warmed me more than the borrowed hoodie.

Steadily, the landscape rose. I wasn't certain exactly how long we traveled, but we had left the county road and took twists and turns down roads that often were little more than a single lane. Kael glanced at the map on his phone once again and pulled over to the side of the road.

"Won't be able to get the car up through there." He jerked his head toward my window, and I followed his line of sight.

It was mostly evergreens, still green even in the colder months, with a few bare trees here and there. All of them were too close to allow for a vehicle.

"Walking it is," I agreed.

I peered down at my boots. Thankfully, they were perfect for all types of conditions, and were well broken in without the sacrifice of worn tread.

A lot of women spent money on high-dollar heels. I spent mine on boots that would survive an apocalypse.

I handed Kael his hoodie, and he tried to refuse it. I shoved it onto his lap.

"I can't wear it. It'll swallow me. I need to be able to move if there's a fight."

He hesitated, but took the hoodie and put it back on before leaving the car. The cold was more intense up in the mountains, and true to my thoughts, it had been snowing. It continued to snow as we headed up into the forest, the icy wind sending the snow in from the side so it hit against our cheeks.

I squinted against the onslaught. "Won't Vehrin sense me coming?"

Kael managed to walk through the snow silently and with envy-worthy grace. I had to pick up my feet high with every step in the deep snow. "Most likely, but we have to hope he will want you enough to confront us."

"Wonderful. I love being bait," I muttered, more to myself. "Old habits die hard."

Huffing out a sharp sigh, Kael grabbed my shoulder and pulled me to a stop. His face was creased with anger, but I could also see the worry in his frown. Was he remembering that I had attempted to sacrifice myself to the mage in an attempt to bind him? Admittedly, the thought had occurred to me, as well. This situation was just too familiar to keep those thoughts from resurfacing.

A crow cawed somewhere above us, but I was too trapped in Kael's intense gaze to let it draw my attention.

"You aren't bait. You're not here to sacrifice yourself." Another crow cawed, quickly followed by a third. Kael shook his head. "Don't do anything stupid."

I put my hand on a cocked hip, and opened my mouth to protest, but the sound of the crows had grown much louder. I glanced up, and my eyes grew round.

There had to be dozens of the birds. They were sitting on the branches above and around us, with more flying in every second.

"That's…" I glanced at Kael, who was watching the birds with suspicion. "That's weird, right?"

The trees were growing so heavy with crows, it was a wonder the branches weren't breaking under the weight.

I shuffled through the snow and closer to Kael, and as I did, the crows fell silent. Every single one peered at us with eyes white and glittering as the snow at our feet.

Then, the branches rattled as they began to fly.

Straight at us.

CHAPTER 4

I'd always liked birds, but at that moment, I cursed every bird on the planet as the flock of crows dove down at us.

Kael snarled so ferociously as the black wings descended on us that he almost sounded like his jaguar self. I covered my head to protect my face, but their beaks and feet scratched at the backs of my hands.

"Run!" I started through the snowy forest. Maybe if we got far enough away, they would stop.

That hope was quickly snuffed out. We'd only managed to get several feet when the attack increased.

The crows tore at our clothes as they cawed and beat at us with their wings. I could scarcely see where I was going. I was afraid if I took my hands from my face, they would go for my eyes. Never in my life had I seen crows act this viciously before.

It had to be the mage's doing.

A cracking noise sounded beside me, and I peeked from beneath my arms to find Kael had ripped a branch from a tree and was using it to swing at the icy-eyed crows. Small trickles of blood ran down the skin of his arms. Mine likely looked much the same.

I risked a glance around the forest. Vehrin had to be out here somewhere, controlling the crows, but I saw nothing save for a frenzy of ebony wings and the cold forest.

Kael let out another yell beside me, thrashing at the persistent crows with his stick. He managed to smack a few down, but more just took their place.

This didn't make sense. From what I had seen of Vehrin in our last encounter, he enjoyed watching his adversaries in this sort of struggle. He had stood by and watched Kael and me fight that giant panther and those soldiers of his. Why would he send the crows at us, then disappear? Wouldn't he have to be here to control them?

I raised my voice so Kael could hear me over the frenzied cawing of the birds. "I don't think these crows belong to the mage."

My partner took a vicious swing and brought down two crows at once. "Well, they certainly aren't wild."

A painful sting flashed across the back of my hand as a crow latched on. "Ouch!"

I gritted my teeth. *That's it.* My magic warmed through my veins, and I let it curl around my hand. The crow retreated with a surprised squawk. I flung my arm forward and let loose an orb of bright and burning energy.

As soon as my magic collided with one of the crows, the entire flock disappeared.

The forest grew quiet. Kael let out a deep sigh and bent over to rest his hands on his knees.

"Next time, maybe try that first."

I glanced up and around, afraid there would be more, but the branches were bare. What the hell had that been about? And who had done it?

Kael walked over to me, his boots crunching in the snow. Before I could say anything, he took a hold of my chin and tilted my face back and forth.

"I'm all right," I said. He was looking for wounds, no

doubt. "This was the worst of it." I held my hand out to show the mark marring my skin from where the crow had latched on.

He let go of my chin and lifted my hand, inspecting it. "Want me to wrap it?"

"No." I shrugged. "I've had worse." I jerked my head toward his arms. "You look like you could use some bandaging."

"I'll be fine. We need to head out before more of them come back." Kael tilted his head. "Are you sure this wasn't Vehrin? Seems like too much of a coincidence."

I didn't answer him, at first. Instead, I closed my eyes, magic still writhing through my fingers. I swore I could sense *something*, though I couldn't put my finger on what, exactly. One thing was for certain: whatever I was sensing, it definitely wasn't Vehrin. I would know his vile and destructive aura anywhere.

"I think it's someone else."

"Someone working for the mage?"

I shrugged. "I don't know, but"—I adjusted my bag and started through the trees, taking the lead—"whoever or whatever sent those crows this way."

Kael hurried to catch up with me. It was disconcerting how quiet and still the forest had grown. Our breaths rose in fine mist in front of our faces as we trekked through the snow. I wiggled my toes in my boots in an attempt to keep them warm. I hated cold weather, and couldn't help but wish I was in the damp and humid jungles of India with my team.

I could use my magic to warm myself, like a built-in heater, but I didn't want to waste energy I may need to use in the event of another attack.

"How much farther?" Kael asked. His voice was quiet, shoulders tense. The blood on his arms was drying, the scratches and tears slowly healing.

I could still sense the foreign magic. It wasn't ancient and wild, like mine, or dark and deadly like Vehrin's. Whoever it belonged to, it was stronger now.

"I think we're getting close."

Kael nodded. "Maybe you should get behind—"

"If you tell me to get behind you, Kael, I swear I'll stick you head first in the snow and leave you there."

He glanced at me, and I wiggled my fingers at him, letting a bit of magic swirl around my hand. He laughed softly and continued on his way. I scowled as he muttered what sounded like "ridiculous stubborn woman."

Overprotective shifter.

From beside me, Kael's hand smacked back into my chest.

"Ow! Kael, what the hell?"

"Ssh!" He held a finger up to his lips and pointed.

Ahead, the trees opened to a clearing. An adorable little cabin was nestled in the center, looking so much like it was plucked from a fairytale that I half-expected to see Goldilocks sneaking up to it.

"Do you think bear shifters live there?"

Kael gave me an odd look. "No, I'd smell them. Why do you say that?"

I shrugged. "Just a thought."

Together, we crept closer through the trees until we were at the edge of the clearing. The door opened, and a woman stepped out.

As soon as my eyes fell on her, I knew she was the one I was sensing. "She sent the crows."

"Witch." Kael spat the word like a foul taste in his mouth.

Before I could reprimand him for his prejudices, a fierce and sudden wind bore down on us. The ice in the breeze was so intense it took my breath away. Kael grabbed my arm and steadied me as the force of it threatened to knock me over.

I peered at the woman through squinted eyes. I could barely see her through the flurry of snow the wind was kicking up. Why was she doing this?

First, the crows, and now this. Clearly, she didn't want us getting to her cabin. Could she be hiding the mage inside?

Vehrin was more than capable of taking care of himself, though, so why was she being so defensive?

I started forward. The earth before me groaned, and a thick spear of ice rushed upward. Kael pulled me back. One step farther and I would have been impaled. I jerked free of Kael's grip and rushed around the ice. Kael cursed behind me, but I could hear him following as I continued forward. More spears of ice shot from the ground.

The pair of us darted around the ice and fought through the snow and biting wind. My breath came quick and sharp, the cold freezing my throat. My muscles burned with each step as we tried to close the distance between us and the cabin.

The cabin?

I squinted. Where had it gone? I couldn't see through the wall of snow and ice and wind around us. Pulling in a deep breath, I spread my hands out in front of me.

My magic seared hot from my veins, and I found myself relishing the sensation. It burned from my hands, unfettered and bent on destruction. The ice and snow before me melted. The wind died down. The way before us cleared, and I found myself staring at the witch standing a mere few feet away.

Take down the threat, that dark and wild part of me seemed to say. *Destroy the ones who stand in your way*.

My brow furrowed, and my magic burned hotter.

Kael's hand landed on my shoulder, and squeezed.

I didn't turn to him, but I could feel his concerned gaze. I swallowed and let the magic slip back to the shadows.

My eyes found the witch's. They were a peculiar silver, icy and cold as the crows had been. The woman glanced behind us, and her fingers knotted on the front of the dark blue dress she was wearing.

"Who are you?" she asked.

"Olivia Perez. I'm an archaeologist from Yale." I was still

an archaeologist, despite spending all this time on a magical goose chase. I jerked my head to Kael. "This is Agent Rivera, from PITO."

Perhaps we would be able to glean more information from this woman if she knew this was an official, and serious, visit.

Her lips pursed thoughtfully. They seemed torn, as if she had been chewing on them too hard.

"Well, what do you want?"

Kael stepped closer to her. His posture was tall and stiff. I couldn't help but admire the imposing figure.

"We're looking for someone," he said. "A dark mage."

The witch's left eye twitched. *She knew.*

"He was here?" I asked.

The woman jerked a nod. "He was."

"What did he want?" It was clear to me that, though he had been in this area not long before according to Kael's agency, he was no longer here.

"Information."

Kael's voice was low. "What kind of information?"

For a long moment, the witch fixed us with a weighing gaze. "Come inside. We'll have tea."

"No, thank you." Kael nearly growled the words.

The witch raised an eyebrow. "*You* may not freeze to death, shifter, but your pretty companion might."

Kael glanced down at me. Now that we weren't running from crows or magical blizzards, the sweat chilled against my skin under my clothes. I tried to warm myself with my magic, but after that last bout of energy I released, I was exhausted.

He let out a sharp breath. "Fine." His golden-brown gaze was sharp on the witch. "But if you try anything…"

Though his voice trailed off, his threat hung heavy in the air.

The witch opened the door and led us into the cabin. We were immediately met with a warmth so lovely I couldn't help but sigh. Kael pulled his stare from the witch as she went through a small doorway that led into a quaint kitchen.

"Cold?" he asked.

"Just a bit."

Kael cupped his hands around his mouth and breathed into them, then reached down and grabbed my hands. His strong fingers wrapped around my hands, warming them. He was always so gruff that the gentle gesture surprised me.

"Thanks," I murmured.

His hair was wet from the ice and snow we had fought through, and it sent water rolling down his cheek as he lifted his lips into a small smile. "You're welcome."

A throat cleared behind us, and I quickly stepped away from Kael, though I missed the warmth of his hands.

"My name is Emily," the witch said. She set down a tray holding three steaming beverages.

I took my cup eagerly and wrapped my fingers around the warm porcelain. Kael left his on the tray. There were only two chairs around the small coffee table where Emily had set the tray. She sat in one, and Kael gestured for me to sit in the other. I sank into it, and he sat on the arm. He appeared at ease, but I noted the way he was shifted to be able to easily jolt to his feet if the need arose.

"You are not a witch." Emily lifted her own cup to her lips and watched me over the brim.

"I am not." I offered no further information. I didn't know this woman, and until I knew if she was a friend or foe, I would keep certain things to myself. "Why did you attack us?"

The woman's back went straight. "I've had unfortunate encounters with visitors as of late. If you were me, you would understand the caution."

"What did the mage want to know?" Kael asked.

Emily's startling eyes swept to my partner. "Are you a friend of his?"

I scoffed. "Absolutely not." It was my turn to be pinned

with an icy stare. “I assure you, Emily, we are the farthest thing from being a friend to Vehrin.”

She blinked. “You know his name?” She set down her cup. “Interesting.”

“We know he was here,” I said. “Why?’

Emily turned to stare into the fireplace spreading warmth around the room. Her hands clenched her knees, and it was then that I noticed her fingers were raw and red, the skin flaking in some places. It was as if they had been…burned.

“He wanted to know where to find the other key.”

The other key?

I turned to Kael, his confused stare fixated on my own. Vehrin already knew I held the two keys. My body went cold, despite the fire and the warm cup in my hands. I turned to the witch and leaned forward.

“Are you saying there is a third key?”

CHAPTER 5

THE CABIN HAD GONE QUIET. Even the flames licking the logs in the fireplace seemed to be holding their crackling breath. My mind was screaming in protest and frustration. There couldn't be another key...could there? Emily had to be mistaken.

The witch finally broke the silence. "What do you mean, *third* key?" She spoke softly, her words so hushed I almost didn't catch them.

I leaned forward to set my cup of steaming tea back on the tray. Slowly, I pulled the pair of keys out from the front of my shirt. Kael was tense beside me as Emily's gaze locked on the keys. I saw his hand drift toward his side, where I knew he had a pistol holstered.

Kael didn't trust the witch, and I really hoped she didn't do anything to attack me, because my partner would not hesitate to pull that pistol out if she did.

"Where did you get those?" Emily asked.

"It doesn't matter where I got them, just that they are in my possession and not the mage's."

Her eyes narrowed slightly, and it offered more bite and

emotion than I had yet to see from the woman. "How old are you?"

The question threw me off. "Huh?"

"Your magic...it's unusual." Emily rubbed a hand up her bare arm, as if she could feel my magic on her skin. "It is ancient, nearly as ancient as…as his." She shuddered and crossed her arms, shrinking in on herself.

I glanced at her burned fingers again. The supernatural world was still new to me, and I barely knew anything that I hadn't always believed as myth. Burning witches at the stake used to be a thing, right? Even if the witch hunter were wrong most of the time. Did that mean a touch of fire was disastrous to a witch?

"What happened here, with the mage?" I asked.

Emily swallowed and shook her head. "I should have known he would come. I always believed someone would, but I hadn't expected the likes of him." Her eyes were round, frantic when she peered back up at us. "He broke through my defenses so easily, so quickly. I didn't have a chance to escape."

"He took a key from here?" Kael asked.

"No. Not a key. He took information."

I leaned forward. "What kind of information?"

"My lineage has always known the whereabouts of the key, but we have never held it ourselves. We were ordered to protect the information at all costs."

Kael got to his feet, then grew cold and still as a statue. "And did you protect that information at all costs?"

"The fire." Emily's voice trembled. Her fingers curled into tight, shaking fists. "He held my hands in the fire."

"So, you told him where to find this key." Kael's voice was rough, and a bit disgusted.

I sliced him with a glare. "Kael."

"Some protector you are," he said.

"I seem to recall a certain jaguar who let a human woman

slip past his defenses to steal a key he was supposed to be protecting with his life."

Emily's stare swept between Kael and myself at my chastising words, no doubt trying to piece together a story. The shifter fell silent. I shouldn't goad him, or make him feel incompetent because he truly wasn't, but he also shouldn't be scorning a woman who had just been tortured.

I gave Emily an apologetic smile on behalf of my friend. "I know you've been through an ordeal, but could you tell us the information you gave the mage?"

The witch stood. "I am afraid I cannot offer much. I told him everything I knew, and it was far less than he was pleased with." Emily took a deep breath. "You will need to find a man by the name of Lor."

I ran the name through my mind, though of course it didn't sound familiar. The wind blew sharply outside and brought with it the remembrance of how chilled I still felt. The tea in front of me swirled with steam, warm and inviting, despite the length it had been sitting untouched. I reached for it, but Kael leaned down to snatch my wrist.

Miffed, I threw him a look of exasperation, but his gaze was locked on Emily. He pulled me up to stand beside him before I could protest.

Kael didn't release my wrist as he spoke to the witch. "What sort of being is this Lor?"

"A warlock."

My partner scowled, and that look of detestation hurt me. How could he dislike all magical beings so much, when I was now one of them myself?

"Do you know anything of the key?" I asked, hoping to get answers before Kael did anything else rude. "Why would Vehrin want it?"

Emily shook her head. "I know nothing, only that if it were to fall in the wrong hands, it would be disastrous." She frowned, guilt flashing over her sullen features. A deep breath rocked her frame, and I pitied her so much, I wanted to wrap my arms around her and hug her. Suddenly, she looked up. "Although…"

She trailed off and narrowed her eyes at the keys on my chest.

I pulled my wrist from Kael's grip. "What is it?"

"If it isn't too much trouble, may I have a closer look?" Emily offered a fraction of a smile. "Perhaps it could help me discern why the mage would want the third key."

I nodded, and she walked around the edge of the coffee table to stand before me. For the longest moment, she stared, and I held my breath. When Emily finally spoke again, her words were not what I was expecting.

Her eyes lifted to mine, and the ice in them made my heart lurch. "He took something from me."

Kael put an arm between myself and the witch and swept me back a few steps.

The atmosphere in the room had shifted. No longer did it feel like a cozy refuge from a winter storm. It felt like a trap. Like a prison.

I glanced at the tea cups, still steaming, still impossibly inviting. I wondered then if they were poisoned.

"What did he take?" My voice was calm, despite the unease unfurling in my gut.

Emily glanced over her shoulder. "My Baron."

I followed her gaze to the corner of the room. A perch sat there that I hadn't noticed before. It was clearly for a bird, and a few ebony feathers sat on the floor beneath it.

"Her familiar," Kael said. His eyebrows were knit in concentration, golden-brown eyes sharp. His feet had drifted slightly apart, and I recognized the stance as one ready for attack.

Thankfully, my knowledge of the supernatural was well enough to understand what a familiar was, and meant, to witches. Usually in the form of animals, they were like domestic companions that often held their own magic and served as spies and helpers to the witch with whom they were bonded.

"I am so sorry." I wasn't really certain what else to say.

Emily seemed not to have heard me. She was staring at the keys again. She pointed. "There is power in that key."

I pulled in a deep breath. She was pointing at the first key, the one I had plucked from the Amazon. The one bound to my soul.

"It holds the same power as you, and more." Emily's cold gaze bore into mine. "There is something dark and dangerous there. Something that you now have, as well. You are soul-bound to it."

A plank on the wooden floor creaked slightly as Kael inched a bit more in front of me.

Emily's nostrils flared. "With that magic, I would never be defeated again. I can take back what the mage stole from me. I could bring Baron home again."

"Why would Vehrin take your bird in the first place?" Kael asked.

The witch's fingers twitched at her side. "He said there would be those following him, searching for him. He said he would give Baron back if…if..."

My pulse began to quicken. "If what?"

Kael nudged me back a bit. "Olivia."

The witch's lips quirked. I couldn't tell if she were holding back from crying or sneering.

"If I killed you."

The fire snuffed out, and the cabin grew so cold it was as if every shred of warmth had suddenly been sucked out. The walls groaned, and the ceiling shuddered. Kael reached for the pistol on his side, but as soon as he held it up, frost quickly crawled over it. He dropped it with a hiss, and I noticed red on his hand, as if he had been suddenly frostbitten.

"Now, Olivia."

Now what? I glanced at him, and he jerked his head toward her.

Understanding broke through to me as the cabin continued to shudder around us. My magic. I could attack her, kill her before she killed us. It uncoiled inside of me, that power. Eager, ready for blood.

I held my hand up and stared at Emily's face.

Her forehead was creased and jaw tight with clenched teeth, but tears ran down her cheeks. I hesitated.

"Olivia!"

I tried to force myself to unleash my magic on her. I had to. We could be killed. Instead, I just stood there and wondered at her tears of loss.

"Damn it, Olivia, now!"

I pulled in a shuddering breath, and it blew back out into a scream. Something rushed forward from the witch and punched me in the stomach. I stumbled back so hard, I slammed into the closed door. Kael was suddenly there. He wrenched it open and tugged me through it. I could hardly catch up to what was going on as he pulled the door closed with one hand and shoved me toward the snow with the other.

"Don't just stand there," he barked. "Run!"

I started through the snow and back toward the forest in what I hoped was the direction we had come. I had only gone several steps when I halted, Kael nearly bowling me over in the process. Several loud and broken howls pierced through the trees ahead. The sound traced a chill down my neck.

Wolves stepped from the trees, all white and shimmery, as if they had been pulled from the very snow they walked through. Their eyes were the same ice as the crows had been. These were no shifters. These were from the witch.

"This way." I swiveled. I grabbed a hold of Kael's arm and urged him through the blanket of white.

Running through the deep snow was difficult. A hurried peek over my shoulder showed the wolves were gaining on us quickly. I had no idea where Emily had gone, but as we darted past her cabin, I was certain I saw her silhouette in the window.

Howls pierced through the frigid air again. The wolves, all cold and winter fury, pursued us with unbridled vengeance. I couldn't help but feel like a fox dashing for her life from the blood-thirsty hounds.

I had assumed the forest continued behind the witch's cabin, and we could at least attempt to break up the wolves' pursuit. We rushed as quickly as we could into the forest, but after several steps, the trees fell away to reveal a deep slope of the mountainside.

There was so much snow clinging to the surface, it was difficult to tell where there may be sudden drop-offs or sharp rocks to break our bones.

Emily's wolves had reached the trees. It was either risk the climb down, or be torn apart.

A shredding noise beside me alerted me that Kael had torn through the fabric of his clothing. His jaguar now stood in the snow.

No matter how many times I had seen this form, I could never get over the beauty and raw power of it. His sides heaved with deep breaths, the pattern of dark spots across his golden-yellow fur shifting with the movement.

Kael let out a vicious snarl. If I had been one of those wolves, I would have halted at the ferocious and heart-hammering sound, but they didn't falter a step.

My partner backed toward the slope, keeping his eye on the oncoming attackers, and I started picking my way down as quickly as I could without breaking an ankle. My hand clenched onto the fur of his shoulder as I turned to find the wolves had reached the top.

A gasp flew up my throat as something gave way beneath me, and I slipped. Kael turned toward me as I tried to keep my footing, but I pitched forward and tumbled through the snow.

The mountain rolled me down her face, beating me from every side. Finally, I managed to halt my momentum. I whirled around and caught sight of Kael as the wolves descended on him.

One lurched into his side, and his pained snarl split the air. Another latched onto a hind leg, tugging, pulling him down. They were going to tear him apart.

Anger burned hot through me. The cold snow around my feet and the unforgiving mountain face fell away as magic seared up through my veins. I flung a powerful attack at the wolves and hit my mark. The one on Kael's leg yelped, twitched violently, then fell to its side, but the other wolves didn't stop. If anything, they tore at Kael with more fervor.

"Kael!" I struggled up through the snow, ready to launch another attack.

A massive rumbling reached me. My gaze lifted from Kael, upward.

It took me a moment to realize it wasn't a cloud rolling toward us.

It was an avalanche.

There was no time to warn him, to call out his name again. I hardly drew a breath when he was overtaken. I turned, some frenzied part of my mind telling me that I could outrun it.

A wall slammed into me, pushing out every breath of air from my lungs, and I pitched forward into darkness.

CHAPTER 6

A STRAINED GASP sucked in past my lips, and my eyes flew open. There was nothing but darkness. I tried to get up and see where I was, but I couldn't move.

My heart raced. Where was I? Why couldn't I move? It was difficult to string my thoughts together, but eventually everything clicked together in my jumbled mind.

The avalanche.

I was buried under who knew how many feet of snow.

It was difficult, but I was able to wiggle just a bit to tilt my head in an attempt to look around. There was no way of telling which way was up. Even if I could eventually start digging, I could very well end up tunneling in the wrong direction.

I huffed out a sigh and shifted my weight around to try and shove some of the heavy snow farther away and give myself room. The air was already beginning to grow thin. If I didn't hurry, I could suffocate.

Just as I was able to make enough room to start clawing at the snow with my fingers, I heard something.

I paused. It was muffled, and difficult to judge the distance, but it was a crunching noise. Footsteps.

Kael was looking for me.

I yelled for him as loud as I could. The footsteps quickened. I could make out the sound of snow being pushed away. Slowly, the darkness receded and the light around me grew grayer.

Finally, I squinted as snow fell on my face and the sky broke open before me. My eyes grew wide. Kael wasn't my rescuer.

Renathe?

I blinked a few times to assure myself he wasn't an illusion. I had forgotten how unearthly beautiful he was until that moment. What was the owner of the Pinnacle nightclub doing here, on a mountainside in Colorado? How did he find me? Why had he been searching me out?

"I feel like a popsicle." That wasn't what I'd meant to say. My brain still felt as if it were churning.

Ren let out a soft laugh from where he was crouched beside me. "A popsicle?"

"Yeah. Stiff. Cold."

"Lickable?" A devilish grin spread across Ren's face, and the shots of silver in his unusual teal eyes seemed to sparkle.

Even as the embodiment of a frozen treat, I could scowl.

Ren chuckled again and started scooping aside handfuls of snow. "Let's get you out of there." I groaned as I wiggled free. I was going to be sore for a while, but I didn't think anything was broken.

"Apologies, Olivia. I hadn't meant for it to be quite that effective."

Brushing snow from myself, I said, "What do you mean?"

The fae man gestured around to the snow as if it were obvious.

It took me a moment before it clicked. "You caused the avalanche? Why?"

"To help you, of course. Those wolves were already tearing into your shifter and—"

I gasped and whipped my head to peer farther up the mountainside. *Kael!*

There he was, already free of the snow and bounding toward me. It didn't take him long to reach us. He snarled and swiped sharp claws at Renathe, who looked annoyed but scooted back a few feet.

Kael stared at Ren for a few seconds longer with his lips pulled up to reveal his teeth before he turned to me.

"You're okay," I said, my voice trembling.

Give or take a few scratches and bites that stained his spotted fur red, he didn't seem too injured considering he'd been fighting off a pack of magic-wrought wolves.

He let out a soft huff and closed his eyes. He bumped his head against mine. At first, I was shocked at his closeness, but then relief lifted my arms. I ran my hands down the side of his neck, then wrapped my arms around him. He curled his neck around mine and hung his head over my shoulder, as if he were returning the embrace.

"Oh God, Kael. You're so warm."

How could he be so warm after being covered in snow? I wanted to cling to his fur forever, but he pulled back. Though he was in his jaguar form, I could see the concern in his golden eyes.

"I'm fine." I pulled my bag around, thinking it was a miracle I still had it across my shoulder, and pulled out a spare set of clothes for him.

While he shifted back and changed, I turned to Ren. "What are you doing here?"

He had settled cross-legged, watching me with amusement and looking perfectly at ease in the snow and sharp wind. "I was curious as to why you were suddenly running off to Colorado."

I narrowed my eyes. "I didn't tell you where I was going." Ren could be a bit invasive at times, mostly, I think, because he saw me as some sort of magical mystery to figure out. At the moment, he was giving me stalker vibes. "How did you know where I was?"

As an answer, he reached down and took my hand. He pushed my sleeve back a bit to reveal a bracelet. A small, crystal charm in the shape of a snowflake dangled from it. He had given me the charm on the date he had gotten out of me on our bargain. Ren touched the charm with a sly grin.

Connecting the dots came quickly. "You—" I had to fight to get the words out, I was so angry "—you're tracking me? What the hell, Ren!"

Oh, I was definitely getting major stalker vibes. Who did he think he was?

"I have my reasons." He was so calm and blasé. It was irritating.

Kael was suddenly at my shoulder, clothed and in his human form again. "You had no right." His voice was so rough it was nearly a growl.

Ren's face went hard, and his eyes narrowed. "I have every right. The mage is not only a threat to you, but to my kind, as well. Already his presence is beginning to affect us. Olivia is the only one who will be able to find and stop him. Of course I am keeping track of her. And it's a good thing I was, or you'd *both* be dead!"

His words were harsh and made me feel a bit like a bloodhound sent to chase out rabbits, but I understood. He was worried about his fellow fae, just as I wanted to save all of humanity from the mage.

I stood. "Well, you still could have told me instead of being sneaky about it."

Ren laughed and pointed at his chest. "Fae, remember?"

I rolled my eyes. "How did you get here so fast, anyway?"

"Private jet."

Private jet. Giving gifts of crystal charms. Collecting rare vehicles. There was no way Ren made that much money from his night club. He had to have some family money, or was a lottery winner or something.

I glanced up the mountain, half-expecting another attack of wolves or crows to come bearing down on us. Had the witch given up? I certainly hoped so. "We should get out of here."

"I agree," Kael said. "But where do we go?"

I thought back to our conversation with Emily in the cabin. She had said to find a man by the name of Lor, and not just any man. A warlock.

"We have to find Lor."

Ren brushed snow from his pants, then peered at me. "The warlock?"

My eyes widened. "You know him?"

"I make it my business to know of all powerful, magical beings."

This all seemed too convenient to me. What were the chances that he knew the man the mage was going after next? How had Ren found me so quickly? Either he was more invested in stopping the mage than I had first believed, or he was on the wrong side.

I would wait, though. The idea that Ren, who I considered a friend, may just be working with the mage, made me a bit too uneasy to accept as truth without evidence.

Ren straightened his jacket as the silence stretched on. I really hoped he wasn't going to ask for another bargain for this information. Finally, he dug into his pocket and pulled out a phone. He quickly tapped a message, and my cell buzzed inside my bag.

"His location," Ren said.

I pulled out my phone and clicked the text.

Chicago?

My team member and friend, Sarah, was from Chicago. While we all worked for Elizabeth Andrews at Yale, we didn't all live in the area. Our dig team was from all over the world, but sometimes we met up outside of digs, too. I'd visited Sarah in her hometown a couple of times, and I didn't hear the word Chicago without immediately thinking of her.

But now, thinking of her also made me think of the dig she was on in India, and a wistful sigh escaped me.

"Thinking of some deep-dish pizza?" Kael asked.

The mention of food made my stomach growl. I didn't want to let on that I was moping about not being on an archaeological dig, so I just nodded.

Making our way down the mountain was difficult, especially since Ren had blanketed the rocky outcrops and cliffs in deep snow. The fae went first, with all the ease of a man taking a Sunday afternoon stroll through the park. Kael went next, telling me it was safer that way in case Ren missed a drop or jagged rock.

I found it just a tad annoying that they were both so graceful trekking through the snow, while I was dinosaur-stomping through it with snow soaking the insides of my boots. At least I had a good sense of direction, which was lucky because Kael's fancy PITO-issued phone didn't have a great enough signal for his map to pull up.

It was a relief to reach trees again. "Hope Emily doesn't have any more attack crows waiting."

Ren raised an eyebrow, but I didn't elaborate.

"Speaking of that witch..." Kael put a hand on my shoulder to stop me beneath a pine. The sun was shining over the canopy, sending tiny slivers of light dancing across his tight jawline. "Why didn't you attack her when I asked you to?"

His question threw me off guard, and I stared at him for a long moment. "I don't know. I just...felt bad for her, I guess. She'd just lost someone she loved and wanted to get him back. Vehrin had *tortured* her. More than likely she wasn't even in her right mind. I wasn't even sure she would go through with it, that she would want to. Why else would she have waited so long, told us so much? Attacking her didn't sit right with me. I can't punish someone for doing something for a person, or being, or pet, or whatever, that they love. That just seems…cruel."

Kael's features softened a little. "You don't know what her right mind could be. Vehrin has allies, just as we do. We can't afford to take chances." He stepped a bit closer. "Livvie, there will come times when you have to make decisions that are hard, that go against everything you are, but sometimes, it is necessary."

A strange sense of foreboding shivered through me at his words, and I suddenly felt colder than I already had been.

"Always so cheerful," Ren remarked. He was leaning casually against a tree several feet away.

Surprisingly, Kael didn't growl something back to him. Instead, he kept his attention on me. "I mean it, Livvie. Next time, you need to fight. If you don't, it may end up being too late."

A heavy weight seemed to drop on my shoulder, and I sighed. "All right. I understand where you're coming from."

I didn't outright agree with him—a slight tick in his cheek told me he noticed, too—but I would think about it. Kael may be a shoot first, ask questions later kind of guy, but something like that would be difficult for me.

That is, unless I let my magic do the thinking for me, and that was something I certainly wasn't prepared to do.

CHAPTER 7

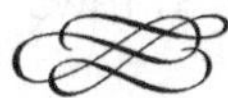

I ROLLED my shoulders as Kael stood in line to rent us a car at the airport. I hadn't slept much on the flight, and the sky outside of the windows was the deep velvet of night. It was preferable, really. The dark skies and deep shadows would help to cloak us as we made our way to find Lor the warlock.

That is, if Vehrin hadn't found him first.

Kael and I had hurried from the mountains as quickly as we could and caught the first flight heading toward Chicago. Ren had left with barely more than a good luck. I'd tried to give the bracelet back to him, but he said giving a gift back from a fae was rude. He'd also told me I never knew when I'd need his help again.

I peered down at the snowflake charm. It felt heavier on my wrist now that I knew Renathe could track me with it. He was right, though. He had helped me out of a tight spot, literally, and this wasn't just mine and Kael's fight. This involved all manner of beings that could fall under the dark mage if we didn't stop him, first. Renathe had every right to want to keep tabs on how I was doing, seeing as I was the frontrunner in this fight.

Kael glanced back at me as the woman behind the desk

tapped at a keyboard. His smile was weary, and I should have been just as exhausted as he was, only I wasn't. It was like electricity was tapping along my veins. My magic prickled beneath my skin, eager, wanting to be set loose. It made me feel like I'd had about four cups of coffee too many. I was jittery. I needed to *do* something.

When Kael finally walked toward me with a set of keys, I exhaled with relief.

"Ready?" he asked.

"Absolutely."

We hefted our bags and walked out of the airport.

The white sedan was certainly less exciting than the Jeep we got to drive into the mountains. Kael mumbled something about its lack of horsepower as I ran my fingers over the keys around my neck. As my touch ran down the length of the golden key from the Amazon ruins, I felt a feathering sensation down my own body. It still made me uneasy, knowing that my soul was bound with the key, and anyone who had it could control me...and my magic.

"Stop worrying."

I turned to Kael as we made our way around the outskirts of Chicago. I tucked the keys back inside my shirt. "I'm not worrying."

"You are worrying. You're about to chew off your bottom lip."

Stupid, bad habit. I purposefully puffed my lip out, which made Kael laugh. Then he went quiet as he checked the directions Ren had given us.

"No one is going to get a hold of that key, or you."

I glanced outside as the streetlights flashed by. People walked on sidewalks. Silhouettes flitted through houses. "We're up against an awful lot right now. Not just the mage. Others want me, too."

Kael's hand tightened on the steering wheel, but he gave

me a smile. "I don't think anyone realizes what they're up against when they try to take us down."

Us.

He made 'us' sound like a more concrete team than just the convenient partnership we'd been when we first started hunting the mage. The thought made something warm flutter inside of me. It also made me uncomfortable, because I wasn't quite sure what to do with that feeling.

The rest of the ride, I sorted through my bag, organizing the things that had become jumbled and taking stock of supplies. I paused with the knife handle, now missing the blade, in my hand. I needed another weapon—something I could rely on besides the blood-thirsty magic tapping for release in my veins.

"I think this is close to where we need to be," Kael said.

I blinked from my wistful thoughts and zipped up my bag, then peered out the window. Kael was pulling up to stop beside a very large park. The expanse of fields dotted with playground equipment and soccer nets glistened under the moon. It must have rained recently. I got out of the car and settled my bag onto my shoulder, the magic in me humming.

"This is the place?"

There were no houses around, only a few businesses with darkened windows on the other side of the street.

Kael shrugged. "Perhaps it's on the other side of the park."

I squinted through the darkness, but couldn't see the other side. "Yeah, maybe."

I wasn't convinced.

Together, we walked under the arched, stone entryway of the park. It was empty of others, and though I was thankful because I didn't want any innocents getting caught in the crossfire if a fight came up with the mage, it was also a bit eerie. Almost *too* quiet. Even the noise of the city seemed to have fallen away as we stepped across the damp grass.

A sudden, uncomfortable itch scattered between my shoulder blades. I peered behind us and didn't see anyone, but the sensation didn't go away.

"I think we're being followed," I whispered.

Kael looked at me, then glanced back. His nostrils flared. "I don't smell or sense anyone."

His steps hadn't slowed, though he still adopted the smooth grace of a predator stalking prey. He may not sense anyone, but he certainly wasn't letting his guard down.

I tried to brush it off. I needed to stop being so paranoid. I wrinkled my nose and ran a finger under my nostrils in an attempt to dislodge a tickle threatening to make me sneeze. Hairs stood on the back of my neck, and I couldn't help but glance behind us again.

A figure jumped out of the shadows.

I yelled as a man reached for me. He was already so close, and by instinct, I threw my elbow at him. A sharp pain ran up my arm as my elbow collided with his head. He stumbled to the side, but more figures emerged from the dark.

They moved across the ground with a silent, deadly grace. Their bodies, though almost human in shape, writhed and swirled like shadows. I could see little of their faces, except for their eyes, which burned like hot coals in the darkness.

Kael whirled around. Out of my peripheral, I saw him pull his pistol from his side. I turned back to the man who had tried to grab me. He had recovered and stalked around me, the outline of his body shifting and blurring with each step he took.

A gunshot rang out as some of the attackers converged on Kael. Just as I started to release the magic within me, the shadowy man slithered across the grass and disappeared. Suddenly, I was grabbed from behind. My nostrils burned, and goosebumps scattered across my skin.

Ice dripped down my neck as my assailant spoke, his lips nearly brushing my ear. "I want your power, little one. I can sense it calling to me, tempting me. I will drain it from you until you are sucked dry. Then, I will feast on you, until you are nothing more than agony and screams."

My gut twisted, and I tried to break free of his hold. These had to be more demons, called from wherever they dwelled by the mage's dark power. Like moths to a flame, they were drawn to my magic, as well.

More writhing shadows passed in front of me as the demon holding me tugged me across the ground. I tried to dig my heels in, but my boots couldn't find purchase on the wet grass. Through the flickering shreds of darkness around me, I saw where the demon was taking me.

Several feet away was a black hole in the ground, swirling like a pool of jet ink.

I didn't know where it led, but I had the horrible feeling if the demon managed to get me there, I would be taken to a place that was unreachable for even Renathe and Kael to rescue me.

My magic was ablaze inside me, ripping at my skin, tearing for release. The power inside of me wanted to burn, and rip, and destroy.

I took a deep breath, then let it free.

A sharp and piercing shriek filled my ears as heat flared up my arms. The demon at my back released me, and the stench of burning flesh assaulted my nostrils. I turned to find gray smoke now swirling with the shadows that wreathed him.

My eyebrows furrowed and my teeth ground together as I drew on more magic. The sizzling energy rushed down my fingers to wrap around his body. His screams intensified. The demon thrashed and tore at himself as if he could wrench free the magic coiling around him.

I do not show mercy to my enemies.

The thought whispered up from deep cracks in my mind, shaking itself free of dust and bearing an ancient resonance that felt a part of me, yet wholly different.

Something flashed through me, a fierce and jagged heat, like a bolt of lightning. The demon before me was gone, and in his place was a man. He was not wreathed in shadow, but was naked. He knelt with his head bowed. His hands were braced on the rough, sun-kissed stone below him. The muscles of his arms trembled, and I scoffed at his weakness.

"I do not show mercy to my enemies," I said. My voice was strong, the voice of a queen who would not tolerate failure.

The air was heavy with the recent rains, and the trees of the jungle shone and dripped with beads of water. Everything else was silent. Even the birds had gone quiet, as if afraid to disturb me.

The man stared at the ground, his face obscured by sweat-slick hair. "I don't understand," he said. His voice shook. "You are on our side."

There was a low growl behind me so deep it rumbled through my chest. The shadow of the massive jaguar passed over the bent man, the cat's padded footfalls silent as he guarded my back.

A finger of magic snaked under the man's chin and tilted his face upward. His brown eyes were pleading under his dark eyebrows. He would find no mercy today.

"Vehrin is the betrayer, not I. It is unfortunate you did not see that before coming here in an attempt to destroy me."

He opened his mouth, but whatever he had planned to say grew into screams as my magic wrapped around him. It reveled in the blood boiling in his veins, at the cries of agony filling his lungs. He fell at my feet and grew still. I watched as the last flickers of life dimmed in his wide gaze.

I do not show mercy to my enemies.

I GASPED as the demon fell to the ground, dead. He was hardly more than a sizzling pile of darkness. My magic faded back into myself, seemingly satisfied. I braced my hands on my knees, and my arms shook as I gulped in deep breaths of air.

Flickers of the memory, of my memory, still whispered through me. I quickly picked it apart with a sense of guilt and apprehension. The man had said I was on his side, his and Vehrin's. What had he meant?

I found a small bit of solace in the fact I had apparently broken alliance with Vehrin, though it hadn't done anything to stop what I saw as merciless cruelty.

I latched onto another bit of the vision. Guarding my back had been a massive cat, a jaguar…

"Olivia!"

Kael ran up. His wide chest heaved with the exertion of the battle. A quick glance behind him showed a few shadowy figures crumpled and still on the grass.

"I'm fine," I said. I knew he was about to ask.

His sharp gaze ran up and down me, then settled on my face. His forehead puckered. "Something's wrong."

I straightened. "Nothing's wrong."

"I don't believe you."

"I said I'm fine, Kael!" The edge of dark magic within myself hummed at my anger, as if it were feeding off of it. I took a deep breath and worked my voice into calmer tones. "Really, I'm fine. Let's just find this warlock before something worse creeps from the shadows."

Kael looked like he wanted to argue, but he nodded. "Yeah, but where is he? I can't imagine he's just squatting in the park somewhere."

"Can't you track the mage with your PITO tech?" I tried to keep the sarcasm from my voice.

The shifter shook his head. "I tried. There is so much energy swirling around here it's messing things up."

I pursed my lips and looked around. Then my gaze stopped at a stone archway similar to the one at the park entrance. I caught the shapes of headstones in the distance.

A cemetery.

"There." I pointed. "That's where Lor the warlock is hiding."

Something was tugging at me, beckoning me. I didn't know if the source of the sensation was something good, or something evil, but we were about to find out.

CHAPTER 8

The stone archway leading to the cemetery loomed before us. I could feel Kael's skeptical gaze tracing up between my shoulder blades as I squinted into the night-cloaked headstones.

"How do you know this warlock is in there?" Kael asked.

I shrugged, then made my way under the archway. "I don't know." My voice was hushed. I was uncertain if there were more demons about, or even dark-cast minions of Vehrin, and I didn't want to draw attention to us. "I just sense that there is *something* calling me in here."

Kael's hand grabbed my shoulder, and he pulled me to a stop. "Livvie, that doesn't mean this is helpful. For all we know, it's Vehrin. This could be a trap."

I sighed and brushed his hand away. "Well, we'll never know until we try."

He crossed his muscled arms across his wide chest and opened his mouth to argue, but at that moment, I caught sight of something over his shoulder that made my heart jump.

I shoved past him and knelt down at the base of the archway I'd just crossed under. There, near the bottom, in a scrawl so worn by wind and rain, was a rune.

Anyone else would have overlooked the angles that seemed almost a part of the stones, but the ancient eyes peering from my soul could read the blocky character.

Kael squatted beside me. "What is it?"

My fingers brushed over the rune. "This."

"Okay, and what is it supposed to be?" He squinted, then tilted his head as if it would help him to better make out what I saw.

"It says *gateway*."

The shifter scoffed and straightened to his feet. "How original. I expect there's one over there that says 'seat'?" He pointed to a bench a couple of yards away.

I rolled my eyes and stood. "It doesn't mean a physical gateway. It's like…" I drifted and tapped my fingers against my thigh as I thought of a way to explain what the rune meant. "It's like an opening to something different. Something ethereal."

"So, what you're saying is there is something otherworldly in here?"

"Or magical," I said. "And ancient."

Whatever this place held, I could sense *something* starting to prickle across my skin like static.

Kael frowned, and I could tell by the way his hand drifted toward his hip, and his pistol, that he didn't like that one bit.

I shrugged a shoulder. "Seems like the perfect place for the warlock, I guess, though why ancient magic is hiding in a cemetery in Chicago, I have no idea." I grinned at Kael. "Shall we?"

I strode off deeper into the cemetery. Kael grumbled something incoherent at my back, and my smile deepened. I couldn't help it. Sometimes I liked to ruffle his feathers, or fur, a bit.

The shifter kept a wary eye out for any more attackers, while I searched for any clues as to where Lor the warlock could be. I tried to follow the ancient magic permeating the cemetery, but it seemed to whisper to me from every shadow. A part of me wanted to give in, but I kept a hold of myself and continued to study the headstones for any unusual markings.

My gaze slid over a glossy, granite tomb and then eased back. It was much newer than any of the other tombs and headstones, whose faces were stained and weathered with age. Surely, that wouldn't be the source of the magic permeating this place? It would have made more sense if it was coming from one of the older tombs, and yet…

I drifted away from Kael and over to the tomb. It was black, almost blending into the night-wrapped cemetery, and barely rose to my chin. I ran my fingers over the cool surface as I inspected it.

There was no plaque or inscription, nothing to indicate who may be inside. I took a step back and scanned the grass, wondering if perhaps there was a plaque on the ground. Then, I caught sight of a small imperfection near the base.

I got down on one knee and pulled away some of the grass to find a small rune on the surface of the tomb and nearly buried in the dirt. Try as I might, I couldn't place the meaning. Perhaps it was a name or something non-specific in the ancient vocabulary.

"Kael." My hushed voice carried to him several feet away. "This is the place."

He loped over and stood beside me. We stared at each other, but apparently we were both at a loss for what to do next. Was Lor inside? I couldn't see how…unless he was dead.

"Maybe I can lift the top off?" Kael suggested.

I crossed my arms, prepared to tell him how unlikely that was, when he braced his hands on the top edge and began to shove. I gasped as he grimaced and groaned, the lid of the tomb scraping. The lid tilted and dropped to the ground. Kael stepped back with a triumphant smile tugging at his lips.

"It wasn't as heavy as it looked," he said.

My teeth clicked as I snapped shut my gaping mouth and peered into the tomb. The inside was walled with rough and weathered stone. It was at that moment I realized the outside was merely a case to hide the true tomb, probably to throw off nosy people like us. A steep and narrow set of stairs led down into pitch black.

"Hello?" My shout was swallowed up by the cold dark.

Kael let out a short chuckle. "Did you honestly think that would work?"

I put my hands on the tomb and gave a little hop, then settled on the edge.

"Bet you would've died if someone actually answered back." Kael laughed at his own joke.

I dropped to the top step. My palm warmed, and I let a trickle of magic come to the surface. Not much, but enough for fuchsia swirls of energy to lick my fingers and light our way.

"Are you sure this is a good idea?" he asked.

"Do you have a better one?" I made room for Kael as he swung into the tomb. He didn't answer me, but peered down into the depths with pinched brows.

"It isn't very wide," he noted.

I followed his line of sight. True, the way was narrow. He'd barely be able to get through without brushing the sides. I shrugged. I'd been in tighter spaces.

"Come on, Shoulders," I said. "You got this."

Kael quirked an eyebrow. "Shoulders?"

I held my hand out in front of me, the light from my magic spilling down the old, gray steps. "Don't act like you don't know you have Herculean shoulders."

"I hadn't realized you admired them so much." His voice was touched with amusement.

I nearly missed a step. "Your shoulders are just good in a fight. That's all. Don't let it get to your head or you really won't be able to fit through here."

He let out a low chuckle behind me, and I turned my attention to keeping my footing on the steep steps.

It had been a while since I'd found myself in a tomb. Though this place was unknown to me, the close press of ancient stone and stale air was familiar.

Excitement pulsed quicker through my veins. *This* was me. This is what I was meant to do, exploring the forgotten places beneath the earth. Being cursed with magic and pursuing a dark mage was just a hiccup.

I hoped.

"How much farther?" Kael grumbled.

"How am I supposed to know?"

There was a long pause as we turned a corner and Kael had to wiggle a bit to get through the curve. He let out an impatient huff. "This is ridiculous. What if we get stuck down here?"

"One time, I was in a tomb in central America, and it collapsed. I was stuck in there for two days with nothing but a canteen, bugs, and a four-thousand-year-old Mayan corpse."

"That doesn't really make me feel better."

Kael's voice was tight, and I turned to study him. His face was taut, there was a sheen of sweat across his forehead, and he kept swallowing.

"You're claustrophobic," I said.

His lips were pulled back, and he was practically snarling at me. "I don't like feeling trapped."

I tried not to take his snarl personally. He was a shifter, the genes of an animal ran through his veins, and animals always showed their teeth when they were frightened.

"What about in Scotland?" I asked. We had gone underground together in those long-hidden ruins.

"We were desperate, and trying to find the other key. This trip, on the other hand, could be either pointless or a suicide mission."

I reached beneath my shirt and grabbed a hold of the key

that looked as if it were carved from bone, the one that had been given to me by the druids in a Scottish mountain. "We're trying to find some warlock. And he might be down here."

"Might," Kael muttered.

But there was something else, too. Something more calling me down here. The farther we went into the cold tomb, the more I grew certain that something ancient waited for us in its depths.

Kael had gone quiet, and I wondered if he was concentrating on not freaking out in the closeness of the tomb. In an attempt to distract him, I kept up a string of chatter about some of my favorite digs I had been on.

"This one time, I was in Mongolia, and it was freezing. I'd wandered off from my team and—" I gasped as a step crumbled beneath my foot.

Kael's arms wrapped around me and kept me from falling fully onto my backside. The movement cost him his footing, however, and the pair of us tilted backward. My partner grunted as I landed on top of him, and we slid a few steps.

"Sorry," I muttered. "Thanks for catching me."

"No problem."

His breath brushed against the nape of my neck. His arms were still wrapped around me, and it was difficult not to think about the way those firm muscles held me close.

I cleared my throat. "Um, can I get up?"

Kael tilted me forward, though his hands lingered on my ribcage as he helped me up. I couldn't bring myself to look over my shoulder at him as he got to his feet. My cheeks were already warm enough. Instead, I surged onward, taking a bit more precautions on the steps below my boots.

It wasn't long after that my boots hit solid ground. The air was cool, and I didn't mind too much when Kael stopped close beside me. He was so close I could feel his warmth, tempting me to close the few inches of distance between us.

I swiveled and peered through the small, square room.

The magic licking my fingers sent light flickering across the walls, picking out pock-marked stone and shining trails of moisture.

"There's a door." Kael pointed to one corner of the room.

The door was wooden, and a gray so weathered it nearly blended in with the stone. Footprints led to the doorway.

Who had disturbed the thick layer of dust on the floor?

I crept across the floor, and Kael's prowling shadow behind me reminded me of the pacing jaguar in my memory.

I stared at the door. Should I knock? What did a warlock do when you trespassed? There was no doorknob, but I reached for the rusted iron handle. I barely gave it a tug when I paused.

This wasn't right. I withdrew my hand.

Something inside of me gave a little tug, and I glanced behind me. My gaze slid around my waiting partner to the back wall.

"What are you doing?" Kael asked as I stepped around him.

I didn't answer him. The closer I got to the wall, the more I was certain I was close to the source of the ancient power I had sensed along the way. Ignoring Kael's impatient sigh, I scanned the wall. My heart leapt as my eyes fell on a small rune.

I lifted my magic-wreathed hand and touched the rune. My breath caught in my throat. As I traced the rune with my fingertip, I could have sworn it had been put there for *me*. A tug jerked on me again, so strong, and almost painful, that I gasped.

Suddenly, the writhing energy around my hand spider-webbed across the wall. I jumped back as the stone began to crumble. Kael grabbed my shoulders in a tight grip, ready to pull me from harm's way. I coughed and waved a hand in front of my face in an attempt to wave away the cloud of dust that had been stirred up by the falling stones.

It grew quiet, and the dust began to settle. I stared in front of me. Through the swirl of motes dancing in the light of my magic, I caught the silhouette of a figure.

"There you are," a voice said. "Do you have any idea how long I've been waiting on you…Olivia Perez?"

CHAPTER 9

I STOOD FROZEN in place as the silhouette sharpened into a man sitting on a low bench. A strange, golden light lit the room, and though it was poor, it was enough for me to make out his features.

His hair was startlingly white, but the face beneath was one of a man no more than twenty years old, at best. His eyes were a brilliant green that reminded me of sunlight through a rich, jungle canopy. The clothes he wore were odd, robes that swirled with patterns of blues and greens. An impatient frown corrupted his face, though his vibrant eyes danced with amusement.

Lor.

I took a step forward, and Kael growled a low warning in my ear. I ignored him and continued farther into the low-ceilinged room. A bundle sat on the warlock's lap, wrapped in aged fabric that seemed to have once been a rich brown, but was now the muted color of drying mud.

A few feet in front of him, I paused and squinted as I ran my gaze over his features. There was something tickling in the back of my mind—a sense of familiarity.

"Do I…do I know you?" The question seemed absurd. I

certainly didn't know any warlocks, that I was aware of, but Lor seemed very familiar.

Lor smiled, and though his face was young, something about the gesture seemed old, and weary. "Once, long ago."

My heart jumped. *I had known him in my past.* An uneasy sensation unfurled in my stomach. If he was as ancient as myself and Vehrin, was this warlock a friend, or foe?

"You were a friend of mine?"

His stare drank me in. "A student."

Student? "I was your teacher?"

The man gave a short nod, his hair shifting over one of his eyes. "Yes, though I fear I was not the talented pupil of magic you had hoped for. Still, I think I managed to do my duty well enough."

I shared a glance with Kael. I had been teaching him magic?

"What do you mean, you've done your duty?" I asked.

Lor's green eyes went vacant; was he seeing something, some memory from the past that Kael and I couldn't see? "When things began to crash around us, and you knew you would lose yourself to stop Vehrin, you gave me this for safekeeping."

He pulled the muted, brown fabric from his lap and dropped it to the floor. My lips parted at what lay beneath. There, stretched across his lap, was a sword.

The blade curved ever so slightly, and the hilt gleamed with a blend of gold and green hues, like the jungle light itself had been forged into it.

"You've been here all this time?" Kael's voice soaked into the stone around us.

Lor turned to peer at him. I still had my eyes on the sword. My fingers itched to grab it.

"I am where I was meant to be," Lor said.

The words snapped my attention from the weapon. "What do you mean?"

"Because the place you need to go, the clue that you need, is in the library." His bone-weary smile lifted a bit more at our silence. "I always did love finding the answers I needed in between the pages of books."

Kael stepped closer to him. "Has Vehrin been here?"

It was easy for me to read between the lines. What Kael really meant was *Did you give Vehrin this same information?*

"No." Lor's gaze flicked over my shoulder. "But his friends are in the other room."

Indeed, at that moment, I could hear a commotion behind us: low voices, muffled footsteps, and what seemed like the noise of boxes being rifled through.

"You had best be going," Lor said. He looked at Kael, then back to me. "Keep your guardian close, as you've always done." He lifted the sword.

I started to reach for it, then paused. "How did Renathe know where to find you?"

A crooked grin lifted one cheek. "Ah, him. He came snooping once. Be sure to ask him about the scar he has for doing so."

"Olivia, we need to go." Kael was looking back toward the other room.

I reached down and took the sword. It was warm to the touch, despite the cold air around us. My fingers wrapped around the green and gold handle, and my hand fit as if it had been molded just for me.

I knew this sword. As I studied the blade, the metal gleaming like quicksilver even in the poor lighting, a name fell from my lips.

"Soulsbane." I could have sworn the sword hummed in my grasp with approval.

Lor's piercing gaze danced. "A slayer of souls, indeed. Just be sure you know which souls to end, and which to let breathe." Another glance behind us. "Best you be going."

The warlock smiled at me one last time. It was a smile of

friendship, though it seemed sad to me, as if he were saying goodbye for good. Then, he began to meld into the shadows behind him, his body shifting and fading, before disappearing altogether. Silence and darkness filled the room.

"Your friends are weird, Livvie."

I quirked my eyebrow as I turned to Kael. "You would know."

He smirked, then jerked his head to the doorway. "Let's go. Not sure who else is down here, but I'd rather not find out if we can avoid it."

I nodded. We left the place where Lor had been waiting, and just as we entered the other room, the door on the other side opened. I caught a glance at what appeared to be simple living quarters: a bed with a torn mattress and an overturned dresser being the only details I could see before a small group of people came out.

The vile and malevolent auras swirling around them gave me no doubt they had been sent to this place by the dark mage.

Kael growled in the almost jaguar way he had and shifted his stance, ready for a fight. My magic purred inside of me, and I grinned, finding myself eager for the confrontation.

With quick steps, the men charged forward. I couldn't get an exact count in the darkness, but I guessed there were maybe three or four. One ran straight at me, a hulking figure with wide shoulders and long arms.

Energy burned through my veins and bloomed across my skin. My magic lit the room and licked up the gleaming sword in my hand, the sword I now turned toward the enemy.

My movements were sure and smooth, not a flick or twitch out of place. It was as if my muscles were tied to the memories of how to use the weapon in my hands. It only took moments before Soulsbane cut a deep line across the man's thigh. I finished the whirling move by sinking my blade into his chest.

As he fell to the floor, I stepped back and turned, seeking another opponent. He came out of nowhere. The only warning I had were his ruby eyes burning in his shadowy face. I let out a sharp yell as he collided into me. My back hit the wall. My bones shook, and I nearly lost my grip on the sword.

"You're coming with me." His breath rolled across my face and brought with it the nauseating stench of sulphur and putrid meat. I couldn't tell if he wanted to bring me to his master, or if the key with my soul tethered to it was tempting him. Either way, I wasn't going to wait to find out.

He was so preoccupied with trying to keep my sword arm from him, he didn't notice my left fist swinging up in a sharp hook until it collided with his jaw. He stumbled, and I swung my sword, magic still crackling up it like it was an extension of me.

His screams turned to gurgles as blood sprayed from his throat. He hit his knees, and his fingers scrabbled at the wound I'd left there. I swallowed burning bile at the sight and stepped away. His drowning screams continued until a gunshot rang out. He fell silent and folded the rest of the way to the floor.

Kael lowered his pistol. The third man lay in a still heap by his feet. My partner had an impatient scowl on his face.

"What?" I snapped.

"You can't let things like that bother you. They're the enemy."

I pulled in a deep breath and let my magic dim a bit, withdrawing from my sword to kiss at my knuckles.

"Well, it was creepy. Who the hell can still scream like that when their throat has been cut out?"

I was playing it off with sarcasm. The truth was, I found it disconcerting just how easily killing them with the sword had been. Kael's gaze dropped to the weapon in my hand, as if he were just now realizing it, as well.

"Livvie—"

"Quiet." I tilted my head, certain I'd heard something.

"I just want to—"

I waved my hand at Kael, and he scowled. "No, *listen*."

The noise in the darkness was subtle, like a pebble being dropped to the floor. Then, I heard it again, and again. The walls groaned around us, and dust drifted from the ceiling above. A rock the size of a softball fell loose from the wall, and dirt spilled onto the floor. My breath caught in my throat.

The tomb was going to collapse.

Kael darted over and grabbed my arm. He urged me toward the steps that would lead us up to safety. I shook my head and whirled behind him.

"You go first," I said.

He started to argue, and I gave him a hard shove.

"You'll have more trouble," I said. "If the walls start closing in behind us, you'll never get through."

He looked over his shoulder at me. "But what if—"

"Just shut up, and move!" I gave him another hard shove, hard enough that he stumbled up the first couple of steps.

He snarled. "You're impossible."

Still, he started to make his way up the steps.

I stayed close behind him and used the light from my magic to help light our way. Dust continued to fall as the ceiling and narrow walls shook and groaned. I blink my eyes against the debris as it rained down around us.

Kael's breathing quickened. He didn't like tight spaces. This had to be a nightmare for him, being trapped in a collapsing tomb.

"You got this," I said. My shoulder scraped roughly against the wall as it hugged us closer. "You can get us out."

He didn't say anything as he surged forward. I gasped as the steps underfoot began to give. Kael reached back and grabbed my arm in a tight grip.

Had it taken this long to get down here? I couldn't remember. The steps seemed to go up and up with no end.

Perhaps Lor had been working with Vehrin after all, and his words were just some nefarious joke.

Rock from the ceiling fell. Kael pushed himself harder, and I stumbled after him. Something hit our clasped hands and nearly broke our grip, but he held fast and didn't let go. My muscles burned, and my skin stung where it had been scraped by the walls.

We weren't going to make it.

I'd finally managed to find myself in a tomb I wouldn't get out of.

Fresh air teased me from the distance as the walls and ceiling groaned louder, their final push to bring us to an early grave.

Then, I was in the open, and Kael was pulling me up and over the edge of the tomb. We both stumbled back as it collapsed in on itself, leaving nothing but a pile of cracked and broken black marble.

The pair of us stood, bruised and breathing heavily, and stared at what had nearly been our demise.

"That," Kael said. He swallowed. "That is why I don't like tight spaces."

I tried to come up with a witty remark, if only to ease the tension, but I couldn't find the breath for it. He squeezed my hand, still held tight in his, as if to tell me he understood.

I turned away from the tomb, and inspected my sword. Thankfully, it hadn't been damaged.

"I don't know why, but it suits you."

I glanced at Kael. He was studying the sword with approval.

I shrugged. "Yeah, but now what? I can't go walking around Chicago carrying something like this."

If only I could hide it somehow.

In the next moment, Soulsbane *disappeared*. Instead, a braided bracelet hugged my wrist, the same green and gold color of the sword. My pulse quickened, and I thought about drawing the sword out, as if from an invisible sheath. It appeared in my hand again, as solid and real as it had been a moment before. I gasped as I let it swirl back into a bracelet again.

"Well, that is extraordinarily convenient," I said, twisting my arm and studying the bracelet.

Kael just shook his head as if he could expect nothing less from me. I was already a reborn ancient entity with my soul tied to a cursed key and the ability to conjure supernatural powers. What was a magical sword compared to that?

"Now what?" Kael asked.

I raised up on my toes and reached for his head. I wiggled my fingers through his hair, shaking dust loose. Then, I smiled.

"Now, we go to the library."

CHAPTER 10

I PEERED at the brick building smashed between a law office and what used to be a suite of offices for some sort of business, but now had a faded "For Sale" sign on the door.

It certainly wasn't the fanciest library I had seen. I almost felt bad for the poor thing. It looked decrepit and forgotten, the only sign of life being the sign on the front that told us it wouldn't be open until nine the following morning.

We walked up the steps, and Kael gave a jerk on the door handle. Locked. He shrugged. "Maybe there is a door in the back that isn't locked?"

It wasn't likely, but it was worth a try. We had to round the law office before we discovered a narrow, trash-littered alley running along the back side of the buildings. I wrinkled my nose at the stench of garbage coming from a nearby dumpster. It seemed an unusual place to find a clue. Where were the guards, or anyone looking after such knowledge?

We reached the back of the library, and Kael tensed in front of me.

"What's the matter?"

As an answer, he toed a piece of jagged glass on the ground with his boot, then pointed. I followed his gesture to find a broken window. My breath caught. Someone had already broken in.

Were we too late to find the clue that would lead us to the third key? I hurried forward.

Kael grabbed my jacket and hauled me back a step. "Wait a minute. What are you doing?"

My brows pinched in annoyance. "What does it look like? I'm going in."

"Listen, I can appreciate your whole charge in like a chivalrous warrior type of thing, but maybe you should let the agent who is actually trained in these situations go first?"

I let out a sharp sigh. He was right, I supposed. I held my hands up. "Fine. Do your thing, Agent Rivera."

He smirked at me, and I realized it was the first time I'd ever called him by his proper title. It did sound good rolling off the tongue, even if I had done it in mocking.

Kael walked to the window. Bits of broken glass still stuck up along the edges like sharp teeth.

"Hand me that," he said, pointing at a brick that had come loose from the building.

I handed it to him, and he knocked the glass away so we wouldn't get cut to ribbons climbing through the window. He hauled himself through, and then pulled me up.

Glass cracked and crunched as we stepped inside. Immediately, the scent of aged paper hit me, along with the smell of wooden shelves. There was even a slight scent of lemon, as if someone had cleaned in the past day or so. Decrepit library, or not, someone was attempting to keep it going.

I glanced around at the shelves spilling with books. It reminded me of my study, and I felt a tinge of homesickness. I shook it off and told myself I would get back there someday.

The pair of us headed cautiously toward a soft yellow light down a hall. Kael's nostrils flared as he attempted to pick up any scents that would be out of place. He grimaced and rubbed at his nose as we drew closer to the light.

"What is it?" I asked.

"Nothing."

Clearly, it was something, but he wasn't going to tell me. I rolled my eyes, but didn't press the issue. As we reached the light, we found it was a desk lamp on a spindly table. A few books had fallen to the floor nearby. Kael walked over and started to pick them up carefully. He eyed the titles, then scanned the shelves. He started putting them back in their proper place.

"What are you doing?" Now really wasn't the time for Kael to be playing librarian.

He carefully stuck a thick volume beside its brethren. "Books don't deserve to be on the floor."

I laughed. "Kael, I didn't know you were such a nerd." He shook his head, and I suddenly found him more endearing. I had no idea the warrior shifter who had been my companion for a while had such a fondness for books. "You know, I think I like you more now."

Kael gave me a glance that I couldn't read, then cleared his throat and shuffled by. If I didn't know any better, I'd say he was embarrassed. I followed after him, grinning like a cat.

We headed down the narrow aisle in between row after row of shelves in search of clues. I told him we should split up, and he agreed after some persuasion. After all, we couldn't spend all night in this place. Kael headed off to the right, and I turned left.

As I walked among the shelves, I kept a lookout for runes that may help lead me to where I needed to go, but I found none. Then, in the heavy silence of the dark library, I heard a scuffle. Kael was on the opposite end, so I knew he hadn't made the noise. With quiet steps, I made my way toward the source.

I passed a few more rows of shelves, then found more

books spilled onto the floor. Not wanting to be outshone by Kael, I bent down to replace them on the shelves, then paused. On the floor was a few drops of something dark red.

Blood.

Slowly, I straightened. There was more blood, and I followed the trail. It led to a desk beneath a window. A combination of moonlight and a flickering streetlight shone through the window. Old newspapers were scattered over the desk and onto the floor. The papers were in shreds and much of it was soaked in blood.

As I edged closer, my wide gaze fell on a being the likes of which I had never seen.

The dull eyes were large, almost insectile on the face of what belonged to a female of whatever sort of species she was. Her skin was a pale yellow-brown that reminded me of old parchment. Her hair, a silky black like ink, was in tangled disarray around her.

I drew in a shuddering breath and touched her shoulder. I could feel the coldness of her skin, even through the fabric of her garment.

"Kael." I didn't yell his name, but I knew his keen shifter ears would hear me. He was beside me in a matter of seconds.

"She's a type of lesser faerie," he explained. He crouched beside me to examine her. "Her kind are drawn to knowledge and books. She likely frequented this place at night to avoid detection from humans."

I frowned at her with pity. If only we had been here sooner.

Kael got to his feet. "Whoever did this was obviously looking for something." His sharp eyes narrowed. "No doubt they are still here, unless they already found what they were looking for."

I let Kael keep an eye out while I carefully filtered through the newspapers. I winced every time I touched a piece that was damp with blood, and swallowed the bile burning in my throat. It wasn't the first time I had been around the dead body of an innocent, but my encounters were never so…fresh.

A crumpled piece of paper shoved under the desk caught my eye. It was crammed between the leg and a small trash can. If I hadn't been angled just right, I would have missed it. I grabbed it and did my best to smooth it out without tearing it. My heart rate accelerated.

"Kael, I think I found something."

I walked to his shoulder and showed him the newspaper article. There was no date, but by the yellow of the paper, I knew it wasn't recent.

"A rare artifact was donated today by Alastor Glenhaven to the…" I trailed, trying to read the location, but it was darkened with blood. I let out a frustrated huff and continued. "The piece will be examined and then put on public display within the next few weeks."

It went on to talk about the importance of such artifacts in the preservation of history.

"I know that man," Kael said. "He's a fae."

I twisted my bag around my shoulder and started digging through my bag. "I'll call Ren. Maybe he knows where we can find him."

Kael grabbed my wrist. "No need. I know where he is."

"How?"

"Alastor Glenhaven is a collector of both rare and dangerous magical objects, so PITO keeps a close eye on him. We can drop in for a visit." Kael tapped the paper in my hands. "If this is what we are searching for, and I have a feeling it is, he can tell us where he donated it."

"Great," I said. "Let's get out of this place before—"

My words were cut short as the bookshelves around us shuddered. Books toppled to the floor, and an uneasy sensation unfurled in my stomach.

"I thought I smelled something when we arrived," Kael

said through clenched teeth. His grimace deepened as three figures came into view.

Even in the poor light, I could see the pitch-black eyes in their faces. They had been sent by the mage. I could sense it in the malevolent power swirling around them. My gaze dropped to the one in the front. He had blood on his hands, blood I knew belonged to the poor, dead faerie behind me who had only come to the library to read. My brow furrowed, and I joined Kael in a snarl at the newcomers.

The aisle was too narrow to fight with my new sword, so I called forth my magic. I let it burn the torn and stained article in my hands, then smiled with satisfaction. That was one secret no one else would learn. The ashes drifted to the floor, and as the man in front watched their fall, I charged forward.

The concept of mercy fell from my being, and I didn't hesitate. I loosed a powerful surge of energy forward. I missed the man in front as he dodged quickly to the side, but I managed to hit one of his comrades square in the chest. He screamed, and tore at his clothes as my magic ravaged over his body.

The smell of burning skin made me gag. I tried to breathe through my mouth to help with the assault, but I could almost taste the mage's soldier as he thrashed to the floor. My magic quickly consumed him, leaving little more than a pile of charred bones.

The third man took one look at what I had done, and fled. Kael surged after him. I locked my eyes on the man I assumed was leading this attack. He ran toward me, and as my magic licked my fingers, I heard the angry snarling of Kael's jaguar form a little way down.

I wasn't expecting the man to have his own magic.

A twisting darkness shot from his hand like a serpent and wrapped around my legs. My feet were jerked out from under me and my back hit the floor. I grunted and kicked my feet, but couldn't break the hold.

With gritted teeth, I hurled my magic at the writhing blackness cutting the circulation from my knees down. It sent up hissing sparks, and I could sense the wrongness in the black magic as my own tried to break through it.

The man laughed at my struggle, and something about the grating sound strengthened me. Who did he think he was? I had fought against Vehrin himself. I was powerful and strong. I was deadly.

I gave him a fierce grin as I unleashed the dark, tainted part within me. That power rejoiced at being set free, and the hold he had on me evaporated. I jumped lithely to my feet. Suddenly, the man before me seemed hardly more than a pesky fly, one that would be easy to squash into oblivion.

His eyes grew round, surprised by my sudden confidence as I strode toward him. He was little more than a blur: there one second, and gone the next. Some sort of power given to him by Vehrin, no doubt.

Anger seethed through me. The dark shade of magic inside me begged for more freedom, yearned to set flesh ablaze to every person near.

We need to kill them, before they kill us, it whispered to me. *We have to be strong, we have to be powerful.*

A warm touch landed on my cheeks, and I blinked. Kael was standing before me, somehow already in his clothes again.

"Breathe," he ordered. "Control it. You are not that kind of magic. Fight it."

I did as he said. I fought it, and though it was a struggle, I bottled it back up. I let out a shaky breath.

"He got away," I said.

Kael shook his head. "Doesn't matter. Are you all right?"

"Yes, I think so."

Kael still hadn't let go of my face. I lifted my hands to his, and suddenly found I didn't want him to pull away. His touch was comforting. I didn't want it to end.

"Livvie." The sound of my name on his lips was soft, and

his deep voice brought an unexpected tremor through me. He was much closer than I'd realized.

Kael was beginning to get to me in a way that made me feel safe. Comforted. And I wasn't sure if I should feel that way.

I couldn't let my guard down. Feeling safe with Kael could get me killed.

I stepped away. "Let's go find this hoarding fae of yours."

I tried to ignore the hurt that flickered over Kael's face as I brushed past him.

CHAPTER 11

I HAD TO ADMIT, after surviving an avalanche, enduring a long flight, taking a romp through a cemetery, and getting into a fight at a library, I was utterly exhausted.

I sat on the bed in our hotel room and toweled my freshly washed hair. The news was on, but I was only halfway watching it. My mind was wandering uneasily toward what we would find at Alastor Glenhaven's place.

Please don't let this fae be dead and the relic stolen.

I had wanted to go there straight away, but Kael insisted we wait until morning. The man wouldn't open his gates to us at night, and besides, we had needed the rest. I'd been so tired, I hadn't put up much of an argument.

The bathroom door squeaked, and I turned to find Kael exiting in a billow of steam. All he had on was a towel tucked tightly around his bottom half. His hair still dripped, and sent beads of water rolling down his sculpted chest.

I swallowed, then berated myself. It wasn't as if I hadn't seen him naked numerous times, and this certainly wouldn't be the last. I gazed back at the T.V. and told myself it wasn't just for a distraction.

Kael rifled through his bag for some clothes, and I

reached for the remote, then froze. A story came up that had me scooting to the edge of the bed. I turned up the volume.

"...and her team have been on an archeological dig in this remote part of India." The news reporter pointed to a highlighted section of a map. "Yesterday, the team emerged with a brand new relic, the likes of which has not been seen before."

A photo popped up of a disc the color of coffee grounds, but runes were etched in the surface in stark white. I squinted to try to decipher them, but then they flipped to an image of my team.

Sarah, who was apparently the head of the expedition, had her arms around my other colleagues and was grinning widely. The report continued to say the relic would be taken back to the university for examination to further attempt to uncover its history.

A mixture of jealousy and excitement for my friends hit me, but also a confusing sense of dread. I didn't know why I felt them finding that disc was bad news, but I couldn't shake it. Perhaps I should call Sarah and warn her.

I shook my head, wet strands of hair falling into my face. I pushed them back behind my ear impatiently. I was being silly. Not every hidden and long forgotten item in this earth was magical. If I kept this up, I'd start looking at things like toasters and umbrellas with scrutiny.

"Is something bothering you?" Kael asked.

The man was wearing nothing but a pair of boxer briefs that left nothing to the imagination. It was an effort to lift my gaze to his face.

"I'm not sure," I said honestly. "It's probably nothing."

Kael stepped closer, and I wished he wouldn't because he was distracting my already frenzied thoughts. "Livvie, if there is something bothering you, tell me."

There was a sudden knock on the door. "That would be

our pizza." I hopped off the bed and hurried past Kael. "Put some pants on," I hissed at him.

My partner grinned as if he knew it had been bothering me. I scowled and opened the door a bit more roughly than I'd meant. The teenager on the other side looked startled to find an angry woman scowling at him.

I cleared my throat and smoothed my features. "Sorry," I said. My stomach growled at the scents of sauce, cheese, and Italian seasonings wafted to me. I handed him a wad of cash. "Keep the change."

The youth hurried off, and I shut the door.

"Finally," Kael said. "I'm starving."

Despite his smirk, he had put on a pair of lounge-type pants, similar to the ones I was wearing, loose and plaid.

I sat on the bed as he reached for the box on the top. I smacked his hand. "Ladies first."

We didn't have plates, so we sat there trying not to drip sauce on the coverlet while moaning about the deliciousness of the pizza. I'd only managed to get down four slices, but Kael didn't put the boxes on the nearby table until he'd eaten eight.

A large yawn cracked my jaw, and I peered longingly at the pillow behind me.

"We'd better get a couple hours of sleep while we can. We'll head out to Alastor's place in a few hours."

Kael stood and grabbed the other pillow from the bed, then headed toward a chair settled in the corner by the window.

"You know you won't get any rest if you try to sleep in a chair," I said.

"I'm not going to make you sleep in the chair."

I laughed. "I meant, you can share the bed with me."

It wasn't as if it were the first time we'd slept beside each other. The memory of me sleeping in his arms on a chilly night in the Scottish highlands came to mind.

Kael didn't move from where he stood by the chair. "You don't mind?"

"Why would I?" Of course, my tired voice chose *that* exact moment to break. I hurried to shimmy under the cover.

The shifter climbed in next to me. I kicked my feet to dislodge the sheet and blanket where it was tucked in tightly under the edge of the mattress.

"Why are you abusing the bed?"

"Just because I unearth mummies doesn't mean I want to sleep like one," I said.

Kael chuckled. "Goodnight, Livvie."

"Goodnight, Kael." I rolled over, and tried my best to ignore the man mere inches from me.

Kael may be a jaguar shifter, but he snored like a grizzly bear in the midst of hibernation. I contemplated smothering him with my pillow for what was probably an unhealthy amount of time before I resigned myself to not being able to sleep. Instead, I let my mind wander to thoughts of magic and mages.

My partner made a particularly loud snort, mumbled something incoherent, and then rolled over. I stilled as he draped his arm over me. His hot breath brushed evenly across the back of my neck. I thought about telling him off, but despite not wanting to get involved with him, especially while the mage was still running around, I couldn't help but enjoy the feel of his embrace.

Suddenly, the alarm on the table next to me blared. I closed my eyes and pretended to be asleep. Kael jerked awake and hurriedly leaned over me to turn off the alarm. He stayed in that position, hovering over me, for what seemed to be an eternity.

Why wasn't he moving? What was he looking at?

My heartbeat picked up pace, and I really hoped he couldn't hear it. Finally, he eased back and shook my shoulder.

I blinked my eyes and did my best to look momentarily confused.

"Huh?"

He smiled at me. "Time to get up and get going."

I made a play of groaning about how it felt as if I'd just fallen asleep and stretching my arms above my head.

"Why are you pretending you were sleeping?" he asked as he changed his pants.

"What?"

He straightened and pulled on a shift. "Come on, Livvie. I know you were awake."

I frowned and shook my head. "I was dead asleep," I lied. "Right in the middle of a dream."

"Huh," he said, clearly not buying it. He threw me a change of clothes. "Must have been having quite a dream then. Your heart was going crazy."

"Really?" I said. I shuffled out of the covers and was thankful I was facing away from him. "I don't remember."

Before I headed to the bathroom to change, I glanced at Kael. He was watching me with a knowing sparkle in his eyes. Not wanting to know what *he* knew, I hurried inside the bathroom.

Once I was dressed and ready to go, we took a rental car to the outskirts of the city. Thankfully, the traffic was light and it didn't take us long, especially with Kael's crazy, frightening driving.

When we pulled up to a manor that looked like it should belong to some celebrity in Hollywood, my mouth dropped open. A massive, iron gate barred our way. Kael rolled down his window, jabbed his finger into a call button on a box, and waited.

"What is it?" a voice answered.

"My name is Kael Rivera. I'm with PITO and would like to ask you a few questions."

There was a pause. "I am not due for an inspection for quite some time."

"This is not an inspection. We are on a very time-sensitive mission. However, if you would like, I'd be happy to make a call to headquarters and ask if an impromptu inspection is in order."

Wow. Kael wasn't pulling any punches. Straight to the threat.

"Fine. But be quick about it. I have appointments to keep."

The gates swung open, and we drove inside. We rounded a massive fountain, though no water flowed at this time of year. We exited the car, I hunched my shoulders against the stiff breeze, and the pair of us strode between the columns lining the front and to the large doors. Before Kael could raise his hand to knock, the door eased open.

A pair of gorgeous green eyes peered down at us, eyes that I knew were often filled with curiosity and wonder. Where Renathe seemed to have been born in a fancy suit, this man wore casual clothes, loose khaki pants, and an untucked shirt. He certainly didn't look as if he belonged to this manor.

"Are you Alastor Glenhaven?" I asked.

He narrowed his eyes. "Who are you?"

I stuck my hand out. "Olivia Perez. I found an article about you in a library and was wondering if I may ask you about it?"

He opened the door wider to let us in. Once inside, I could see why he would need a home so large. Antiquities, relics, maps, and trinkets covered nearly every surface. Some were similar to many of the items I had found on digs, but others, like a strange-looking object that was a cube but seemed to glow red when I was staring straight at it, were obviously magical in some way.

"Well, sit down." Alastor waved impatiently at a few chairs

not far off the entryway. He sat, too, and crossed his arms over his chest. "So, what article are you referring to?"

"The one where you donated an item, a sort of artifact, somewhere."

The fae let out a short laugh. "Girl, I have donated hundreds of items to many different places."

"This one is rare," Kael said. "And likely dangerous."

"Again, I have donated many such items."

I was closest to Alastor, and I reached into the front of my shirt and tugged out the pair of keys. His emerald eyes grew round.

"The relic would be similar to these," I said.

He leaned forward. "Where did you get those?"

Behind me, Kael let out a vicious snarl of warning. The fae withdrew his hand.

"Forgive me, I just hadn't heard more had been discovered."

"They have, and it's quite the tale, but I'm afraid we are short on time. If you would like to hear more, I suggest you seek out a fae named Renathe."

The man nodded slowly, clearly interested, but not quite willing to press the issue. "If you want the relic, you will need to break into a museum."

Break into a museum?

"I'm not a thief," I said.

He shrugged. "If you truly want it, then you will. However, I must warn you, it is heavily guarded by the supernatural. It may look like a tourist attraction for humans by day, but in reality, it holds some of the world's most deadly magical objects. That is why I donated the key in the first place. I knew there it would be better protected."

I looked to Kael. "Could you ask your superiors for permission to take the item?"

Kael frowned. "I think the less people who know about things from here on out, the better."

"Fine. Thievery, it is." I turned back to Alastor. "Where exactly is this museum?"

His green eyes danced, as if he knew the answer to some joke we were missing.

My breath whooshed out of me in surprise when he told us, and suddenly, the third key seemed like it would be impossible to steal.

We would be heading to Paris, to break into the Louvre.

CHAPTER 12

I TOOK a bite of the warm pastry and moaned as it practically melted in my mouth. I couldn't remember the name of the delicacy—Kael had handed me a paper sack of them—but I would definitely be getting more.

I sat on the bench and continued to nibble while I turned a glare toward a flock of pigeons that wanted to partake in my breakfast, as well. In a flurry of gray and white feathers, the birds took off as the jaguar shifter strode through them.

Kael held up a pair of tickets. "Let's do this thing."

I stuffed the last pastry into my mouth and gave him a thumbs up before throwing the sack into a nearby trash can. I adjusted the slouchy, beanie-style hat on my head before hurrying to catch up to Kael.

We had opted for new clothing that would blend in more with the local tourists. Leggings weren't really my thing, but I had to admit, the light gray fabric looked great with the cute, black boots I'd splurged on.

Kael, though he always did look casual, had stepped it up with simple jeans and a sweater. I'd tried to get him to buy one with the Eiffel tower stitched on the front, but he'd adamantly refused.

My lips twitched into a grin as we neared the massive metal and glass pyramid standing in front of the Louvre. Behind the pyramid, three huge wings made up the building which had once been a castle before being converted into the most famous museum in the world.

After waiting in line for what felt like ages, I was practically bouncing on the toes of my new boots as we showed the woman at the entrance our tickets. Visiting this place had been near the top of my bucket-list since the moment my father had shown pictures of him and my mother here years ago. I had always been so busy skipping around other places of the world on digs, I'd never gotten the chance.

Kael tugged on the collar of his mocha-colored sweater with a sour expression.

"I told you that one looked itchy," I said.

He frowned. "You also told me it brings out the color of my eyes."

"It does." I grinned. "I'm glad to know you take my opinion so seriously. Who would have known you were the type to suffer for vanity?"

Kael growled under his breath and peered around. "I always thought this place was an art museum."

"It is," I said. "For the most part. It has works like the Mona Lisa and The Coronation of Napoleon. Many historians consider certain discovered artifacts to be art, like jewelry, engraved pottery—" I gave him a smile. "—and, of course, keys."

"Right," he said. "So where do we start?"

I jerked my head toward a kiosk with pamphlets, fliers, and maps. I found a map that had labels and directions in English, took two, and handed one to Kael.

The man behind the desk informed us the museum offered guided tours, if we wished, but I gave him a smile and explained getting lost was half the fun. He merely smiled and nodded, then he turned to a family with a pair of unenthusiastic teens in tow.

We moved to a corner out of the way, and Kael took a pen from his pocket. I caught his golden eyes glancing around the room. Then he began putting little dots on the map.

It was easy to figure out what he was marking…guard placements. I took my turn studying the map in my hands and tried to sort out the best place to search for the key. There were three main wings in the Louvre, and while the archeologist and historian in me wanted to peruse every inch of the place, we wouldn't have time.

When we had left Alastor's place, we'd given him a warning about the dark mage. We hadn't heard any bad news, but that didn't mean the mage hadn't gotten to him. It could be only a matter of time before Vehrin learned the same information we had that led us here.

"Well," Kael said. "Do you have any ideas on where to start?"

I pursed my lips as I studied the map. "This is the Denon wing," I said, pointing to the wing behind us. "I think we can dismiss this one. It mostly houses Italian Renaissance paintings and other pieces from that point in history. I feel like the keys, so far, have been more ancient. We should focus mainly on the Sully wing, which houses the Egyptian relics and pieces from Middle-Eastern culture, and perhaps the Richelieu wing, home to artifacts from the middle-ages."

Kael waved a hand forward. "All right, professor. Lead the way."

"Professor?" I scoffed. "Hardly. My dad was, but being trapped behind a desk isn't my thing."

"Clearly. If it was, your life would be decidedly less exciting."

"That's the truth," I muttered.

I soaked in the wonder around me as we strolled toward the Sully wing. Paintings and sculptures were everywhere, most of them hundreds of years old, and pieces I'd never dreamed of seeing with my own eyes.

The pair of us walked around for a while, and even though we were on a mission, I couldn't help but stop to soak in some of the items on display. A few times, Kael had to tug on my arm and tell me we'd never get through this place if I stopped to gawk at every little thing.

The next room we entered was dedicated to Near-Eastern antiquities. Kael drifted off to one side of the room while I headed toward the right. Sculptures and other large items lined the walls, with glass cases placed here and there around the center of the room.

I had yet to see anything that seemed like it was dangerous or magical, but I suspected I wouldn't be able to tell, anyway. After all, I hadn't known the key I'd plucked from the Amazon was cursed until later. I could have walked right past some powerful artifact and never known. It was an exciting concept, and I told myself I would return one day when I wasn't on the hunt to save a relic and stop a dark mage.

I ran my finger along the red rope stretched in front of a figure of an ancient Hittite god, the small statue burnished to a warm bronze, when a nearby glass case caught my eye. I sauntered over to it. Inside was a collection of beaded necklaces, bracelets decorated with small gems, and there, nestled on a white pillow, was a key.

It was dark in color, and I couldn't guess without touching it what it could possibly be made of, but it matched the description Alastor had given us. My heart raced with excitement as I pulled my phone from my pocket and snapped a picture of the key.

The single guard in the room turned my way as I lowered my phone, but his eyes didn't linger. Many of the visitors took photos on their tours through the Louvre, so it wasn't as if I'd done anything unusual.

Kael was still meandering on the other side of the room.

He glanced my way, and I smiled brightly. He raised an eyebrow in question, and I gave him a little nod, trying to tell him in the small gesture that I had found what we were looking for.

For some reason, I could sense the guard's gaze on me again. I didn't dare turn to peer at him to be sure, but I was certain he was watching me. Was he one of the supernatural beings set to guard the magical artifacts held in the Louvre?

I continued toward Kael and wondered if the man could sense the magic in *me*. Or maybe he could sense there was a shifter in his midst? Perhaps the guard was a shifter himself.

I reached Kael and twined my fingers through his. He gave me a strange look, but didn't withdraw his hand.

"I'm hungry," I said. "Maybe we can go out and get a bite to eat." I squeezed his hand.

"Sure." He tugged me out of the room. I half-expected the guard to follow, but thankfully, he remained at his post. Perhaps I had thrown off the suspicions I was certain were there.

We headed out to the Tuileries Gardens, an expansive garden that bordered the back side of the Louvre. I imagined it was usually splashed with more color, but at this time of year, only the evergreen shrubs were vibrant.

Kael chugged a bottle of water like it was his last, but I was too excited to do more than merely sip on mine. I pulled out my phone and showed Kael the photo.

"Here. This has to be it. It matches the description Alastor gave us." I stared at the Louvre, and while I admired the architecture consisting of arched windows and the intricate figures carved along its face, I also thought it looked impossible to infiltrate. "How are we going to get in?"

"From what I have seen, the guards run on a steady schedule of rotation. I saw two such shift changes. The first time there was a twenty-second window of time when a guard wasn't at his post, and the second was thirty."

I set the bottle of water beside me on the bench. "That isn't much time."

"No, it isn't, but it's the best we have. We can make it work."

"There was a guard in the room with the key. He was watching me closely."

Kael nodded. "I noticed. It was likely out of curiosity. Shifters are perfectly free to live just as humans do, visiting museums and monuments, but we tend not to do so frequently. He smelled like some sort of cat shifter, a panther, maybe." He frowned. "Still, we need to be cautious. Blend in the best we can. Shifters are suspicious by nature. Even if he was merely curious about us, I doubt he would forget our presence quickly if something seemed at all unusual."

As if to prove his point, a guard strolled by on the path before us. Kael stretched his arms out, then settled one around me. I didn't have to pretend too hard to lean into his side with a sigh.

The guard gave us a nod as he continued on his way. Kael didn't remove his arm. Was it in an effort to blend in, or did he really just want to have his arm around me?

"So, back to the issue at hand," I said. "How are we going to get in?"

"I think our best option would be to hide out here." He waved lazily around the expansive garden.

I laughed. "What do you want us to do, squat in some shrubbery?"

Kael shrugged. "Do you have a better idea?"

"I suppose not. Still, just because we'll be on the grounds doesn't mean we would be able to get into the building."

With a smirk, Kael pulled a guard's ID badge out of his pocket. "This acts as a key card."

My mouth popped open. "How did you get that?"

When had he gotten it?

"Jaguar shifters can easily go unnoticed."

I knew jaguars were able to ghost unseen in the Amazon, but it amazed me, given Kael's size, that he was capable of being just as stealthy in the real world as well.

"Perhaps I should keep a closer eye on my wallet," I mumbled.

Kael chuckled, then stood and pulled me up off the bench.

"Let's go back to the hotel, finalize our plans, and get some rest."

Great. I was embarking on a mission of theft from what was likely one of the most protected places in the world. This was, of course, after being on the run after it had appeared we'd murdered the witch sisters in Scotland the last time we were pursuing the mage. I supposed next it would be grand theft auto in Italy.

I shifted my bag onto my shoulder as we headed toward the open gates. "So, planning, rest, and then…?"

"We come back later this evening before they close, hide, and hope we don't get caught."

CHAPTER 13

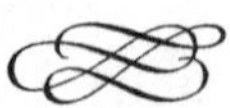

I GRUMBLED as I crawled out from underneath the evergreen. This was absolutely ridiculous. I crouched beside the shrub and picked bits of twig and needles from my hair as I waited for Kael. A moment later, he came strolling up as if hiding in fancy gardens were a regular occurrence for him.

"Something wrong?" he asked.

I straightened to my feet and moaned as my back protested. "Oh, no, not at all. This was so fun I think I may pick up this *hide-and-seek: danger version* as a new hobby." I glared at him as he let out a quiet chuckle. "What are you doing just waltzing around? I thought we were supposed to be stealthy?"

"I was only several feet away," he said. He pointed at a large, cone-shaped tree.

"Well, yours looks roomier. How come I got stuck hiding in this thing?" I kicked lightly at the juniper beside me.

Kael shook his head. "Do you honestly want to argue about this or shall we get going?"

I tilted my chin in the air and started toward the museum. Kael's hand landed on my shoulder, and he pulled me to a halt.

"Hang on a second. I have better eyesight in the dark. I'm going first."

I didn't like being bossed around, but I couldn't really argue with his logic. As a jaguar shifter, his eyesight was better than mine. He would be able to keep a better lookout on the guards.

The pair of us stayed away from the walkways and instead ghosted across the manicured lawns, letting the grass cushion our steps.

"Isn't there likely cameras?" I squinted through the darkness toward the building, but if there were, I couldn't see them from where we were.

"Probably, but we have to take the chance they aren't keeping a close enough eye on it. It's not like there's a perfect way to sneak in. Besides, seriously, who would try to break into the Louvre?"

I rolled my eyes. "Um, us?"

This was certainly shaky ground we were traversing, but Kael was right: we didn't have much of a choice. Getting caught was a risk we had to take in order to get the key before Vehrin did. Together, we slipped from shrub to shrub, or ducked behind statues and fountains.

At one point, I managed to catch the muffled footsteps of a security guard just before we rounded a corner. I clutched the back of Kael's shirt and tugged. We hid, and I held my breath as the guard walked by. Kael's breathing also went silent until the guard had passed.

Walking across the garden seemed to take an hour, instead of mere minutes, and I let out a sigh of relief when we finally neared the door which would lead us straight into the Sully wing of the museum. We crouched as the guard outside the door glanced at his watch and then left.

"We'll have twenty to thirty seconds," Kael whispered. When the guard walked away, he touched my hand. "Now."

My heart nearly jumped in my throat as Kael took off

toward the door. The guard was still in sight. All he had to do was glance back and he would see us.

I ran as quietly as I could and shouldered up to Kael without incident.

The shifter took the key card from his pocket, placed it at the top of the slot near the door handle, and slid it down. A glaring, red light of denial burned in the dark.

It hadn't worked.

The other guard would be at his post any second. If we tried to back out now, we'd be caught for sure. We only had maybe ten seconds now to get in the door.

The sound of footsteps reached me. We were nearly out of time.

"Try again," I said.

Kael slid the card into the slot once more, and a quiet click sounded. I wanted to cry in relief as he turned the handle and pushed the door open. I eased the door shut behind me, and we waited. On the other side of the door, we heard the guard walk up. Then, silence.

I smiled at Kael. "We did it," I said quietly. "I don't think he saw us."

"Good." My partner started toward the stretch of hall that would lead us to the Middle-eastern antiquities room, and the third key.

We hadn't gone a dozen steps when an alarm started blaring. I covered my ears and turned to Kael with wide eyes. He stood rooted to his spot for a heartbeat, then swore, grabbed my hand, and started running.

"How did they know? I could have sworn we weren't seen."

"This place is guarded," Kael said. We paused beside a water fountain.

"Yeah, no kidding. We saw the guards, remember?"

"Not just those kinds of guards. I think there's—" The

braying sound of dogs suddenly fractured the quiet of the sleeping museum. Kael grimaced. "Hell hounds."

I blinked. "Excuse me? Hellhounds? Did you just say hell hounds?"

The dogs were getting closer by the sound of their frenzied howling.

"Yes." Kael had his hand on mine again and was practically dragging me. "Don't let them bite you. You'll burn to death."

"Well, they sound like delightful pets. Why would they have something like that here? Aren't hell hounds, you know, evil or something?"

"They guard the demon realms and keep demons from getting out. Also, apparently, they are being put to use in other ways."

I raised my hand not being crushed in his grip. "We can beat fire with fire."

"*No*. Don't use your magic in here. We don't know what kind of cursed or magical objects this place holds, but there could be something that would feed off your power, amplify it, or even steal it completely. It's too risky."

Great. Now what was I supposed to do? "Kael…"

Toenails clacking on the shining floor caught my attention. I turned and found myself facing a pack of hellhounds. I hadn't spent much time in my life wondering what hellhounds looked like, not believing in such things, but if I had, I would have said they were black beasts built like Rottweilers with red eyes and jaws dripping with smoke and flame.

I was way off.

These hounds were tall, and their wiry gray fur almost reminded me of an Irish wolfhound. Their eyes weren't red, but the piercing silver of starlight. Instead of fiery wrath, these hellhounds seemed all cold fury. Even their teeth gleamed like shards of ice as they growled at us.

Kael was already shucking off his clothes. "Use your

sword," he said. "The less people know you have magic, the better."

Without another word, he twisted and shifted into his jaguar form.

I pulled in a quick breath and imagined the sword in my hand, the feel of the handle in my grasp. The bracelet tingled on my wrist, and then I was holding the weapon. I shifted my feet into an offensive position, held the blade in front of me, and braced myself for the nearest hound.

The creature leaped at me with its lips peeled back. I slashed, and my sword cut through nothing but air as the hound easily dodged my strike. Kael snarled, and in that vicious sound, I could almost hear him berating me to be faster. He sprung toward one of the hounds and clung to its back, narrowly avoiding its snapping jaws as it twisted its neck.

I let out a growl of frustration as I stepped back from tearing teeth. It was easy for Kael to be quick, but I wasn't a jungle cat. The hound jumped at me again, and this time, I gave myself into those deep-rooted instincts.

Just as I had done in the cemetery in Chicago, my memories seemed to take over my limbs. My movements were smoother, more precise. I stepped quickly to the side and swung the sword in a downward arc to catch the hound on the back of the neck. I winced as it let out a painful bellow. It dropped to the floor, kicked for a moment, and then grew still.

Another quickly replaced it, and I pivoted just in time to avoid the gnashing teeth. Instead, the creature's jaws latched onto my bag. I let out a shriek as it jerked me to the floor. My elbow cracked against the cool tile and sent a jarring sensation up my arm. The sword fell from my hand.

The hound released my bag and stalked toward me with its icy gaze locked on me. I reached back, trying to find my weapon. I had no choice—I had to use my magic.

My palm started to burn when suddenly Kael jumped over me. With a clash of snarls and teeth, the two fought. I sat, unmoving. Kael's skill never ceased to amaze me. I found him sort of beautiful as he attacked. His form was fluid and graceful, even in such violence.

The battle was over quickly. I twisted to find my sword as Kael shifted back. My weapon had only been a foot farther than I'd thought. I grabbed the sword and let it turn back into a bracelet.

"We need to hurry." Kael tugged his shirt over his head. "The guards won't be far behind."

I nodded. Already, urgent voices were echoing through the museum in addition to the alarm. They were close. If this had been daytime, when there were more guards on staff, this never would have worked.

Harsh voices rang out, and a group of security guards rounded the corner. They yelled at us, but I couldn't understand what they were saying. My heart raced as Kael swore. What were we going to do now? I didn't want to hurt these people. They were innocent. They were only doing their jobs. I already regretted killing the hounds, horrifying as they'd been. I would not add innocent human lives to the list.

"Run." I tugged on Kael's arm and headed down the left corridor. Shouts and footsteps chased us.

"We can't outrun them. We need to fight."

"Against how many?" I said. "There were, what, four back there? You know there will be more. How many innocent people do you want to kill, Kael?"

"I don't want to kill anyone, but—"

"In here." I pulled Kael into a room dedicated to ancient Egypt. My eyes quickly scanned the room, and then fell on a pair of sarcophaguses on display across the room. "No more excuses. Look for a solution."

I hurried across the room with Kael on my heels. Each one had hinges added, no doubt to make it easy to open each day so visitors had a chance to see inside of them. I opened one, and jerked my head at the other.

"You've got to be kidding me," Kael said.

Right. He was claustrophobic. "Just get in. You'll be okay." I didn't give him a chance to argue before I climbed into the sarcophagus and eased the lid almost shut. "Just don't shut it all the—" I heard a click beside me "—way." I sighed sharply. I really hoped it hadn't locked on him. I'd once spent two weeks trying to figure out how to get one open.

I slowed my breathing and strained to listen over the blood pounding in my ears. I could hear voices, and then footsteps entered the room. What if there were shifters among them? Kael could catch the scent of others, and I was certain other shifters would be able to, as well.

I bit my lip as footsteps neared and a voice spoke right in front of me. I really wished I'd bothered to learn French at some point in my life.

Minutes seemed to stretch on, and I didn't dare crack open the lid until I was certain the room was empty. I stepped out and tapped on the sarcophagus hiding my partner.

"Kael," I whispered. "Are you okay?"

"Please, get me out of here."

I stifled a laugh. Luckily, I only had to twist a small lever for the lid to spring open. Kael stepped out and immediately started brushing himself off with a look of disgust. I glanced behind him. Whoops. His had already been occupied. I pulled my gaze from the mummy and gave Kael an apologetic smile.

"Sorry," I said.

"Let's just go," he said gruffly.

The room with the middle-eastern antiquities was the next one over. The pair of us eased our way as quietly as we could down the short stretch. I let out a breath when we entered the room unnoticed, but my relief was short-lived.

I crossed over to the case which held the key. "How are we going to get it out without drawing attention?"

Kael shook his head. "We can't. We just have to grab the key and run for it."

“Fantastic.” I frowned, then glanced at Kael. “Well, go ahead, Shoulders. I certainly can’t do it.”

He gave me a grin. “Watch your face.”

He cocked his elbow back. I winced as the glass shattered. There was no way the guards hadn’t heard.

I reached in, grabbed the key from the pillow, and turned. We started to rush from the room when I slowed and peered down at the key. My brows knit together.

“Uh, Kael…”

He stopped and looked back. “What? Come on, we have to get out of here.”

“We have a problem.”

With a sharp sigh, he stepped over to me. “What kind of problem?”

I held up the key. “This is not what we’re looking for.” The two keys around my neck held an almost magical aura about them. This key was…nothing. I peered up at Kael. “It’s a fake. This isn’t it.”

Voices reached us again.

“Put it back,” Kael said. “We can’t let them know what we were after.”

I hurried to do so. Where was the real key? My gaze locked on a little sign next to the key. I quickly pulled out my phone and snapped a picture. It was our only clue.

“Let’s get out of here.” My stomach twisted. All of this trouble and planning had been for nothing.

Fortunately, Kael managed to find a window that was unlocked, and I wondered if that had been his backup plan all along...or the entry and escape route taken by whoever got to the key first. The pair of us slipped quietly to the ground outside and ghosted our way across the grounds. I wasn’t about to spend the night in the gardens, so Kael and I scaled the tall fence and jumped out.

We didn’t stop running until we reached our hotel.

"Get your phone out," I said. "I need you to translate this."

I held up the picture of the key in the museum and zoomed in on the sign beneath.

Kael squinted at the photo and quickly tapped it into a translation tool. "It says that while the key had been found in what was formerly Anatolia, now modern-day Turkey, it is believed to have originated in what is now…Kenya."

I moaned. So the real key hadn't been stolen. It just hadn't been there to begin with. This one was a replica, perhaps even switched out years ago before it came to the museum. And the real relic was most likely in Africa.

Kael sagged onto the mattress of the bed. "I can't believe it wasn't there."

"Yeah."

Which meant, Alastor either hadn't known his relic had been a fake all along, or he had known, and had sent us on a wild goose chase. If that was the case, Vehrin may already know the true whereabouts of the third key.

And for all we knew, he may have already beaten us to it.

CHAPTER 14

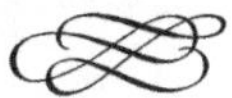

A constant babble of voices drifted in on hot air through the open window of our hotel room. The bed creaked beneath me as I shifted, while Kael paced the room.

Aidan's deep voice carried through the phone at my partner's ear, loud enough for me to hear even from across the room. It made me miss the bear shifter who had been my sparring partner and impromptu trainer back at the PITO headquarters. I hoped I'd have a chance to go back there someday, even if it was for a short visit. Aidan had grown on me.

I turned my attention back to my bag in my lap and dug around in it until I found my phone. I frowned. The signal wasn't the greatest here in Nairobi, Kenya, and likely wouldn't be anywhere in Africa, but I scrolled through my contacts until I found Renathe. I hadn't checked in with him since before we infiltrated the Louvre.

Hey. Alastor is either incompetent, or a traitor, I tapped out on my cell.

He answered me almost immediately. *You know, I've never waited so long for a date before.*

I rolled my eyes. *Can't you read? Alastor may be a traitor. The key in the museum was a fake. He may be working for the mage.*

I'll look into it, sweetheart.

Now he was just trying to aggravate me. I could almost see the smirk on his face.

A little smile quirked at my own lips. *Yes, you do that, darling, and be careful. I'd hate for my date to be taken out before we can get together.*

There was a longer delay than usual before the next text come through: *Tease.*

I laughed. I did enjoy our little conversations. *I need to get ready to traipse across Africa. Seriously, be careful of Alastor.*

Don't get eaten by a hippo. The man added a kissing face emoji.

I grinned and stuffed my phone back into my bag. My attention swung back to Kael.

"No, we don't know what he was doing in the Louvre, but we're hot on his tail." Kael still hadn't mentioned there was a third key. He'd said it was safer not to divulge such information, but it made me wonder why he didn't trust his superiors. Did he just not want to tell them until he was sure we'd get the key? His brow pinched as he listened to Aidan ramble on about something. "Oh. Really?" He glanced at me quickly, then turned away.

My eyes narrowed in suspicion. What was that about? Were they talking about me?

He spoke for a couple of minutes longer, then hung up and sank into the single worn chair in the room with a heavy sigh.

"What's wrong?" I asked.

He looked tired, and while all of the travel lately would certainly do that to a person, it seemed deeper than the flights and car rides and lack of sleep.

Kael offered me a weary smile. "It's nothing."

"It didn't seem like nothing. Did Aidan give you some bad

news?"

He shook his head and leaned back against the chair, closing his eyes. There was obviously something bothering him, and the fact he didn't want to tell me stung. Didn't he trust me? Weren't we partners on this endeavor? Weren't we friends?

"Fine." My tone was short, something he wouldn't be able to easily miss. "You don't have to tell me anything."

I turned to peer out of the window. The sun was bright and the sky clear, but the atmosphere was marred by the amount of noise. The road beneath was packed with people, most of them shouting about one thing or another they were selling, trying to accost tourists and missionaries. The honking of cars only added to the harsh sounds.

"Livvie." Kael had come over to the bed. I scooted over as he sank onto the squeaky mattress beside me. "It is not that I don't trust you. I trust you with my life."

The intensity in his gaze, and his words, made my pulse quicken a bit. If it wasn't an issue of trust, then there would only be one other reason he wasn't telling me. "Is it about me?"

"Not exactly." He pressed his lips together and sighed before continuing. "It's about your friend, the one heading your team."

I sat up straighter. "Sarah? What's wrong? Is she all right?"

Kael waved a hand to settle me down. "She's fine, but apparently that object they uncovered on the dig in India may be, while not cursed, magical."

"Magical?" How many ancient relics existed in this world that were more than meets the eye? I started to reach for my phone. "I need to warn her."

"No need. PITO has agents looking into the matter."

"Looking into the matter? Aren't they going to take it away? What if it hurts her?"

Kael let out a sharp sigh. "This is why I didn't want to say anything. I didn't want you worrying for nothing. PITO has their eye on the situation. They will step in if need be. Your friend will be fine." He tapped my temple. "You need to keep your head in your own game."

I dropped my phone onto my bag with a huff. He was right. I couldn't worry about Sarah and Vehrin at the same time. If she had PITO watching her, she was in good hands. I nudged Kael's shoulder with mine.

"Hey, thanks for trusting me. You're a good friend." My gaze turned to the carpet that I was certain used to be a rich brown but had been soiled by so many shoes and stains over the years it looked like mud. "Probably the best friend I've ever had."

My words nearly rushed past my lips, but it was the truth. I had good friends, like Sarah, but I'd never had anyone I trusted more than the man beside me.

Kael was silent for so long I began to wonder if he'd heard me, and I started to hope he hadn't. Heat crawled up the back of my neck. It had been a silly thing to say.

"You know," he finally said. "Surprisingly, I'd have to say the same to you." He shrugged. "I mean, I never thought I'd find such a good friend in a stubborn, magic-cursed woman, but—"

I shoved him. "Stop it. I am not stubborn."

He leaned closer to me. "As a mule."

My breath caught. I couldn't help myself. The man was practically flush up against me. He must have heard my lungs hitch, because his gaze dropped to my lips as if wondering what was keeping me from bringing air in. His hand lifted to glide up my arm, and I panicked. What was he doing? Why was he staring at me like that?

"Kael?"

He opened his mouth, and then a loud knock echoed through the small room. Both of our stares shifted to the door.

"Your friend?" I asked. Kael had an acquaintance who may be able to help us figure out which direction Vehrin was heading, and hopefully get the third key before he had a chance to claim it.

Kael stood slowly. "Yeah." He glanced at me. "He's a bit odd, just so you know."

He didn't say anything else as he strode to the door. I rubbed my arm where he had feathered his fingers up my skin. It felt warm.

I got to my feet as Kael opened the door. A loud, boisterous laugh bounced through the room. "Kael! It's been too long, brother!"

My partner was quickly swept into the arms of his friend at the door. Kael grunted in the grasp, and then shoved away.

"As exuberant as ever," he said. He rubbed at the back of his neck as he stepped from the doorway and motioned his friend inside.

Kael's term of exuberant seemed to be a vast understatement. The man was tall, but gangly, as if he hadn't grown out of his teenage years despite his face showing he was in his mid-twenties, at least. A wide grin split his face, and his dark eyes danced with amusement. The man wore nothing but a pair of worn sneakers and athletic shorts that were a vibrant orange. The way he moved as he stepped past Kael gave me the sense he wanted to jump into action at any moment. He had a fast, almost twitchy energy about him. His grin, impossibly, widened as he found me.

He glanced between myself and Kael. "Kael! You did not tell me you found a mate!"

I nearly choked on the sharp breath I sucked in at his words. His mate? It was a preposterous notion, but it also curled inside of me in an unexpectedly delightful way.

Kael shut the door and shook his head. "She's not my mate. She's my friend. I told you as much on the phone." He glared at his friend, who was still staring at me.

His friend shrugged. "If you say so, brother."

My partner let out a sharp sigh. "Olivia, this is my friend, David."

David held out his hand, and I took it. "David Ortege," he said. He had a funny sound to his voice, as if he were constantly trying not to laugh.

I glanced at Kael. "Brother?"

"A term of affection. David is a cheetah shifter, and we're both cats, so…" Kael shrugged as if that explained it.

I studied David. His long limbs and buzzing energy certainly made sense for a cheetah shifter. He released my hand and proceeded to rock back and forth on his heels.

"So, Kael, what brings you and your lady here, exactly?"

Kael scowled. "I told you, she's not my—"

David waved a hand. "Semantics." His eyes glittered as he winked at me.

"We're seeking an object. It's magical in nature, possibly cursed, and very ancient." Clearly, Kael wanted to ignore his friend's baiting. "It could be dangerous, and we need to uncover its whereabouts quickly."

The tall man pursed his lips. "And why are you asking me this instead of using the resources of your organization, my friend? Do you not trust your own comrades?"

"With the object we're seeking, I trust myself and Olivia alone. And now, you."

David raised an eyebrow. "Indeed?" He paused, but if he was waiting for an elaboration from Kael or myself, he received none. He continued. "Very well. There is one who may be able to help you. She lives west of here. She is not easy to find, and those that do find her, often wished they had not."

"What do you mean?" I asked.

"She is a prophetess, of sorts, and most do not like what she has to say."

Kael grunted. "We'll take the risk. Where do we find her?"

David gave us loose directions—apparently the woman

didn't stay in the exact same area often.

"Can you just show us the way?" I asked. Surely, David knew the area much better than we did. The last thing we needed right now was to get lost in the African wilderness.

He shook his head. "You could not pay me enough to step foot anywhere near her." Then, he turned to leave with no more explanations. He paused in the doorway, then glanced back at me. "I do hope you live, Olivia. I wouldn't mind seeing what becomes of you and Kael in the end."

After the door closed and I was certain David was beyond earshot, I turned to Kael. "Your friend is charming."

Weird was more like it. What did he think was going on between Kael and myself? We were just friends.

For some reason, it nearly sounded as if I were lying to myself.

"Come on. No point in wasting any time." Kael started to gather our supplies, and I hurried to help him.

The din outside was even stronger as we left the small hotel. The streets were so packed with people that it was nearly impossible not to be jostled by shoulders or hips. Much of the street was crowded with people shouting out trinkets to the obvious tourists in the area. Tables were heavy with necklaces of brightly colored, wooden beads; small paddle drums of stretched skin with zebras or giraffes painted on them and painted decorative plates with scenes of elephants or acacia trees. We had to tell people over and over again that we weren't interested in anything they were selling. More than a few were quite forceful.

A prickle suddenly dripped between my shoulder blades, and I glanced behind me. I was certain someone was watching me, but I could see nothing out of the ordinary. Still, I voiced my unease to Kael. His jaw tightened, and his nostrils flared. His gaze darted to me, and I knew in the brief glance I had been right.

We were being followed.

Kael quickened his step as best he could in the throng, and it took quite a bit of effort to push through the crowds. Eventually, we broke from them, though, and Kael darted into an alley.

"This way. Quick," he said.

I followed him, continuing to check behind us. There was nothing. No one.

"I think we lost whoever it was," I said. I shook my head as something fell onto my hair.

Bits of grit rained down. I glanced up, then gasped. Before I could warn Kael, a pair of figures descended toward us.

The stench reached me first, like meat rotting on a hot summer day, and it twisted my gut. I had to fight back the bile burning up my throat. These were no henchman of Vehrin's, but demons drawn to the power of the keys around my neck and drawn to *me*.

With long limbs, they scuttled down the building like spiders, and as they neared, I caught excited clicking noises. The demons reached toward us with long, curved talons.

Kael snarled and leapt at them. One of them lurched to the side and hurtled toward me. I summoned my sword, and brought it down in an arc. The speed at which the creature dodged was startling, and suddenly it was rushing past me.

I pivoted, refusing to let it at my back, and brought my blade aloft. The demon issued out more clicking noises, this time accompanied by a strange hissing I was certain was laughter.

My brow furrowed, and with gritted teeth, I dashed at the monster. It seemed surprised I would come toward it and shifted back ever so slightly. I couldn't stop my momentum, and my blade moved straight at its abdomen. The strange, black casing that made up its skin was hard, and while my sword marred the surface, it glanced off to the side without penetrating.

The creature swiped at me as I continued to move

forward, and I winced as I felt a small sting at my side. Thankfully, I fell hard and fast enough that I missed most of the long talon. I hit the ground with a grunt and rolled. I couldn't see Kael, though a terrible shrieking told me he likely had the upper hand in his fight.

My heart pounded as the demon stared down at me with large, glittering, bulbous eyes. My veins warmed and pulsed with my magic. Letting it loose here could do more harm than good, especially if Vehrin or any of his minions were in the area. The monster descended, and I had no choice. My palm warmed as I shoved it toward the creature and sent up a blast of energy. My magic slammed into it, and the thing cartwheeled backward.

Kael was suddenly beside me and hauling me to my feet. Without a word, he tugged me down the alley. We didn't stop running until we had left the town. I bent over and braced my hands on my knees, trying to catch my breath.

"Are they dead?" I asked.

"I'm not sure about the one you hit with magic. The other one is, for sure." He put a hand on my shoulder. "Are you all right?"

I nodded and straightened. A sharp pain stung at my side. I waited until Kael was searching through his pack to inspect it. There was a small tear in my shirt, and I quickly lifted it.

A scratch, barely more than a couple of inches, ran along my right ribcage. It wasn't deep, and was hardly red with blood. I'd gotten worse pruning roses at my home. I hurriedly covered it back up.

"Water?" Kael held out a canteen.

I took a gulp and handed it back. "Now what?"

Kael gestured to the expanse of grass and trees before us.

I nodded. "All right. Camping trip, it is."

We shouldered our packs, then headed out into the African wilderness with demons behind, a dark mage ahead, and the untamed elements to survive in between.

CHAPTER 15

THIS WAS by far the worst hike I had ever been on. Most would think a trek through Africa would be like an exotic safari, with giraffes, and elephants, and herds of gazelles to awe at. All we had found was heat, scratchy grass, and some rather annoying birds that had taken up the habit of screeching at us every few minutes.

I had no idea how long we had been walking, but it seemed like hours. My collar was sticky with sweat from the midday sun glaring on us. The landscape hadn't changed in a while. There was nothing but the brown grass and the occasional sprinkling of acacia trees. Surely, we should have found the person we were seeking out by now? Yet we'd seen no sign of civilization since we'd fled the town from the demons.

Kael paused and squinted back in the direction we'd come. He'd been doing so at regular intervals, I assumed trying to catch the sounds, or even scents, of any demons that may still be pursuing us. He seemed convinced they wouldn't have given up so easily.

"Anything?" I asked.

"No." He turned and continued.

We had found a narrow path cutting through the grass, though whether it was made by people or animals, I didn't know. It made the walking a bit easier, but if we wanted to avoid being followed, we wouldn't be able to stay on the trail for long. I pulled in a deep breath and winced slightly at the stinging pain in my side at the movement.

The scratch had not lessoned in pain with the growing of the day. It had worsened. I told myself it was likely from the chafing of my shirt, and next time we took a break I was going to put some ointment and a bandage on it. It seemed silly, worrying about such a small scratch, but something at the back of my mind told me the stinging was a cause to be anxious.

I shook my head. Fretting over such a tiny scratch. Kael would probably laugh at me if I told him. I frowned. No, he likely wouldn't. If anything, he'd probably berate me for not telling him about it in the first place.

My pace had slowed, I realized, and I picked up the pace to get back into step with Kael. He glanced behind us again, and his brow furrowed.

"I think it's time we get off this path," he said. "I don't think we're being followed, but something is nagging at me."

"Sure, let's go." I wasn't going to argue with him, even though trekking through the itchy grass was the last thing I wanted to do. He could have some sort of shifter instincts warning him for all I knew, and it would be smart not to argue with them. After all, I'd never prided myself to be someone who argued for argument's sake. I was more of a "choose your battles" kind of woman.

We veered from the path, and quickly left it behind. My breath was beginning to labor. I hadn't realized I'd gotten so out of shape. I used to be able to hike, climb, and trek all day without becoming winded. Perhaps it was the glaring heat.

The burbling of water caught my attention, and we soon came up on a small stream. There was a rocky outcrop nearby that cast a small shadow at its base. Kael led us to it, and I was never so happy to sink down to the ground beneath some shade. My partner folded to the ground beside me, and though he appeared to be the picture of ease, I knew he was still listening and watching for danger.

I settled back against the rock. It was cool after the heat. As we sat, a herd of water buffalo made their way to the opposite bank. Their dark coats were peppered with little birds picking bugs from their hides. Kael watched the herd as we rested, and I pulled my pack from my shoulder. I rifled through it until I found my ointment and some Band-Aids.

The cut was red and stung as I smeared antibacterial ointment across it. Kael didn't notice what I was doing until I had finished pressing the bandage to my skin.

"What's that?" he asked.

"Just a little scratch, but out in this wilderness and in this heat, I don't want to risk an infection." I pulled my shirt down and gave him a smile. "Don't worry, I'm fine."

Kael nodded, and I was thankful he was as unworried about it as myself. He pulled out the water and some trail mix. We spent several minutes taking careful sips and munching on the mix of nuts and dried fruit.

"Which way from here?" I hadn't wanted to ask him before, but I had a suspicion we were lost. Either that, or the woman had already traveled to a different location and we had missed her.

Kael stood and studied the wild landscape. "Let's continue the way we've been going." He jerked his head in a westerly direction. He held a hand down to help me up. "We'll find her."

I hoped he was right, and I hoped he trusted in the advice of his friend. After Alastor had pointed us to a false key, I was suspicious about directions from sources I didn't know.

Time stretched on, and I was beginning to think we'd never find the woman, and never stop walking. The day seemed to grow warmer by the minute. I was down to a tank top, and was seriously considering cutting off the bottom half of my pants, even if it did further expose me to bugs and scratchy weeds. My head had been throbbing for the past hour, despite the water I'd been drinking.

My energy was quickly sapping, and I tripped a few times with feet that had grown heavy. The third time I stumbled, I hit my knees. I leaned over and braced my hands on the grass. A shadow fell over the grass in front of my face.

"Livvie?"

I glanced up to find Kael's face pinched with concern. "Hey."

He grabbed me under my shoulders and settled me back on my butt. I didn't even have the energy to protest being handled like a child. His hand paused on my arm, and he frowned.

"You're really hot," he said.

Really hot? I stared at him. If he was going to compliment me, did he have to do it with such an uneasy look on his face?

"Now isn't the time for that," I said.

It was beyond me why Kael thought being lost in the African wilderness would be a good time for flirting. Wait. *Was* he flirting?

I squeezed my eyes shut for a second. It felt like someone was tapping my skull with a tiny hammer.

"No," he said slowly. I opened my eyes, and he gave me a tight smile, and though a tiny spark of amusement lit in his eyes, his brow remained furrowed. "I mean you feel hot, like feverish."

I pushed him away from me and blinked. Kael was a sturdy guy, but it had been like trying to push a truck out of my way. "It's impossible not to be hot in this climate, Kael."

He let out a sharp breath and stood. He bent down to help me up. As I climbed to my feet, a sudden pain licked my side. I grabbed it with a gasp.

Before I could say anything, Kael grabbed the bottom of my tank and lifted it. His nostrils flared. I glanced down to see what he was staring at. The skin around the scratch was red and inflamed. It was starting to burn a little. Still, I pulled my shirt from Kael's fingers and yanked it down.

"I'll be fine," I said. Judging by his silent stare, he obviously wasn't convinced.

Kael's lips pressed into a thin line. After a moment, he said, "Perhaps we should find a place to rest. Tomorrow we can continue our search."

I couldn't help but scoff. "Where are we supposed to rest?"

Aside from the grass and scattered trees, there was nowhere we could hunker down where we wouldn't be exposed to the elements, wild beasts, or worse, demons.

Kael squinted as he peered around. Then, he paused and pointed. "There."

I followed his gaze to a slight rise in the horizon that looked to be a forest.

"We can go for that," he said.

So, the pair of us continued through the endless sea of grass, the silence broken occasionally by the indignant, territorial birds. After a while, the sky turned from blue to gray, followed by a blush of pink and orange. Kael's steps were quick, obviously in a hurry to get to the forest before nightfall.

The pain at my ribs had worsened. It burned, growing hotter with each step, as if someone were teasing me with a red-hot poker. I gritted my teeth and concentrated on putting one foot in front of the other.

Left. Right. Left. Left.

I stumbled, and only quick footwork kept my face from meeting the ground.

Kael glanced back at me, and I gave him what I hoped was a reassuring smile. He frowned, but continued on his way.

Minutes dragged on. A strange fuzziness flickered in my

mind. I shook my head and tried to clear it, but the sensation persisted. I glanced up from my boots shuffling through the grass to find Kael had gotten quite a bit ahead of me.

"Kael," I called. My voice sounded strange, as if my mouth were full of cotton.

Something hard hit my back end, and I realized after a moment it was the ground.

Grass and sky spun around me, and I closed my eyes against the dizziness. A warmth pressed against my face, and I wished it would stop. I was so hot.

"Livvie."

I opened my eyes. Kael had his hand pressed to my face. Why did he look so worried?

"Kael?" The word was hardly more than a whisper from my dry lips.

He dropped his hand from my face and lifted my shirt. His breath hissed in, and I flinched as he yanked off the bandage. The wound at my ribs was an angry red, with bluish-green tendrils spreading across my skin like spiderwebs. I peered up at Kael, and wondered if I had the same panic in my eyes that stared from his.

"Where did this wound come from?" he asked. His voice was tight, and I couldn't tell if he was angry or scared. Maybe both.

Strangely, it took me a minute to recall where I had gotten the scratch in the first place.

"One of the demons," I said.

A muscle ticked at his jaw, and I wondered if he was trying not to yell at me. He put his arm around my back. "We'll find some help, but we need to get to the forest so you can rest."

Kael glanced up. When had night fallen? He started to help me to my feet, when his head snapped to peer behind me. A low growl rumbled through his chest. I didn't have to ask to know what he had seen or heard.

Demons.

Without a word, he hauled me to my feet. The forest was ahead of us. If we hurried, we could reach the trees and maybe find shelter. Kael kept his arm around me, but even with his support, I was having difficulty. Every step and breath I took brought more pain. I couldn't get my feet to work right, and my vision faded in and out. Hairs rose on the back of my neck.

The demons were drawing closer. We weren't going to make it into the forest in time.

Magic. I could use my magic.

I glanced behind me into the darkness, expecting a group of demons to race toward us at any second. I pulled at my magic, but the more I tried to summon the power that could save us, the more my stomach churned. It wasn't working.

Pain lashed at me, and tears pricked my eyes. The agony ripped through me, and my muscles gave out as we neared the forest. My legs bent. I tried to clutch at Kael. He caught me before I fell and, tightening his grip, he swung me up into his arms.

My head bounced against Kael's shoulder as he ran. He glanced back and swore. We reached the trees, and he bent to ease me onto the ground. Grass and twigs tickled at my cheek as I lay wishing I had a softer place to put my head.

I twisted as best I could to stare up at Kael. His face was pale, but determined, as he stared forward. I tilted my head just enough to be able to see a dozen pairs of eyes, burning like coals in the dark.

I pulled the necklaces from beneath my shirt and closed the keys in my fingers. I tried to tell Kael we would be all right, but a moan came from my lips instead at the pain that sliced at my side. If I could reach for him, get his attention, maybe he would understand. My muscles wouldn't hardly work, however, and my vision started to fade.

A sudden deep rumbling carried from the trees and reverberated in my chest. Something heavy thumped from somewhere behind me, like the footsteps of a giant. Shrieking came from in front of us, and I winced at the horrid sound. The indignant cries faded.

Were the demons fleeing? Why?

Kael crouched and hovered over me protectively. Had another demon come? A bigger, more terrible demon?

"What is this that has stumbled into my home, and brought demons to my doorstep?"

I tried to crane my neck to see who had spoken, but the pain enveloped me, and dragged me down with relentless claws.

CHAPTER 16

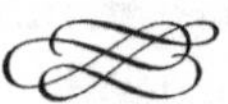

A SOFT SENSATION floated from my forehead and over the crown of my head. Once. Twice. Then, over and over again. It was nice, and drew a small moan from me. The feeling paused, and I could have sworn someone said my name from the darkness weighing me down.

I tried to find a light, but I was wrapped in shadow. If I could reach out, maybe I could find my way out of the dark, but my limbs felt heavy and sluggish. A warmth touched my cheek, and I tilted my head to lean into it.

"Livvie? Can you hear me?"

Yes, I wanted to say, but when I opened my mouth to speak, only a small, pitiful noise came out.

"She needs more rest. Leave her be, or you can wait outside."

I didn't recognize the deep, chiding voice. Who else was in the darkness with me? I fought and clawed my way out of the depths and slowly opened my eyes.

At first, Kael's face was nothing more than a blur, but after a few moments, the lines of his jaw, the golden-brown of his eyes, and his puckered forehead sharpened into view.

"Kael," I breathed.

"See? Now you've done it, you baboon." There was a heavy sigh. "I will get some tea for her."

There was that voice again. I tried to look around, but Kael had trapped my head in his hands.

"Are you all right?" His tone was tight, and scratchy, as if he hadn't slept or drank in days.

"I…" Truthfully, I wasn't really sure. It took a moment for the memories to drag back into my muddled mind, and even then, I couldn't recall much. "I was hurt?"

Yes, that sounded right. I started to reach down toward my ribs, but Kael caught my hand.

His eyes closed, and he lifted my hand to his lips. "You are all right." He mumbled the words, heavy with relief, against my fingers. Then, he leaned down and rested his forehead against my own. "You are all right."

He sounded more like he was trying to convince himself than he was trying to convince me.

Kael's breath tickled my face, his lips a hairsbreadth from mine. I had a sudden, crazy urge to close the distance between them. Before I could, he straightened. The man looked like he was trying to put himself back together.

"Kael?" My throat was raw and scratchy, and I cleared it before continuing. "Are *you* okay?"

His eyes were wide. "You almost died." The way he said those words, it was as if his universe had been swept out from under him.

"I did?" Honestly, I couldn't remember much except that I had a wound festering on my side and a pack of demons on our tail. I was fairly certain we'd reached the forest, but after that, I couldn't recall anything.

Kael nodded. "You were feverish and screaming about being on fire." He reached down and touched my side. "It was the scratch from the demon. Some of them have poisonous claws, and you were unlucky enough to encounter one."

I leaned up. My ears rang a bit. I was covered in a blanket

to my waist and wearing nothing but my sports bra. A bandage had been placed on my side, so I couldn't tell what the actual wound looked like, but the skin around it held a healthy glow. My gaze slid from myself to my surroundings.

I was laying on a low cot in a small room. The ceiling was nearly dome-shaped, if peaked slightly at the top, and the walls were a rich brown. Kael was leaning on a brightly covered woven rug sitting on a floor of stone. There was no window, but bright light filtered through a beaded curtain doorway behind my partner's back.

My stare swung back to Kael. God, he looked exhausted. When was the last time he slept? How long had *I* been out?

"What happened to the demons?" I asked. If we were safe, perhaps he could now get some much needed rest.

"They are waiting for you outside of my forest."

The beaded curtain parted, and a woman walked in. I froze as I stared at her. It was as if a goddess had just strolled into the room. Not only was she beautiful, even with the fine lines of age, but something about her presence commanded respect, even reverence.

She wore a brightly-colored dress and plain brown sandals. Earrings that looked to be the very tips of an elephant's tusks hung at her ears. White dots, running a path from the top of her forehead and down to the tip of her nose, stood in stark contrast to her dark complexion.

But it wasn't her feminine stature, or her perfectly sculpted face that had me unmoving on the cot.

It was her eyes.

They were gray, almost non-descript compared to the rest of her beauty, but her gaze was heavy with more wisdom than I could ever hope to possess.

We had found the prophetess.

She strode over and nudged Kael to the side with her hip.She held out a plain white teacup. Steam swirled up from the dark liquid. "Here, child, drink this."

I took the cup, glanced at Kael who was staring at the woman with an annoyed frown, and took a careful sip. My face scrunched as something akin to sour ditchwater flowed over my tongue.

The woman nodded. "Yes, I know. It is awful stuff, but will help you to heal faster. You are fortunate you found me when you did. Another ten minutes, and you would be gone."

She climbed to her feet, muttering something about foolish girls and demon poison.

I sat up and was glad to find the movement only hurt a little. I took another sip of the horrid concoction and motioned for Kael to come and sit beside me. The woman settled cross-legged in the corner with a wooden bowl in her lap and started tearing up what seemed to be an assortment of herbs.

"What's your name?" I asked.

"Most call me Bibi." She looked up from her bowl with amusement in her ancient eyes. "It means 'grandmother'." Her gaze narrowed as she stared at me. "You carry some interesting trinkets with you."

I lifted my hand to my collarbone, and panic flashed through when I found the keys were missing.

"Here." Kael pulled them from his pocket and handed them to me. I took them, and the one bound to my soul hummed at the reunion. I placed them back around my neck.

"That one does not trust me," Bibi said. She fixed her steely gaze on my partner.

"I don't mean to offend, but these, and her, are too important to risk." Kael was sitting very close to me, and I could have sworn his hand twitched toward me just a bit. I groaned inwardly. This near-death experience of mine was going to make him hover more than ever.

Bibi did not seem bothered by Kael's explanation. Instead, she jerked her head toward the keys now resting around my neck. "I have not seen the likes of those in many years."

My heart skipped. "Have you seen a key like these before?"

"I have, indeed." She ripped more of the herbs and dropped them into the bowl. "Seen it, held it—" Her gaze swept over the pair of us. "—and gave it away."

This woman *gave away* the third key? "Well, who has it now?"

Bibi's head tilted, and her eyes narrowed.

I squirmed under her shrewd gaze.

"I do not know if I should trust you with such information."

I sputtered. Had she not just chided Kael for being untrustworthy? "But…but we need it."

"And why do you *need* it, child? No one needs objects such as the ones around your neck, unless they are planning something very wicked, or very stupid."

Kael was silent and unhelpful beside me. Trying to stop Vehrin wasn't wicked, it was the opposite.

"Well, I guess we're probably doing something stupid, then," I said. "Stupid, but still the right thing to do."

"You want to stop Vehrin."

I blinked at Bibi's words. How did she know who he was? I nodded slowly.

She set the bowl aside. "And what makes you think you are capable of doing such a thing?"

Before, as with Cordelia, and the witch coven in Scotland, I had shown them my magic as proof of who I was and what I could do. I reached for it, and tried to draw my magic up from inside of me, but my head suddenly buzzed, and my vision blurred at the edges.

"It is the demon's poison. It tampers your magic, but it will wear off."

Bibi's tone held a promise I wanted to believe. "Are you truly a prophetess?"

A big, booming laugh shook from the woman's slight

frame and bounced off the walls. It seemed impossible that such a loud sound came from her.

"Prophetess," she scoffed, though her lips were lifted in a smile. "Most claim I am such a thing, but truly, it is only because the more you know about the past, the more you can read the future."

"And you know much about the past?" Kael asked.

She heaved a heavy sigh, pushing out a few more chuckles. "I have been alive for a very long time." There was a story playing about in her mind. I could see it in the way her eyes dimmed, as if seeing into the past. Suddenly, her gaze flicked to me. "Drink your tea."

I had forgotten about the cup in my hand. It had grown cold, and my nose wrinkled as I downed the rest of the foul drink.

Bibi bobbed her head in satisfaction, then shifted on the floor and faced us. "My grandmother knew of a sorceress across the seas on the other side of the world. She lived in a place of twisted vines, of shadows and heavy rains."

I leaned forward. The rainforest. She had to be talking about the rainforest, and the place I had supposedly lived in my past life.

"The sorceress was a powerful woman, full of great magic, with ties to an equally powerful mage."

I shared a brief glance with Kael. This woman could be the only being on earth besides the mage who knew the true story about the keys.

"They were aligned, for a time. Together, they kept the balance of magic, and life. Eventually, there was a disagreement between them. The mage had grown to rely too heavily on magic, forsaking things which were real, and good. He cared not for the fish in the waters, or the animals of the earth, or the people that followed his and the sorceress's rule. He grew twisted, and dark. There was war, and sacrifice. In the end, both of their lives were forgotten, until now."

Bibi's gray eyes which, at first, I had thought dull compared to the rest of her features, sparked with life.

I swallowed. "I already knew who I had been, in a past life. I know who I am."

"Do you?" Bibi's tone was quiet, and her gaze bore into mine. "Do you really know who you are, Olivia Perez?"

A tingle scattered across my neck and played down my spine. Something about her question made me nervous, because perhaps I *didn't* truly know who I was anymore. I didn't know myself, or what I was capable of doing.

The woman broke her stare and tilted her head toward Kael. "I do hope you will take better care of her this time around."

Kael sat up straighter under her glare. "What do you mean?"

"Why do you think you feel so drawn to protect this girl? Just as she is the descendant of the sorceress, you are the descendant of the fierce warrior who protected her."

I had known this for a while. Vehrin had hinted as much, and besides, something within my soul just knew what Kael truly was, and had been.

But instead of being relieved at the confirmation, my stomach twisted bitterly. Was that why we worked so well together? Were my growing feelings for him some sort of twisted bond we already possessed, and not of my own heart's making?

"Of course I would never let anything happen to her. That has nothing to do with the past. I will protect her with my life."

I turned so sharply toward Kael, I winced at the pain that shot along my wound. "No, you will not protect me with your life. I don't want your sacrifices, Kael. I don't need a knight in shining armor."

Kael's eyes widened at my sharp words. "I only meant—"

"I don't care. I don't want you getting yourself killed

trying to protect me, Kael!" Couldn't he see how much that would hurt me?

"I was unaware I had invited quarreling lovers into my home." Bibi unfolded and rose from the floor.

"We're not lovers," Kael and I insisted simultaneously.

A gleam of amusement sparked in the old woman's eyes.

The whole situation was ridiculous. We weren't here to fight about our relationship, or whatever strange thing was going on between us.

"Where do we find the third key?" I asked.

Bibi headed for the curtained doorway, bowl of herbs in hand, then paused to peer at us over her shoulder. "Long ago, I entrusted the relic to a pack of lion shifters."

My heart raced. So, next we had to find those shifters and get to the key before Vehrin?

"But they will not give up the key without the spear," she added.

"Spear?" Kael shot to his feet. "What spear?"

"I told them if someone made it through a trial to obtain the spear, and presented it to them, they were trustworthy enough to take possession of the key. Tomorrow, you will attempt to claim the spear, so you may trade it for the key."

I stood beside Kael. "Why tomorrow? Why not now? We don't have much time."

As if in answer, a terrible shrieking echoed from outside.

"The demons wait for your return in the night. It will be safer to go in the morning."

I frowned. The last thing I wanted to do was wait, but I also wasn't keen on becoming demon fodder. I nodded.

"Good. Now, come and eat." Bibi strode out with a no-nonsense attitude that had me and Kael following. "Tomorrow, we will see if you are worthy."

CHAPTER 17

"WAKE UP!"

My eyelids fluttered as I tried to drag myself to consciousness. I stared up at the low ceiling, and it took a few blinks for me to remember where we were. Beside me, Kael climbed up from the floor with a groan. I sat up, and my bones ached from sleeping on the stiff cot. My gaze found Bibi, the beaded curtain spilling over her shoulders as she stood in the doorway.

She cast a glance behind her, and I craned my neck to see what she was looking at. "Hurry," she said. "The birds and the beasts are restless. Something is stirring in the wilderness." Her gaze locked on me. "You must complete your task, and quickly."

Without another word, she strode away.

Kael set my bag beside me as I wiggled my feet into my boots and bent over to lace them.

"Did you sleep okay?" he asked.

Shrugging one shoulder, I mumbled, "As well as I could on this ironing board."

He gave me a half-smile, and I remembered he'd spent the night on the floor.

"Sorry," I said. "I'm just feeling…"

I couldn't put a word to the tightness in my heart. Bibi had said something was stirring in the wilderness, and I had to agree. I was restless, and uneasy.

I rose to my feet and slung my bag over my shoulder. With a relieved breath, I realized my magic was swirling inside of me once more. The demon's poison had worn off.

Kael gathered his own things. He checked his pistol with a frown. He was running low on ammo, and he wouldn't likely find anymore until we left the country. He'd have to rely on the strength of his arm, or his teeth and claws.

Kael led the way out of Bibi's home and into the patchy, pale sunlight of early morning. The cries of birds pierced the air, and I caught the fluttering of wings from nearby trees. The entire atmosphere seemed sharp and alive, like electricity was crackling through the air. It was hard not to bounce on my toes with eagerness.

Bibi was waiting for us. She smiled, though it didn't reach her eyes. She pointed deeper into the forest. "That is the path. Once you get farther in the trees, Olivia will know which way to go."

How was I supposed to know which way to go? "What kind of obstacles are we going to meet out there?"

Bibi shook her head. "I cannot say."

"Will I be able to use my magic?" I asked.

The prophetess narrowed her sharp gaze at me. "If you need magic to prove yourself, young mage, perhaps you are not worthy, after all."

Ouch. That was an ego-bruiser. She was right, though. If I had to rely on my magic every time things got difficult, what kind of person would I be in the end?

I nodded and gripped the strap of my bag. "Will we see you again?"

"That remains to be seen." Bibi gestured toward the forest

once again, an obvious invitation to embark on this test of hers.

Kael and I headed into the forest. I peered at the foliage as the birds continued their calling. "You don't think there are animals in here that will attack us, do you?"

My partner gave me a crooked grin. "Why? Scared of monkeys?"

I scowled at him. "Monkeys have teeth, you know."

"So do I." He grinned widely, as if to prove his point.

I rolled my eyes. "Fine. You keep your mighty teeth at the ready, then." I peered up at the branches above, then glanced back to Kael. "What about the demons?"

He shrugged. "I haven't heard or smelled anything. Maybe they gave up and left."

"Maybe."

The pair of us fell silent as we trekked through the forest. As Bibi had said, I could sense where we were supposed to go, as if I was following some sort of invisible tether. We seemed to walk for hours, and I was thankful for the canopy as the day grew hotter.

Kael insisted we stop a couple of times to rest and drink some water. I relented, though I was eager to continue on our way as quickly as possible. The restless aura around us only seemed to be growing more intense, and I didn't know what it meant. Hopefully, it wasn't because the dark mage was near, though my gut told me that was likely the case.

The forest finally opened up to reveal a trio of flat-topped, gray, squatty buildings. They were old, judging by the vines creeping through the cracks on the walls and the stone crumbling at the edges. We walked up to the building in the center.

"Look," I said.

There was an open doorway. Scrawled in the stone along the top and sides were runes, so weathered with age they were difficult to make out. I ran my fingers over the curving lines, and as I did, their meaning bloomed to life in my mind.

"Only one may enter," I said.

Kael grunted in disapproval beside me.

I turned to him. "That's what it says. I'm not sure why, but I think we should follow the directions, don't you?"

He didn't answer me, but he had a growing frown on his face.

"I'll go in," I said.

A heavy sigh blew from Kael's lips. "I knew you were going to say that. Livvie, you just survived demon poison. You nearly died." He paused, and something like pain passed over his face. "Are you sure you can handle this?"

"Have some faith in me, shifter." I smiled to take any sting from my words. "Besides, I can read the runes. What if there are more scrawled down there?" I jerked my head toward the open doorway. I winked at Kael. "Don't worry. I got this."

I squared my shoulders and stepped into the doorway.

"Olivia."

I glanced over my shoulder at Kael as the shadow of the building fell over me. He opened his mouth, hesitated, and then said, "Be careful."

I smiled and then walked farther into the shadow. Thankfully, the cracked stone in the building allowed for slivers of light to pierce into the darkness. The air was stale and touched with the slightest scent of mildew where the cracks in the surface allowed rain inside. For the most part, puffs of dust billowed up with each step I took on the dirt floor.

A big grin pulled at my lips, and my heart swelled unexpectedly. It felt great to be inside ruins again, and a part of me wished I wasn't on a mission so I could explore the history this place had left behind. I missed that part of my life spent in ancient and forgotten places, uncovering relics that weren't magical and unearthing long-forgotten histories.

It would be fun to take Kael on a dig sometime. He'd probably enjoy the adventure of it, if he could get over his dislike of small spaces. I cut the image short as reality seeped in.

Would Kael even still be around when all of this was said and done? What would it mean for us once Vehrin was stopped for good? Kael would likely return to his duties at PITO, and I would have to get back to work for the university.

My heart clenched at the thought of not being around him anymore. I would miss him terribly. It made my throat tighten to think of just how much of a hole there would be once he was no longer an everyday part of my life.

My eyes widened as I continued through the low, dark building. Since when had I started caring for him so much? He was my friend, and maybe starting to be a bit more, but to think I would have a hard time living without him… Was it because we were tied together through some ancient threads of duty and companionship, or was it my own true feelings? Not knowing for certain made me feel even worse, and more uncertain.

A part of me wondered if our connection would remain intact after Vehrin's destruction, and if it didn't, how would I handle it?

I kicked up a puff of dust. Now was a stupid time to think about such things. I was supposed to be taking part in some important test.

So far, I hadn't seen anything of significance—no runes, no paths leading elsewhere. What kind of test was this, anyway? All I'd been doing was walking, and worrying over my relationship with a grumpy shifter.

I passed through another pale slant of sunlight filtering in through a crack in the ceiling, and then halted. There was another doorway in front of me, and I could make out the gray outline of something inside. For a moment, I wondered if I should bring out my sword, but I kept the braided bracelet hugging my wrist. I'd wait until I investigated further.

The room I entered was so cold it nearly sucked the breath from my lungs. Goosebumps rose on my arms as I stepped toward a low dais in the middle of the room, and it wasn't completely because of the temperature.

A spear sat on the dais. Instead of a spearhead being attached to a shaft, it was one solid piece. It was a polished white, and appeared to have been carved from ivory. Stepping closer, I could pick out details carved into the spear, little whorls and patterns entwined together in a maze of perfection and beauty.

My hand hesitated over the spear. Surely, picking up the spear and leaving with it couldn't be so easy. How was all of this tied together? What did this spear have to do with the keys? Was it simply a bargaining chip, or something more? How many other relics were a part of the pattern I'd tangled myself in?

I shook my head, and my cheeks puffed out with a sigh. "Only one way to find out," I muttered.

Slowly, I closed my hand around the smooth spear. It was cool to the touch and nearly seemed to hum beneath my fingers. I lifted it from the dais.

The frenzied cry of birds broke the silence and was joined by the screeching chatter of monkeys. My heart jumped. I tightened my grip on the spear and whirled to the doorway. A gasp filled my throat. The way out was blocked, as if the very stone walls had grown together. I ground my teeth.

I had a feeling my test was just beginning.

I swiveled around. The only way out was a small window. I wasn't certain I would fit, but I hurried toward it. Outside, I could see what appeared to be a courtyard surrounded by buildings. Above the roofs, branches of the forest shivered as birds and beasts scurried about.

I shoved my pack through the window, followed by the

spear. I took a steadying breath, then stuck my arms through the window. It took a lot of wiggling, and the sides of the window scraped at the wound on my side, but I made it through. As I got to my feet, I noticed a trickle of warmth at my side. A quick peek under my shirt showed my wound had broken open and was leaking blood through my bandage.

"Great," I said. "Can't wait for something like a hyena or a jackal to catch wind of that and—"

I paused. Amidst the chirping of birds and monkeys, a new screeching shattered the air.

Demons.

Bits of debris rained down beside me, and I pivoted. Demons were scrambling over the flat roofs of the buildings. My magic writhed inside of me, begging for release as the wicked beings drawn to my soul-bound key surged forward. I started to reach for the power that would destroy them, then hesitated. Bibi had warned against using my magic to complete this task.

I scooped up my bag and the spear, and I ran. A glance over my shoulder revealed hundreds of demons pouring over the buildings, like ants from a disturbed nest. My pulse raced. I had to find a way out. Quickly.

My searching eyes landed on a narrow path between buildings. It was the safest bet. Perhaps it would help slow the onslaught of demons on my heels.

Relief billowed in me as I saw the open forest on the other side of the path. I peeked over my shoulder to find demons fighting their way into the narrow passage. Then, a shadow fell over my way out. My gaze widened.

A massive elephant stepped into the end of the path. Its ears fanned out, and it let out a deep, rumbling sound that vibrated through my chest. Large, white dots ran from the top of the elephant's head, and down its trunk. The animal stared at me with familiar eyes.

Bibi.

The prophetess was an elephant shifter. Why would she be blocking my path? The demons were coming. Any second and they would be upon me. How was I supposed to get out of here if Bibi was blocking my path?

As if in answer, the spear in my grasp tingled against my palm.

Blood pounded in my ears as I was faced with three decisions. One, I could use my magic to take down the demons, though I knew by doing so, I would fail the test. Two, I could throw the spear at the demons. It wouldn't do any good. I would only kill one, at best, and lose the spear in the process. Or three, I could use the spear to take down the elephant.

The logical part of me said the spear would do no good against the elephant, but in my heart, I knew this was no ordinary spear. If I threw it at Bibi, it would kill her.

My throat burned. What kind of sick test was this? I had to kill an innocent person, someone wise and ancient, just to get this spear?

Bibi rumbled again, urging me to make a decision. A glance back showed the demons closing the distance. I could pick out the details of scales, and sharp claws, and eager, gnashing teeth.

I turned my attention back to the prophetess, and I lowered my eyebrows. Kael and I would just have to find some other way to convince the lion pride shifters to relinquish the third key. I refused to kill an innocent being.

With a yell, I drove the spear into the side of the building. To my surprise, it sank in like a knife to butter. Not wasting a breath, I used the spear to brace against as I climbed up onto the roof. I hurried across the cracked stone, stumbling a couple of times as my footing nearly gave way. I didn't turn to see if demons followed. I only focused on getting away from the buildings, back into the waiting arms of the forest, and Kael.

Finally, I reached the edge and jumped down. My teeth clacked together as I rolled through the impact. Pain splintered across my side, and I grabbed it with a slight grimace.

"Olivia!" Footsteps pounded, and then Kael was there, hauling me up. He steadied me, and his hand replaced my own along my ribs. "What happened?"

I stared at the ground. "I failed, Kael. I couldn't pass the test."

"To the contrary…"

Our heads whipped toward Bibi. She was walking from around the buildings, the spear in her hands. A wide smile split her face as she stepped up to us. She held the spear out to me, and I took it slowly.

"I don't understand," I said. "I didn't use the spear on you."

"Exactly." Bibi put her hands on my shoulder. "You chose to give up the one thing that could help you get the key. By doing so, you passed the test."

I glanced behind her. "What about the demons? Where are they?"

Kael stiffened beside me at the mention of demons, and drifted a few feet away, sharp gaze peering into the forest.

"An illusion. You had to have something driving you forward, something that would allow no way of escape."

My mind was reeling. We'd obtained the spear. We could get the third key. I smiled at Bibi. "Where do we find the lion shifters?"

The prophetess gave us directions. She equipped me with fresh bandages for my side and more of that foul-tasting tea to drink when we rested. Then Bibi took off the earrings in the shape of tiny elephant tusks.

"Take these," she said. "They will ward off any wild beasts that may do you harm, and any demons that may be lingering nearby." She wrapped her arms around me as she told us goodbye, and I was so thankful I had chosen not to end the woman's life. She straightened suddenly, and her gaze was piercing as she stared at me. "Olivia, power and sacrifice often go hand in hand. When the time is right, you will know how to use it."

I swallowed and nodded. As Kael and I left, I thought about how I didn't want to sacrifice anything, or anyone, not for all the power in the world.

But the magic humming beneath my skin did not agree.

CHAPTER 18

OUR SECOND TREK through the African wilderness was a bit more enjoyable. Likely it had something to do with the fact I was no longer racing toward my death bed with demon poison in my veins. The sky was overcast, and though it was still hot, my skin wasn't sizzling. There was more wildlife to watch this time. Kael laughed when I waved at a herd of elephants, and I told him it was just in case they knew Bibi.

As we walked, I fingered the tiny elephant tusk earring in my pocket that the prophetess had given me. What would happen if I were to wear it? Kael strode beside me, and as I glanced at him, I tried to picture him wearing the earring in his pocket that was twin to the one I carried. I giggled.

Kael smiled as he peered down at me, though his eyebrows were raised. "What's so funny?"

"Have you ever had your ears pierced?" I asked.

"Not in this lifetime," he said. He shook his head with a laugh.

I pulled my hand out of my pocket to adjust the strap of my bag biting into my shoulder. "This lifetime?"

"Well, apparently this isn't the first time I've been alive, is it? I'm some sort of reborn warrior destined to protect you."

The light-hearted question had taken a turn toward a conversation I wasn't sure I wanted to partake in. I chewed on the inside of my cheek. "How do you feel about that?"

The shifter paused, and I hesitated beside him in the tall brown and yellow grass. "About protecting you?"

"About not really having a choice about it." I shrugged a shoulder. "I mean, it's like you had no choice but to be there at the ruins in the Amazon and ever since, you've been stuck with me. You're risking your job, risking your *life*, for something and someone you had no choice but to encounter."

Kael stepped closer to me, and his hand lifted to curl around my bicep. "I don't think of it like that. I want to be here to protect you."

"I can take care of myself, though. I don't need protecting."

"Everyone needs protecting sometimes, Livvie." A crooked grin twisted his lips. "Even strong, intelligent, independent archaeologists need a hand now and then."

I smiled back, even if my heart wasn't quite in it. I still couldn't shake the feeling I was nothing more than a reborn obligation to Kael. He accompanied me and protected me because he was meant to, not because it had really been a choice for him.

"Besides," he said. "If you hadn't wandered into those ruins in that deep, dangerous jungle in the first place, I would have never had the privilege of meeting you."

When had his hands trapped my shoulders? I lifted my face to find myself suddenly trapped in Kael's intense gaze.

"I want to support and protect you, not because it's my job, or because something is telling me to, but because you've grown to mean a lot to me, Livvie."

The air seemed to press in around us. It had nothing to do with the climate of Africa, and everything to do with the way Kael's chest was mere inches from me. His hands, calloused and strong, feathered up my neck to rest on my jawline.

I swallowed, and Kael's nostrils flared as he pulled in a deep breath.

His eyes widened, and suddenly it wasn't his chest in front of me, but his back. It took me a couple of seconds to realize he'd whirled around and shoved me behind him.

"What…" I leaned over to peer around his shoulder.

A massive lioness prowled from the grass in front of us. Her head was lowered and her gaze steady. Her massive paws padded silently as she closed the distance. A low growl rumbled from her chest. Then another lioness parted through the grass, and another. A young male lion followed, his mane nothing more than a shaggy crest down his neck.

Just as I was about to tap into my magic to avoid becoming lunch, Kael reached back and squeezed my wrist. Then he dropped to one knee, bowing as if in reverence. Confused, I didn't know what else to do but follow suit.

"Forgive us for trespassing," he said. "Bibi sent us."

I glanced up to see the lions turning to look at each other. Were these the lion shifters, then?

Not bothering to wait for instruction from Kael, I rose to my feet and held out the spear. The lioness closest to me snarled, her canines showing as she peeled back her lips.

"We've brought this," I said. "As a sign of good faith." My heart was hammering as the lions' growls echoed in my chest. What if I said something wrong? Surely, they didn't see me as a threat.

Kael straightened beside me, his shoulder nearly brushing mine. If this turned into a fight, his jaguar form, sleek and powerful as it was, wouldn't stand a chance against the group of lions.

The lioness before me turned and headed into the grass. She glanced back and stared at us until I started forward. Clearly, we were supposed to follow her. The rest of the lions spread out. Some were beside us, and others behind. We had no choice but to go deeper into the lion pride's territory.

I tried to soothe my racing pulse and even my breathing as we walked, but it was difficult to do surrounded by the group of capable and deadly predators. Still, I did my best to lose myself in my surroundings. Not much had changed. There was still mostly just grass, with the horizon broken now and then by acacia trees and herds of distant antelope.

The farther we walked, the more I could sense a disturbance in the atmosphere. I rubbed my clammy hands on my pants. It was as if something vile were spreading into the area, soaking into the soil, and tainting the water. Things had become still. There was no breeze or chirping of birds. Goosebumps scattered across my skin, and my stomach curled.

Something was very wrong.

"Kael," I whispered.

He grabbed my hand that wasn't holding the spear and squeezed. "I know."

A sense of relief flashed through me that he could sense something was amiss, as well, and it wasn't just me going crazy.

"Stay close," he murmured.

I nodded. As if I was going to wander off when we were surrounded by a pack of suspicious lion shifters.

I lost track of how long we walked. My side burned a little —not painfully, but enough to be uncomfortable. We'd already changed my bandage once earlier in the day. I'd skipped drinking any of the foul tea, but now I wished I'd drank at least one cup.

Judging by the way Kael's gaze flicked to me constantly and how he hardly kept more than a half of a foot of space between us, I sensed he was worried. My near-death experience with the demon poison must have rattled him, but he needed to give me a bit more credit. I didn't say anything to him, though, and let him hover. He was on edge as much as I was.

The lions led us into a small forest, much like the one near Bibi's home. I thought to find the shifters dwelling beneath the canopy, but we continued through the trees. When we reached the other side, my mouth popped open.

Massive, rocky outcrops broke through the grassy plains. Squares dotted the walls—doors and windows, apparently. A mixture of people and lions were scattered about, partaking in cooking, cleaning, and talking.

The lioness in front led us to a semi-circle of rock. A crowd gathered as she left us on the flat ground in the half circle and disappeared into a dark doorway up ahead. There were equal numbers of men and women; even a group of children were gathered on the right, their wide eyes curious. A few moments later, she re-emerged, followed by a man.

I had seen a great deal of intimidating men in my lifetime. My father had been intimidating in his sternness, I'd had competition in the archaeological field who'd thought they could best me, and even Kael had his moments, but this man…this man had a presence to him that made me want to bow my head. It was as if a king had stepped before us.

The man wasn't incredibly tall, like many of the men that filed out after him, and his dark hair was tinged with gray, but he made up for it in his stature and his granite, unwavering stare. A shaggy lions' mane settled around his shoulder, making him appear wider than he actually was. His chest was bare, all hard, strong lines as if old age had yet to sink into his bones. Though he appeared human, I swear I could almost see the lion prowling beneath his skin. I'd never seen a human wearing a lion's mane before, and that alone stirred a cold pit in my stomach.

This man was unmistakingly the chief, the leader of the lion shifters, and by the hard line of his brow and stiff features, he was not thrilled to see Kael and I standing before him.

Silence permeated the air, as if the very world itself were

holding her breath. I inhaled deeply, then let my breath out slowly. I held my gaze on the chief.

"My name is—"

"I know who you are, *mage*."

The chief's spitting words took me aback, as did the hard, twisting features of his face. It was not suspicion there, as I had first believed. The man peered at me as if I were a deadly viper.

I shook my head. "I am not a—"

The lion shifter took a step forward. "You are not a mage? Do you deny you possess the ability to beckon magic and twist energy to do your bidding?"

I huffed. Would he even let me answer his questions? "I don't deny it, but I'm not..." I hesitated. Could I really deny the fact I was, indeed, a mage? I could summon and control magic, after all.

"We bring you an offering, great chief," Kael said. He waved his hand toward me, indicating the ivory spear still clutched in my right hand. "Bibi sent us."

The chief stepped forward, and the people behind him followed closely. They had weapons, I realized—spears and long knives. Not that they needed them with lions closing in on us.

"I have been expecting you," he said.

Had Bibi sent word ahead of us? But if she had, why were they so suspicious?

The chief continued. "Vehrin warned us of your coming."

"V-Vehrin?" I sputtered. I couldn't help but look around, as if the dark mage would unfold himself from the nearest shadow. "He's here?"

"No. He warned us you would come here, seeking something you have no right to possess."

Kael stepped closer to the leader of the shifters. "We are not the villains. Vehrin is the one you should come together and fight against."

The chief's hard eyes cut to Kael. "Do not speak to me of fighting together, *jaguar*, when your kind prefers to hide alone in the shadows. We do stand together here, and we know those with malicious intent when we see them." His gaze swept back to me. "I know you seek the key, thief, and I will not relinquish it."

"I am not a thief!" I took a step forward to stand beside Kael and held the spear out. "I passed the test. Bibi sent us here to trade this spear for the key. You must give it to us before Vehrin gets a hold of it."

"I see nothing in your hand but proof you have killed Bibi." Something strange flickered in his eyes. It was almost as if a shadow had passed over his gaze. I watched him as Kael spoke.

"Do you smell the scent of blood on the spear?" my partner asked. "We did not kill her. Send some runners to go and ask her if you wish."

I ground my teeth. If we had to wait on the lion shifters to confirm we had no ill intent, we could be too late. It was apparent Vehrin was close. He could seize the opportunity to steal the key any moment.

"That is what you want, isn't it?" the chief asked. "You want my pride to be divided so you can get your thieving hands on this."

The chief pulled a necklace from beneath the shaggy mane nestled on his shoulders. On the chain was a key. It was a deep brownish-black, and though I couldn't really see it in much detail, I could feel it. The air nearly pulsed around me, and as much I wanted to step forward and snatch it, I stood my ground. I reached beneath my shirt and pulled out the two keys already in my possession. I held them up so he could clearly see them.

"Vehrin has been lying to you. He has already tried to steal these. Your key is next. You have to let us have it, before the truly dark mage gets a hold of it. He is the one who wants death and destruction."

"You are the one spewing falsities." The chief bared his teeth, his gaze searing me where I stood. "I've seen what you have done. I've seen who you have murdered to get your hands on the keys around your neck. You may have the power to convince lesser beings, to take down weak witches and old women, but you will not find us easy fodder for your foul intentions."

I was shocked into silence as a shadow seemed to flicker behind the chief's eyes again. Then, I *knew*, and the realization brought with it the sour taste of defeat.

Vehrin had used his power to give the leader of the lion shifters false visions. He had done the same to me, in the beginning, before I grew powerful enough to keep the dark mage out of my head.

I glanced at the other members of the pride. They seemed sound of mind, but why would they have a reason to believe anything but what their leader told them?

Kael's fingers tightened into fists beside me. "Listen, we came here in good faith. Olivia only wants to help, but she is powerful, and we will take the key if we must to keep it out of Vehrin's hands."

Unexpectedly, the chief laughed, a great, booming roar that bounced off the rock around us. "You dare threaten me with your mage and her trinkets? For thieves, you are very uneducated about the items you wish to steal." He held up the dark key in his hand. "This key has the power to override the ones in your possession. Now, tell me, what reason do I have to fear you?"

My heart hammered. If Vehrin got a hold of the third key, would he be able to render me powerless? If he could take my magic, he would easily be able to get the keys from me…along with my soul.

"Leave." The chief's command was loud, harsh.

I tried one last time. "Please. You must listen to me. You have been deceived."

"If you do not leave, your pet shifter will see your blood soaking the ground."

A growl rumbled through Kael, and a few of the lionesses stalked forward, tails twitching and snarls ripping through their open jaws.

I grabbed Kael's arm. "It's all right." I looked at the chief. "We will leave, but I hope you come to see the truth soon." I glanced at the children gathered on the right, and my chest squeezed. "For all your sakes."

I twirled the spear, and a few of the men behind the chief shifted their own weapons toward me. I ground the point into the dirt and left it standing for the lion shifters to do whatever they wished with it. The trial had been useless. I hadn't been able to trade the spear for the key.

Kael and I left, though I could sense the lions prowling behind us for a good mile before they left us alone.

When we reached the shade of a tree, I sat down heavily on the ground. My emotions were all over the place, and I felt like a great weight was grinding me into the dust.

Kael knelt before me and rested his hands on my knees. "Livvie?"

"Why didn't Vehrin take the key already?" I asked. Kael shrugged, and I took a deep breath. "What are we going to do, Kael?"

The pride of lion shifters had forced us out, and with Kael and I out of the way, Vehrin would not hesitate to steal the third key...and kill all who would stand in his way.

CHAPTER 19

Kael had started a small fire, then shifted into his jaguar form and managed to take down a gazelle that was now roasting over the flames. I was still trying to figure out why Vehrin hadn't already taken the chance to snatch the third key.

"I don't know," Kael said, back in human form again. "Given the confidence the chief had that we wouldn't obtain the key, perhaps it has to be freely given."

I crossed my legs as the smoke curl around the sizzling meat. The scent of it made my stomach growl. "That won't stop him," I said.

We had continued for at least another mile after leaving the lion shifter's territory before choosing a spot to rest. The sky was a soft purple as the sun dipped below the horizon. Kael lowered to the ground beside me. He was shirtless and had opted not to put his boots back on in case he needed to shift again.

"No," he said. "It won't."

I tapped fingertips on my knee. "Maybe we should have gone back to Bibi. We could have brought her to the shifters. He would have seen we weren't lying."

"I don't think it would have helped." Kael grabbed a stick and poked at the fire, spreading the coals to even out the heat. "You said Vehrin had likely given them visions with the wrong impression of us. Even if we had brought Bibi, the chief likely would have assumed it was some sort of trick."

Kael was right. Besides...straying too far from the pride's territory would be a risk. The atmosphere was teeming with a sense of *wrong*. I could feel it pressing in on me. It made the air heavy and crackled through our surroundings like a fierce storm about to descend. If we left now, the dark mage would definitely take advantage of our absence to snatch the third key.

The pair of us sat in silence a little longer. The fire hissed as juice from the roasting gazelle dropped to the flames. I'd never eaten gazelle. Would it taste like venison? My mouth was watering as Kael carefully lifted the meat from the sticks he'd assembled over the flames. As he pulled the meat from it, I wondered if the only reason he'd roasted it was for my benefit. Surely he could have just eaten while in his jaguar form.

Kael handed me a sizeable chunk of the meat, and I shifted the portion from one hand to the other as I waited for it to cool down.

"Do you ever eat raw meat while in your jaguar form?" I asked.

"I have," Kael said. He pulled in a quick sniff of the meat. "I prefer cooked, though. The flavor is better." He tentatively bit a piece off, chewed, then nodded. "The hunt itself is fun, but it's hard to explain."

I tried my own meat. It had a very gamey taste and could definitely use a bit of seasoning, but it wasn't too bad. "I could see that," I said. "Tackling a deer or antelope is probably akin to me plucking a bit of ancient treasure from a pile of earth and dust."

A crooked grin lifted one of Kael's cheeks. "Maybe, though my method of hunting is likely a lot less dangerous."

"Probably." I laughed. "Let's hope you never accidentally take down a cursed zebra."

"Let's hope." Kael chuckled, and bit off more meat.

I stared at him for a moment, watching the muscles work as he chewed and noticing the stubble shadowing his jaw. "Do you prefer to be in your human form, or would you rather give in to your primal nature?"

Kael studied the piece of bone in his hand, already stripped of meat. "I wouldn't say it is my primal nature. It's just nature. You, as a human, don't get up and take a shower because it's primal. You do it because it's just something you do. Shifting isn't me tapping into some primal piece of me, it's just who I am." He tilted his head and studied me. "Why do you ask?"

I shrugged. "Just curious, I guess."

I took another bite to spare myself from needing to give him any further explanation. In truth, I was wondering because my own ancient, dark nature moved inside me like a restless shadow, and it was nothing but primal. I had hoped Kael could give me an insight on controlling a feral part of yourself, but it didn't appear he would have any pointers on what was troubling me.

"You know, when I first shifted, my mother had to chase after me for two days," Kael said. He tossed the bone away and tore off seconds from the roasted gazelle. Instead of biting into it, this time he merely tore off little pieces. "I had never felt anything like it, and I just wanted to run, climb, and hunt. I grew so lost in my sleek new muscles and sharpened senses that when she finally caught up to me, she took me by surprise, and I put a clawful of scratches across her face."

"You attacked your own mother?"

Kael gave me a frown. "I wasn't myself. She convinced me to change back, and I apologized. My point is, I had to learn to control my shift. I had to learn to let it be a part of me, and not something I had to set loose."

It was then I realized he was giving me advice by way of a story from his past. "Thanks for telling me. I'm sure your mom is a wonderful woman."

He nodded. "Are you going to eat that?" He pointed at the remainder of the meat.

"Nope." I still had some to finish, but after the first several bites, I'd begun to lose my appetite. "Eat away, kitty cat."

Kael snorted. "That's a nickname I could do without."

As he finished eating, I rifled through my pack to take stock of supplies. There was only one spare set of clothes left for Kael, so I really hoped he would be careful with his shifts. We had a canteen each, but one was only about a quarter full. Some bandaging was still left over from Bibi, and I had a couple of small knives. Aside from that was only a handful of granola bars and a set of clothes for me. If something wasn't figured out soon with the pride, we would have no choice but to turn back to civilization.

A sudden thought occurred to me. "Kael, couldn't you just contact PITO and tell them to have the pride hand over the key? You're all shifters, after all, and protecting relics is what you do. Wouldn't they have to listen?"

Kael shifted and angled himself toward me. "It doesn't work like that. True, we are all shifters, but that doesn't mean we all follow the same government. PITO is an organization, not a monarchy. Your FBI can't go to another country and make demands without cutting through red tape and jumping through loopholes." He looked away, his gaze sweeping across the darkening landscape. "Besides, I don't want PITO to know about the third key. Not yet, anyway."

"Why? Don't you trust them?"

He took a while to answer, and I wondered if he was afraid to speak against his own organization. "They follow their own rules, for their own reasons, just like everybody else.

These keys, this plot of Vehrin's, is bigger than any of us. His influence likely stretches far, or he wouldn't be taking such risks. I'd rather wait until the key is in our possession and we figure out our next move before letting PITO know anything other than the fact we know where Vehrin is located."

I picked at some dirt lodged in the tread of my boot. "It must be awful to feel like you can't trust the people you work with."

"I don't trust most people."

It was a surprising thing for him to say, but it made sense. Kael had always struck me as a loner. It was in his shifter nature. Jaguars didn't live in prides like lions, or packs like wolves. They dwelled in solitude. He'd always seemed suspicious of the witches and fae we met, but now I wondered if it stretched to people in general, shifters included. It was a sad thing to think about, not being able to trust in anybody.

"Is there anyone you do trust?"

I lifted my gaze to Kael, and he held my stare as he smiled. "I trust you."

For some reason, his words made my stomach flutter. I couldn't help but feel a bit proud that I was someone he was able to put faith in. "Good thing," I said, trying to make light of it. "This whole mission would have been a mess if you didn't."

"It's still been a mess," Kael pointed out. "But at least the company is good."

I grinned. "You're full of compliments tonight."

"It's a good night for compliments, don't you think?" Kael lifted an eyebrow.

"Is it?"

As if in answer, Kael laid back on the ground and laced his hands behind his head. I followed suit, though I used my bag as a makeshift pillow. The stars had come out, and they shone above in an endless sea of diamond dust. I'd never seen the heavens so clear and vast.

Despite the beauty above, the silence around us was disconcerting. We were in the African wilderness. There should be the sound of animals, like the chirping of birds and insects. The quiet in the air was heavy, and wrong.

I scooted a bit closer to Kael, feeling a little vulnerable in the dark, silent open. "Vehrin will return to take the third key."

"I know," Kael said. "We have to get it before he does."

I studied the stars, trying to pick out familiar constellations. "Kael, there is no way that guy is going to hand over the relic. The only way we will be able to get that key is if we steal it, and we can't do that."

"You didn't have a problem stealing it when you thought it was in a famous museum."

A sharp sigh blew past my lips. "That was different. To get the key now, we would have to do it by force."

"There may not be another way, Livvie."

I turned to my side to face Kael and propped my head on my elbow. My eyebrows furrowed. "I don't want to attack innocent people. They have children there, Kael. We can't just tear in there and hurt people."

Kael's features were impassive. How much of his agent identity was he using to steel himself? "We have no choice."

I recalled what he had said to me after we confronted the witch on the mountain after I'd been pummeled by an avalanche. He'd told me there would come times when I had to make decisions that would go against everything I was, but it would be necessary. I rolled over onto my back again.

"I'm afraid," I whispered.

Warm fingers touched the back of my hand—a silent request. I opened my hand, and Kael slid his into mine and gave it a squeeze.

Kael's voice was soft. "Why are you afraid?"

I chewed on the inside of my cheek as I thought about attacking the shifters so we could get the key. I couldn't bring myself to use my sword. The thought of cutting innocent people down made my stomach clench. I would have no choice but to use my magic to incapacitate them.

"If I attack people using my magic, the power inside me may like it too much." I tilted my head to peer at him. "What if I can't stop?" The thought of slaying people, of enjoying it, of dropping body after body, made me shiver.

Kael leaned up on his elbow and stared down at me. "You make your magic, Olivia; it doesn't make you."

He had so much faith in me and so much confidence in my ability to handle myself. What if I failed him?

I looked away. "I'm not so sure."

He laid a warm, rough hand on my cheek. "I'll look after you, Livvie."

My heartbeat quickened, and I knew he could hear it. Kael would look after me, both physically and mentally. He wouldn't let me become a monster. I stared up at him for a moment and breathed in his peculiar rain-and-citrus scent. He was so close I could feel the heat of his bare chest. My gaze found his stubble again, and I wondered how rough it would feel against my skin. My fingers twitched as I thought about wrapping my arms around his neck.

Rational thought caught up to my emotional musings, and I swallowed so hard it came out like a gulp. My cheeks reddened, and I caught Kael's lips twitch in amusement before he eased back.

Now was not the time to be falling for a shifter. Though, was there ever a good time to fall for a shifter? It wasn't as if we would work out, anyway. Didn't shifters have to stick to their own kind? More likely than not, we'd have to go our separate ways eventually.

"What are you going to do when this is all over?" I asked. "Will you be assigned to a different location to protect?"

After all, there would be no point in him being at the ruins in the Amazon since the relic he'd been protecting there was now around my neck. I'd probably be going back to my job at the university, if they'd still take me after my extended vacation.

Kael didn't answer my question. "Get some sleep, Livvie," he said. "We have a fight tomorrow, one way or another."

He rolled over so his back was facing me. I curled my hands against the power inside me waiting to be released, and thought of the shifter pride. I could almost feel the taint of innocent blood already staining my palms.

CHAPTER 20

THE SCENT of woodsmoke was the first thing I noticed when I started to stir the next morning. I could tell it was early, even before I opened my eyes to the pale gray of dawn. A moan hummed up my throat as I rolled to my back. My shoulder was sore, and the healing wound on my ribs panged a bit from sleeping on my bad side. I tilted my head to see if Kael was still asleep, but he was no longer laying beside me. I shifted to lean up on my elbows.

The fire was smoking, but no flames licked the wood remaining in our hand-dug fire pit. I glanced around, expecting my partner to be sitting nearby, but he was nowhere to be seen.

"Kael?"

There was no answer.

A chill prickled over my skin. I sat up and rubbed my arms. What if Vehrin had come in the middle of the night and…

And what? It wasn't as if the dark mage would have attacked Kael and left me unharmed. I did a quick check. The pair of keys still hung around my neck. He definitely wouldn't have left those. Besides, Kael would have made some noise if he were being attacked, and I would have woken.

The sticks Kael had used to hold the meat over the fire the previous night were laying neatly beside it. He'd most likely just gone out to hunt for our breakfast. My stomach churned at the thought of eating when I would most likely be in a fight at some point during the day. I wasn't sure if I'd be able to muster up an appetite.

I twisted around, grabbed my bag, and settled it onto my lap. Maybe I could just munch on a granola bar and let Kael eat a gazelle, or antelope, or whatever unfortunate creature he would manage to take down. He always had a ferocious appetite. I wouldn't be surprised if he skewered a water buffalo over our fire.

My fingers hit a canteen as I dug around for a granola bar and I pulled it out. Staying hydrated was a lesson I'd learned the hard way. I untwisted the cap and took a few swallows. When I was finished, I unwrapped the granola bar. I took a bite, then grabbed a nearby stick. There was a tiny chill in the early morning air, despite what I was certain would be a hot and dry day. I stirred up the ashes, trying to tempt a flame from the smoldering coals. The smoke shifted, as if the wind blew it, and I froze.

There was no wind.

I couldn't see behind me, but I was certain there was someone standing there. It wasn't Kael. I'd know his presence.

I poked at the charred wood in the firepit again as I took a deep breath. Then, I straightened, and as I whirled, I imagined my sword in my hand. The man retreated a step as I pointed the blade at his throat. His hands rose into the air.

"Easy now," he said with a laugh. "You'll want to be careful with that thing."

I narrowed my eyes. He seemed familiar to me. I studied his tall, gangly form and wide smile. I blinked. "You're David, right? Kael's friend."

He'd been the one to tell us how to find Bibi.

The smile faded from his face, though amusement still danced in his dark eyes. "Vehrin knows you are near. He would very much like you to stay away for the time being."

His words surprised me. Vehrin had sent him?

I searched his eyes for a sign he was being deceived, like the lion shifters, but I found nothing that would suggest as much. My pulse started to quicken. David was a traitor.

It angered me, and it wasn't so much the fact he was working for Vehrin, but he was supposed to be a good friend of Kael's. He already had a hard time trusting people, and the last thing he needed was a traitorous friend.

My sword didn't waver as I glowered at him. "You're with Vehrin?"

It didn't seem right. David had seemed so vibrant and happy back at the hotel. He'd said he hoped I lived, and that he wouldn't mind seeing what became of Kael and me. Had his words merely been an act, or had he meant he hoped I lived to this point so he could see our downfall?

David tried to sidestep my blade, but I followed his movement. He sighed. "I can see this is going to take more effort than I had hoped for. I don't suppose there is any chance of you coming quietly?"

"Coming where?" I asked.

"Vehrin is an old friend of yours, I understand, and he wants to spend some time catching up when he is done taking care of the pride."

The thought of that evil mage harming those people for the key around the chief's neck had me baring my teeth in a way that would have made Kael proud. I didn't waste another second. I thrust my sword straight at David's neck, but stumbled as he moved away so fast he was little more than a blur.

Something struck me in the side, and my feet shuffled in an attempt to regain my balance.

"It was a good try," he said.

I whirled around to find him behind me. How had he gotten there so fast? *Right*, I thought. *He's a cheetah shifter. That's just fantastic.*

The man seemed to like to talk. Maybe I could keep him preoccupied until Kael returned. He'd be easier to take down together.

"Why are you with Vehrin? He's evil. He's *wrong*."

A large grin split David's face. "Is he? And how would you know what he is?"

"I probably know better than anyone," I said. "I remember what he is capable of, and believe me, if you knew, you would not want any part of him."

I hoped David wouldn't realize I was bluffing. While fragments of my long-forgotten memory had begun to return, I didn't know the whole story. All I knew was whoever I had been in the past had been in an alliance with Vehrin, before that partnership went sour.

David waved a hand in front of his face. "You cannot sway me. Besides, good and evil is a matter of perception."

I tightened my grip on my sword, and subtly shifted my feet into an offensive stance. "What do you mean?"

The man started to circle me, his gaze watching me as if he were searching for the best opening for attack. "It is time for a change. It is time for magic to be in the open, time for old ways to once again rise." He suddenly looked down, and I followed his gaze to the pile of Kael's neatly folded clothes at his feet. "Shifters used to be held in high regard by all beings. Now we must hide who we truly are from those who would seek to destroy us if they knew what we truly were." His stare lifted back to mine, and there was no longer any mirth in his eyes. "You are young to this world, to this life of secrets, and you cannot understand. We live in a world where beings like us would be considered monsters."

So that was what this was all about. Vehrin wanted magic

to come out of the shadows. I could understand not wanting to live a life in hiding, and even the appeal of being revered, but I couldn't appreciate his way of going about it.

My eyebrows lowered toward David again. "Funny, for someone who has no desire to be a monster, you're very keen on serving one." I flicked my gaze quickly around but saw no sign of Kael. "Why did you send us to the prophetess if you're with Vehrin?"

I didn't mention Bibi's name, just in case the man wasn't aware of it.

He had resumed his circling, his steps calculated. "I needed to assure your mission was believable, but I'd hoped the demons would finish you off first."

So, the demons were likely siding with Vehrin now, not merely breaking out of whatever realm his presence had allowed to weaken.

"I've been tracking you since you left. I found where you had stayed with the prophetess, but she appears to have moved on to a different location."

"Fortunately for you," I said. "I have a feeling she would have done away with you and spit on your bones for your treachery."

David's fingers flexed, and I knew I was running short on time. "It doesn't appear the lions wanted to play with you, but I'm willing to give it a go."

He dashed forward, and I swept my blade up. Only a quick step to the side saved him from his guts spilling to the ground.

"Are you sure you want to play with me?" I said. "Because I tend not to lose." I risked another sweeping glance across the landscape. *Where the hell are you, Kael?*

"You seem distracted," David said. His sharp eyes followed every flicker of movement as I squared up to face him again. He tilted his head. "Wondering where your mate is?"

"He's not my mate." My stomach fluttered, and it had nothing to do with nerves. "Kael's a friend."

My opponent grinned. "Call him what you will. Regardless, he's a bit preoccupied with some friends of mine I brought along."

I strained to hear fighting in the distance, proof that what David said was true, but I heard nothing. Was he bluffing, or was it already too late?

I chided myself. Kael was an excellent fighter and was more than capable of holding his own. His absence just meant I would have to take this joker down on my own.

"Now, since you've shown me your bite, Olivia, it's only fair to show you mine."

David rushed at me, but I'd been expecting as much. I lunged to the side, tucking myself in tight, and rolled away. I rose up to my knee, teeth clenched and hand tight around the handle of my sword. Thank goodness for those deep-rooted instincts, or the move may have had me putting the blade through my own body.

I wouldn't be able to outmaneuver David for long, especially if he decided to shift. I quickly studied my surroundings from my peripheral, and found I was near the firepit again. Its heat brushed against me, and an idea sparked in my mind. I didn't rise from my crouch. Instead, I waited for David to lunge down at me. I reached for the firepit with my free hand and grabbed a piece of wood sticking out of the embers. The end glowed red, and as the cheetah shifter bore down on me, I turned the burning wood toward him.

David screamed, and I wrinkled my nose against the stench of burning flesh as he lurched away from me. He held a hand to his neck with a grimace, then returned his gaze to me. He bared his teeth, and his eyes flashed. Before I could regain my feet, or think to raise my weapon, he was on me.

My back hit the ground, and David's fingers dug into my

biceps. "If you're not going to play nice, then neither am I. Vehrin wants you alive, but he never said anything about you having to be in a perfect state." His tongue ran over his teeth, as if his cheetah self was ready to shift and sink his teeth into me.

This man was crazier than I'd first assumed if he thought he was going to bite me. "Careful, or you're going to wake up something you don't want to tangle with."

David's lips peeled back, showing his white teeth in a fierce smile that was anything but friendly. He leaned down so his face was only a few inches from mine. "I can handle myself just fine."

The piece of wood in my hand had fallen when he'd attacked me. I pulled on my magic, waited until I could feel it tasting my fingertips, then drove my head up into David's face. He cursed and let me go in surprise, and I pressed my magic-soaked hand into his face.

The shifter fell backward, and though my hand was no longer on his face, my magic remained. The energy stuck to his skin like a spiderweb. He clawed at his face, screaming, as the magic consumed him. It was a gruesome sight, his skin burning, his own fingers raking bloodied lines down his face. I scooted back with a disgusted grimace, and quickly bottled up my magic before I did anything else horrific.

It didn't take long for David to fall, dead, his face a twist of unrecognizable features.

As I got to my feet, Kael broke from the grass in his jaguar form. His sides heaved, and blood stained the fur around his mouth. He glanced briefly at the dead man as he passed. He loped over, then he pressed his head against my hip.

"I'm fine," I said, reaching down to pat his head. He made a chuffing noise, so I got down on my knees to peer into his golden eyes. "Kael, I'm fine. Promise."

I ran my gaze down the pattern of spots on his fur,

searching for any injuries. Then, I hugged his neck. He always seemed cuddlier in this form, and I couldn't help myself. "Are you okay?"

Kael sniffed sharply.

Taking that as a 'yes,' I smiled. "You better get your clothes back on."

We both turned to look for his clothes, then I realized I'd dropped a dead man on them. Kael gave me a level, accusatory stare before going to my bag. He started clawing at it as he tried to pull his clothes out. I shoved him away.

"Stop that. You're going to put a hole in it." I drew out his set of clothes. "This is your last set of clothes. If you tear these up, you're going to be making your way back to civilization in your birthday suit."

As Kael shifted and dressed, I gathered our things. Our breakfast would have to wait. My partner came up beside me and jerked his head toward the body. "I see you handled yourself well. Some idiot working for the mage, I suppose?"

I realized Kael couldn't recognize his friend with the damage I'd done to David.

"Yeah, I guess so." I couldn't bring myself to tell him David had betrayed him. Likely, he'd never find out, anyway. Besides, how would he feel if he knew I'd killed his friend?

"We'd better hurry," Kael said. "I have a feeling Vehrin is already back at the pride, or he will be soon."

I hefted my bag onto my shoulder and let my sword weave back into the bracelet around my wrist. "What makes you say that?"

"He wouldn't have sent some of his followers if he didn't want us to stay away."

Together, we trekked back toward the lion shifters. I wasn't certain how close we would be able to get to them before we were confronted, but we had to try.

The horizon turned to a bright orange swept with brilliant

strokes of gold. It was a beautiful day for a battle with a dark mage, but I hoped I wouldn't have to kill innocents in the process.

I'd already killed one man today. How many more would I add to the list before the sun set again?

CHAPTER 21

"What are you thinking so hard about?"

I glanced over at Kael and swallowed the bite of granola bar. "What do you mean?"

He smiled. "Whenever you're thinking hard, you stop chewing your food. You've been eating that granola bar for a good twenty minutes, so that's either the tastiest one you've ever eaten and you're savoring every bite, or you're thinking about something pretty damn hard."

I let out a sharp sigh and stuffed the half-eaten granola bar into my pocket. "It just doesn't make any sense."

"It's all right. There are a lot of people with odd eating habits."

Kael laughed when I sliced a glare at him. "That's not what I'm talking about. I still don't understand why Vehrin hasn't already taken the key. He's a dark mage. He's *the* dark mage. And the chief seems to be on his side."

"True. But the chief still won't give him the key. It's his job to protect it." Kael kicked at a small mound of dirt, then jumped to the side with a curse when ants spilled out of it. I had to look in the opposite direction to keep from laughing as he did an odd sort of shuffle-dance to dislodge the ants and still keep pace with me. "Anyway, what if he was merely trying to draw you to him? He knew you would go after the key."

"But then why would he force those visions on the shifters and make us out to be the bad guys? And why not use that ability to trick them into handing the key over. " I stared out at the sea of grass. "Unless…"

My partner paused to bend over and brush a few stray ants from trying to crawl in his boots. "Unless what?"

"What if Vehrin doesn't want to cause a scene by stealing the key? I have no doubt he is capable of doing so, but think about it. When we confronted him the first time, it was in a secluded, secretive area. There were no humans around to see what was going on. He's been very careful. If he goes and slaughters an entire pride of shifters, someone is bound to notice. Accidents happen. One could slip away, and the next thing you know, other shifters know about what he did. PITO already knows, but I'm betting they aren't letting on about the threat to others. If Vehrin starts making noise, though, soon the whole world will know the truth."

"That's actually a very good point, Livvie." Kael smiled at me, pride shining in his gaze. "Maybe you should come work for PITO."

I laughed. "Me? An agent? No, thanks. Besides, PITO protects magical objects, they don't dig them up. I'd constantly be in trouble."

"I can't argue with that," Kael said. He was silent for a moment. "I think you're right about Vehrin. He can't take on the whole world. Not yet. If he can get the key without bloodshed, he will. Unless a troublemaker comes along." He gave me a wink.

"That's why he convinced the shifters to make us leave. He doesn't want me causing a scene, or being near enough to get the key. He wants me to stay away. That's why he sent those men."

Kael grunted. "He should have known to send better insurance."

"Maybe he couldn't afford the top of the line 'Keep-the-cursed-mage-and-her-shifter-guardian-away' plan." I grinned up at Kael, and his lips started to twitch into a smile.

Then, he stopped. He held an arm out, blocking my path.

Two women rose from the grasses not ten feet in front of us. Their clothing was colorful, bright reds and canary yellows, and I recalled seeing some of the women wearing similar attire with the shifter pack. Their faces, though void of emotion, held a certain fierceness in their quiet staring. These were lionesses. Had they come to stop us?

I started to summon my sword from the bracelet, then paused as the grasses swayed behind them.

Nearly a dozen lion cubs stepped hesitantly out of the foliage. They stared at us, and stuck close to the women. My heart jumped. *Children*. What were they doing out here with children? Had we been too late? Was this all that was left of the lion shifters?

One of the women spoke. "You are returning to the pride."

It wasn't a question. If anything, her tone was accusatory.

I pushed Kael's arm down so he wasn't blocking me and took a step forward. "We are. Is everyone okay? Has Vehrin returned?"

"There is no one there." The fierce woman was several inches taller than her companion, who had remained quiet. She hesitated, and studied us with piercing, golden eyes. "Our leader is not well," she finally said.

I nodded. "I thought as much. I have no doubt Vehrin gave him false visions of our intentions."

"We sensed something was wrong. If he was sound of mind, he would not have turned you away after you offered Bibi's spear. It is an ancient promise, one you fulfilled, and yet he chased you out. It was not right."

The other woman, younger, rounder in the face, edged forward. "We took as many of the young ones as we could, but there are still several that remain. They were too close under his eye to take them to safety."

I dropped my gaze to the cubs, all of whom were in their animal form. Most were very small, with round ears and clumsy paws. They wouldn't stand a chance if things took a turn for the worse. It twisted my gut to think there were still children in danger.

The tall woman came closer, and Kael tensed behind me. I touched his arm with a finger, a silent reassurance.

"If you truly are here with noble intentions, save our pride." She glanced back at her companion and the cubs, then turned back to me. "Save our children."

"Is there a way to get the key?" Kael said.

She grimaced, then shook her head. "That key is supposed to be kept in our guardianship."

"We gave you the spear," I said. "It was a promise, you said as much yourself. If Vehrin gets a hold of that key, your life as you know it will be gone."

The younger woman stepped forward, the cubs shadowing her. "When it is not on our chief's person, he keeps it on an altar in his quarters, but it is heavily guarded."

Kael nodded, and by the way he shuffled forward a step, he was eager to take on the task of stealing the key.

"Wait." The woman nearest me held up her hand. "They are anticipating your return. If you go in the way you first came, they will not hesitate to take you down. Go around, and scale the rocks. You may be able to sneak in that way."

"Thank you," I said. Again, I looked at the children. "Where are you taking them?"

"Someplace safe." She watched me for a moment, and some of her fierceness faded. "Please, save them, our pride, and the young ones."

My brow furrowed and my fingers curled into fists. "I

promise you, no one will lay a finger on any child, unless they want to lose their hand. I will stop Vehrin and save your pride, whether your chief wants it or not."

The woman smiled. It changed her face into something bright and warm, and I couldn't help but wonder, if Vehrin won, how hard would the mothers and aunts and sisters of this world have to grow to protect our most vulnerable?

She turned her attention to Kael. "You are blessed to have such a fierce mate at your side."

Without another word, they left. The cubs followed, and a couple of them rubbed against my legs as they passed. The women were leading them in the direction of Bibi's home, and I knew there would be no safer place for them.

As the shifters melted into the grass, I turned to Kael. "That's the second time someone has called me your mate." I gestured down at myself. "Do I look like a shifter?"

Kael's lips lifted in a crooked grin as we continued on our way, angling our path more to the left.

"Definitely not. They'd be able to smell it."

Why had she said that if she knew I wasn't a shifter? "Is it common for shifters to mate with non-shifters?"

"No, it's actually somewhat rare. It isn't illegal to tie yourself to a human in such a way, but it is looked down upon in many cases."

I frowned. "Why?"

He let a low growl. "It's ridiculous thinking, but it is because mating with a human dilutes the bloodlines, and makes exposure to humans more likely."

I nodded. It made sense to not want all of humanity to know about shifters, but the part about the bloodlines seemed barbaric. I glanced at Kael, imagining him with a jaguar shifter on his arm and adorable little shifter cubs running around in the jungle with him. The thought made my stomach clench.

"I'm sure you will make some shifter female very happy

one day. You are quite the catch." I gave him a smile and hoped he couldn't tell how forced it was.

"I do not want a union with a shifter." Kael held me trapped in his gaze for a very long moment. Then, he continued toward the direction of the pride.

What had he meant by *that*? Kael wasn't anti-human, I knew that, so the prospect of him marrying one wasn't far-fetched. Still, he seemed adamant about not wanting a shifter mate, and the way he had looked at me... I reached back and pulled my hair up away from my neck, letting air get to my sweat-slicked skin.

Kael was an enigma, and he seemed intent on confusing me to death.

Our trek took longer than it had when we were forced to leave, but eventually we caught sight of the rock formations breaking the horizon that belonged to the shifter pride. We made a massive arc in the hopes we could avoid prying eyes. Just as we were nearing a small stream that ran between the grassy plain and the rising rocks, I grabbed Kael's arm.

"Look," I whispered, then pointed to our left.

A male lion, young enough to not have a full mane, watched us from several yards away. Kael froze, and a slight growl rumbled from his chest. The lion watched us for a moment longer before turning and disappearing into the grass.

"Why didn't he try to stop us?"

Kael smiled. "He wasn't a shifter. The pride probably chose this place because it is a popular territory for wild lions. It helps them blend in."

"Glad you know the difference," I said. I stepped over to the stream and looked for a way to cross. A bit to our right, several rocks broke the surface of the water. "Guess we're going rock hopping."

I let Kael go first, just in case there were any loose stones. The man practically floated across them, all grace and ease.

"Show off," I muttered. I made my way across nearly as well as he did. I'd only had to flare my arms out twice to get my balance.

The pair of us quietly made our way to the wall of rock. Thankfully, it wasn't an entirely smooth surface. A few small trees grew up through cracks that would help provide handholds and cover if a shifter happened to be walking by.

I reached up and dug my fingers into the rock. Just as I started to lift myself up, Kael spoke.

"I want to take you out."

I was so surprised by his words I lost my grip and scraped my knee on the rock as I dropped back to the ground. I looked up at him. "Huh?"

Kael rubbed at the back of his neck. "You know, on a date."

Squinting, I wondered if the sun had gotten to him. "You want to take me on a date?"

He nodded.

I threw my hands in the air in frustration. "This is not the best time to talk about this."

He dropped his hand and closed the distance between us. "We may soon be eaten by lion shifters or taken down by a dark mage." He lifted his hand to cup my cheek. "I wanted you to know, if we survive this I'd like to take you on a date."

Kael was often serious, but the intensity in his gaze was unnerving…and intriguing. His look made me want to lean into his touch. It made me want to have his arms around me. What would he do if I rose up on my toes and touched my lips to his? I had to lighten the mood before I did something impulsive.

I cocked a grin. "You know you'll have to get in line behind Ren? I still owe him a date. If I knew I was going to be partaking in so many dates, I would be dress-shopping instead of scaling a mountain."

I expected Kael to be rattled or angry at being dismissed, but while he did drop his hand, a slow grin lifted his lips.

"Livvie, you won't need a dress where I'm taking you."

My heart thumped, and I was overcome with curiosity. Before I could ask for more details, Kael started scaling the rock like a professional climber. Maybe he'd just been trying to distract me so he could go up ahead of me.

I followed after him and tried to put my hands and feet where he had, but he was taller and sometimes I had to compensate. Kael was patient, and a couple of times he reached down to give me a hand. I wished there were birds calling, or insects, anything that would help mask the sound of our breathing and scuffing of boots on rock, but there wasn't. It was still eerily quiet, and I was certain we would be discovered at any moment. We only had a few feet to go before we reached the top. The sky above was a dull bluish-gray, as if it might rain. Kael stretched up to peek over the edge, then quickly ducked back down. He pointed. I rose up on my toes to have a look.

There was a young man standing guard at the top. He was leaning on a spear, and though he looked bored, I knew he could spring into action any second. I ducked back down and flattened against the rock to try to keep from being seen.

Kael made a hushed noise, and I turned to him. He wiggled his fingers at me.

What? I mouthed.

He jerked his head toward the spot where the young man stood. What did he want from me? Kael rolled his eyes. Then, his lips formed the word *magic*.

My breath faltered. He wanted me to use my magic to take down the guard. I clenched my teeth. I wasn't ready to release my magic yet, and certainly not on a boy who looked to be eighteen at best. Biting my lip, I shook my head.

A muscle ticked in Kael's jaw, and he bared his teeth in a *quit fooling around and hurry up* way.

I nodded. Kael was right. I had to do it. I could use my magic to subdue him, maybe just knock him out or something.

Just as my fingertips started to prickle with energy, I heard a commotion. The scuffle of footsteps sounded above, and I pressed my cheek against the rock, closing my eyes. I expected shouts of alarm, but then the footsteps faded.

I risked a peek.

The guard was gone.

I groaned as I looked over at Kael. "I'll bet my life Vehrin has arrived."

"Our lives are exactly what we're betting." He pulled himself up over the ledge and reached down for me. "Come on."

We crouched together on top of the rock. There were trees around us that made it impossible to see below.

"Let's hope the key is on the altar, and not around the chief's neck."

Kael and I started to make our way down the rock and toward the dwellings. We were in a race against time. If the chief had the key, it was likely too late. If it was on the altar, we may be able to get to it first.

Just then, a swirl of dark energy whispered across my skin.

"Vehrin *is* here." I swallowed. "And I'm pretty sure he knows I'm here, too."

CHAPTER 22

KAEL and I started to make our way through the tangle of small trees crowning the rock the lion shifters called home. The dark mage's power slithered over my skin like a viper. He was taunting me, letting me know he was aware I was present. I ground my teeth and glared down toward the base of the cliff. I hoped he could feel my searing stare.

I'm coming after you, Vehrin.

Fortunately, we didn't run into any shifters, and it didn't take long for the trees to grow sparse and our path to open up. The massive rock we were atop sloped steadily at our feet, the surface broken with thick ridges and jutting stone. The terrain would be easy to climb down, if we could stay unnoticed, though I assumed many of the unusual formations protruding from the main cliffs were the dwellings of the shifters.

"Look," Kael whispered beside me. He pointed down.

Through a wedge-shaped crevice, I spotted Vehrin standing in front of the chief. My blood chilled. It would be so easy for him to kill the leader of the lion shifters. A part of me wanted to yell a warning, but that would do no good. The chief was likely still under the influence of Vehrin's dark magic. Our only hope was to get the key. Then, maybe, Vehrin would release his mental hold on the pride chief.

The pair were talking. Vehrin stood casually, and though I couldn't see his face, his robes shifted on a subtle breeze. He looked remarkably out of place and, admittedly, very powerful. Many of the other shifters stood near their leader, some in lion form, but none seemed overly protective like they had seemed when Kael and I had been down there. Were they under Vehrin's spell, too, or were they perhaps afraid of the mage?

The chief shook his head and gestured behind him. Something about the way he had touched his chest, as if he were accustomed to something hanging there, then pointed, told me he was undoubtedly talking about the key.

"I think the relic is on the altar," I said.

Kael shifted his stance where he crouched beside me. "What makes you say that?"

"Just the way he's acting and, I don't know, I just have a feeling he doesn't have it on him. We need to make a move. Now." I chewed on my lip as Vehrin conversed with the chief. Why didn't he just kill him and steal the key? If my guess were true, and the chief had to give it to him willingly, would I really be able to take it from the altar?

My partner leaned toward me. "How are you going to get in his dwelling and to the altar without either of them noticing? Not to mention the other shifters."

"I don't know. I haven't thought that far ahead." A sense of urgency burned through me and tightened my muscles. I needed to get down there. "We have to go."

Kael was silent for a moment. "I can go down as a distraction, and at least try to draw away any guards he may have. You can make your way to the altar."

I blinked. "You want me to fetch the key by myself?"

A smile quirked at the corner of his lips. "Are you objecting?"

"No, just surprised." Kael was usually a lot more protective. I knew it was in his shifter nature, and made stronger by the fact he was my guardian in our former, ancient life, so his willingness to let me sneak down into certain danger alone was a bit of a shocker.

He sighed. "It isn't that I don't want to be there for you, but I trust you. Livvie, I've never met anyone more capable of throwing themselves into peril with the certainty they'll come through unscathed. You've proven yourself many times." He squeezed my shoulder. "You've got this."

"Wow," I said. I smiled. "Kael, that really means a lot to me."

"I'll meet back up with you when I can. Just get that key and get out of there."

I stared at Kael, his amber eyes sharp and fierce. Unease fluttered in my gut. So much could happen so quickly, especially with the dark mage around.

"Be careful," I said. "Please."

Kael took my face in his hands. The calluses on his skin were rough against my cheeks as he leaned in close. My heartbeats quickened. He was a hair's breadth away. The warmth of his skin melted against mine, and with each breath, I pulled in his rain-and-citrus scent, a welcome aroma in the dry, African heat. It would be so easy to lean forward and close the distance. What would his lips feel like on mine? What would he taste like?

I tried to move forward, but Kael held my face so tight between his palms, I couldn't budge.

"When this is over, when you have that key and we are away from this place, we're going to admit there is something here." His breath drew me in, intoxicating me in a way it never had before. "Your lips will be mine, Livvie."

My breath caught, and it took a second to get my lungs working again. "Why not just take them now?"

Kael's mouth was so close to mine I could almost feel his

smile. "Because I want something to look forward to, and something to fight for."

"You better stay safe, then," I whispered.

His fingers tickled behind my ear and drifted down the back of my neck. "Same goes for you."

I started to move forward for a kiss, patience be damned, but his head whipped around.

"Lions are coming."

Kael cast me a searing look over his shoulder, branding me with the need and desire to stay safe, before he leaped in the air. His clothes ripped as his jaguar hit the ground and bolted. I stifled a laugh, staring at the shredded bits of his pants and shirt on the ground. He was going to have to walk back through the African wilderness naked. Those had been the last pair of clothing he had.

I shook off the amusement and got my mind back in the game as I made my way down the rock. There were a few trees clinging to the rough surface, and I tried my best to stay hidden in their scant shadows. I really hoped no one would catch my scent and come investigating, though it appeared as if most of the pride were crowded around the chief and Vehrin.

It didn't take too long for me to reach the dwellings. They jutted from the rock, but also appeared to be part of the cliffs. Small, square holes had been chiseled for windows, and most of the narrow doorways had brightly colored beaded curtains hanging in them. I caught delicious smells of sizzling meats, roasting vegetables, and cooked rice. I pressed a hand to my stomach, trying to calm my sudden hunger. Kael would never let me live it down if my gurgling stomach gave me away.

I crouched in a shadow beneath a window and scanned the homes. The day before, the chief had come out of one at the very bottom of the cliffs, so I assumed that was likely his dwelling. I was about halfway down, but I still couldn't tell where exactly his home would be. I couldn't afford to get lost.

Leaning my shoulder against the rough stone at my side, I closed my eyes and took a deep breath. I reached into the front of my shirt and clutched the keys. They were warm in my fingers, and the one bound to my soul hummed with familiar energy. I concentrated on nothing else but finding the third key. A magnetic sense pulsed in me, and I peered down and to the right. I grinned. There was the relic.

I pushed away from the wall and stealthily followed the tugging sensation. Urgency pulled at me, and I had to force myself to slow my pace and be cautious. I tried to shove away the frantic need to get the key by thinking about Kael. I hadn't heard any roars or commotion. Hopefully he was all right. His final words on top of the cliffs tingled through my mind, and butterflies filled my stomach.

Now isn't the time to be thinking about kissing Kael.

Still, his promise to do so when this was over consumed me. Until he'd said those words, I hadn't realized just how much I had fallen for the jaguar shifter. I had growing feelings for him, I knew that, but the sensation squeezing my heart when I thought of him was stronger. It had taken root, and there was no denying it now.

I was falling in love with Kael Rivera.

He was my partner. We'd bled together and fought together. Apparently, we had quite the history together, too, so maybe we'd been on this track from the moment he'd taken a swipe at me and I'd fallen in those rainforest ruins.

I was so caught up in my thoughts, I nearly ran into someone.

A gasp flew up my throat, and I stumbled back in surprise. "Sorry."

The word came without a thought. *Really*? I chided myself. It wasn't as if I had bumped into someone at the grocery store.

I studied the young man in front of me, who seemed just as surprised as myself. It was the same young man who had been on guard at the top of the small mountain, the one I had been on the verge of attacking with magic. His wide eyes narrowed. I raised my hand to tell him it was okay, but he opened his mouth.

I didn't think. I raised my hand and flicked my fingers. A fraction of magic swirled forward. It whipped around his head like a halo before fading away into nothing.

The young man crumpled to the ground, and my gut clenched. I crouched beside him. His eyes were closed, but his chest steadily rose and fell. I let out a breath of relief. I wasn't certain exactly how I'd managed it, but my quick reaction had merely rendered him unconscious. The last thing I wanted to do was kill an innocent.

I continued on my way, determined to be more careful as I crept between the buildings. Paths twisted in an impossible labyrinth. If I hadn't been following the sensation of the relic, I would have become lost for sure. I made my way down several steps smoothed with age and padded onto flat ground.

Vehrin was close. His magic caressed my skin and brought forth goosebumps. His and the chief's voices carried on the wind, but I couldn't make out what they were saying. At least that meant there was still some distance between us.

There was a dwelling on my right, slightly bigger than most I'd already passed. Magnetic energy pulsed through me. This was the chief's home, and the key was inside. There was a window above where I crouched. With my gaze darting toward the voices, I carefully straightened and braced my hands on the lip of the chiseled opening. I hopped up, then slid through the window.

The chief's home was one large room. The floor was scattered with rugs and woven mats. There was a low bed in one corner and a few tables. One of them held a plate of half-eaten food, as if he had left in a hurry. I swept my gaze through the space three times, but there was no altar, and no key.

I stepped into the center of the room and scanned every corner. I could still sense the key, but the dwelling was so permeated with its presence, I couldn't get an accurate read on its location.

As my gaze swept past a corner with a large chest, something caught my attention. I hurried over. There, near the floor and carved into the rock, was a rune. It was small, and marked in an imperfection of the stone, making it difficult to find.

I knelt beside the tiny rune and traced it. My fingertips grew warm at the familiar marking against my skin. An ancient word rolled off my tongue, and I sat back as the sound of grinding stone shook beneath my feet.

A section of floor beneath the rune tipped downward to reveal a dark opening. I cast a quick glance over my shoulder, hoping no one had heard, before I shuffled forward and slipped in.

My feet hit steady ground. The floor shut above me with the scraping finality of the lid of a tomb being shoved into place, snuffing out the scant light the opening had provided.

I drew on my magic, and the soft fuchsia hugged my fingers. Ahead was a pathway leading to what I assumed would be the third key.

A grin touched my lips. Once again, I found myself in the dark arms of the earth, and I strode forward.

I was in my element, and I was going to get that relic.

Then, I would take Vehrin down.

CHAPTER 23

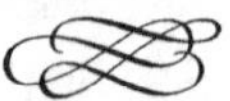

THE SOUND of my footfalls soaked into the rough floor at my feet as I made my way down the narrow path. I strained to catch any sign of pursuit, but I heard nothing except the blood pounding in my ears.

I'd thought for certain the chief would have sent someone after me, and knew it was only a matter of time before I was found out. I just hoped Kael would be able to keep them distracted long enough for me to get the relic, if I was even able to take it from the altar.

I studied the walls of the tunnel as I walked. Every single tomb and ruin I had been in was vastly different, even if they had been made by the same people in the same country. It wasn't solely appearance which made them different, either. It was a feeling. The ancient arms of civilizations had seen different histories, different joyful moments and terrible things. I'd always been able to sense it, like grasping the hand of a person. They all felt different.

My fingertips brushed along the rough wall to my left. It would have been utterly dark down here if not for my magic and the pearly, luminescent stones embedded in the wall. They were a trail of swirls along the surface, not following an exact pattern, but flowing as if they had spread there of their own accord. It was beautiful, and I wished I could snap a picture. My phone had been dead for three days. Perhaps, if this all didn't end in violence with us being chased away, I could come back here someday and study it. Places like this didn't deserve to be forgotten.

The farther I went beneath the mountain home of the shifters, the more energy pulsed from the pores in the stone walls. It pulled at me, beckoning me to hurry. It was so strong it was difficult for me to decipher where, exactly, it was coming from. I knew it was the key I was sensing, but with the sensation billowing all around me, I could only hope I'd be able to pinpoint the relic's location when I grew near it.

I paused as a new sensation found me. Dark magic seeped in through the rock and spread like a stain of ink through the atmosphere around me. I rolled my shoulders in an attempt to free myself of Vehrin's vile claws, but it persisted.

There was no denying it: Vehrin knew exactly where I was and what I was doing.

I had no choice but to continue. His magic wasn't hurting me that I was aware of, merely following me. No doubt so he could keep an eye on what I was doing. I scowled. If he wanted to watch me take the key right out from under his nose, so be it.

I went on my way with nothing but Vehrin's magic and the glowing stones on the wall to keep me company. Just as I was wondering if this tunnel would lead me straight to the key, my path suddenly branched out.

There were three open doorways. The one in the middle was the largest, tall and wide enough for Kael to walk through easily. There was a smaller one on the left. I would have to duck to walk through it, but it would be bearable. The opening on the right was about the size of a doggy door. I'd have to army crawl my way through.

I studied the doorways. It was obvious which one I *wanted*

to go through. The one in front would by far be the easiest, which made me think it was likely not the correct way to go. People tended to take the path of least resistance.

Slowly, I walked past each doorway. I opened my senses further in an attempt to pinpoint the relic's beckoning sensation. My cheeks puffed out in a sigh. It was no use. The feeling was too strong. It saturated the air, and with Vehrin's power now mixing into it, there was no way I would be able to get a handle on it.

I glanced behind me. So far, it didn't seem I was being pursued, but I couldn't linger any longer. Letting out a frustrated growl that would have made Kael proud, I got down on my hands and knees in front of the smallest opening. I shifted my bag around so I could push it in front of me. There was no way I could crawl, the ceiling was too low, so I dropped to my belly and wiggled in.

It was difficult to tell how long this tunnel went. I held one hand aloft with magic warming my skin so I could see and shoved my bag awkwardly in front of me with the other. Dust rained down on me from above, and I kept my eyes squinted in an attempt to keep them clear of debris. My elbows started hurting as I army crawled my way down. A cold sensation wrapped around my ankles, and a chill ran through me.

I tried to glance behind me. Nothing but shadow. A foul taste filled my mouth, like blood and tepid ditch water, and I knew Vehrin's magic had latched onto me.

When I got out of here, I was going to make him wish he'd never touched me.

I continued to crawl and wriggle down the tunnel, then paused at an odd whispering sort of sound. I inched forward slowly, then held my hand up and peered over my bag. My heart jumped.

Snakes.

There had to be at least two dozen of them, their bodies all slithering and twisting together. I was one of those women who weren't the least bit bothered by snakes and insects—it came with the territory of archeology—but I also knew enough about snakes to know the ones ahead of me were venomous.

I caught the flaring head of a cobra as it hissed, its black gaze fixed on me. I couldn't crawl through a nest of cobras. Their venom would affect me in a matter of minutes, and I most certainly wouldn't have time to make it out of this place alive.

I inched back a few feet, putting distance between myself and the deadly hindrance, and let my forehead rest against my bag as I thought. Backing back out of the tunnel would take time and effort I couldn't afford. Besides, there was no guarantee one of the other doorways would lead to the relic. In all likelihood, the snakes were put here on purpose to stop anyone from getting through.

Of course, that didn't explain how they would have put the key down here in the first place. Wouldn't the chief have to go through the snakes, too? Perhaps there was another way, an easier way, to get to the key. But if there was, the leader of the lions would certainly be the only one to know about it. There could be an entirely new doorway that wasn't even located beneath his home. It could be on the other side of the mountain for all I knew. I certainly didn't have time to go looking, especially based on nothing more than speculation. Which meant...

I had to go through the snakes.

I could probably kill them with my magic, but with Vehrin's power nearby, I wasn't certain how that would work out. Besides, unleashing my own power could very well collapse this tunnel on me. Slashing at them with a sword would probably do nothing except piss them off.

I shifted slowly so I would draw the serpents' attention and reached into my pockets in a last-ditch effort to find something to ward them away. I discovered something and rolled the tiny object between my fingers. It was the elephant-tusk-shaped earring Bibi had given me. I held it up in front of me, and the words she told me as she handed it over came back to mind.

Take these. They will ward off any wild beasts that may do you harm.

Did that mean I could get through the cobras without being bitten? I supposed there was only one way to find out.

Clenching the earring in a tight fist so I wouldn't drop it, I shuffled forward. The snakes came back into view. The hissing grew louder as the glowing magic around my fist fell over their dark scales. My heart hammered, and I took a few shaky breaths as I reached the serpents.

Several of them rose up as high as the small space allowed, their horrible hissing filling my ears. I grimaced as I was forced to crawl over their writhing bodies.

"Easy, snakes. It's okay, just passing through." I had to laugh quietly at myself. Talking to snakes. I did odd things when I was nervous.

Several of the heavy, twisting snakes slithered on top of me, crawling up over my shoulders and around my legs. I really hoped one of them wouldn't try to crawl up a pants leg. I winced as tiny tongues flicked out against my face and arms. I kept expecting a painful bite any moment, but none of them did. Finally, the way opened up ahead and I picked up my pace as best I could. I crawled out of the tunnel and hurriedly got to my feet. I flailed my arms and shook out like I was covered in bees.

"That was so gross!" I'd never be able to look at snakes the same way again.

I made sure I was clear of the cobras before putting the earring back in my pocket, then turned my attention to my next obstacle. I craned my neck back and studied the path rising before me. The way almost looked like it could be stairs, but the protruding ledges of rock made no set pattern. I took a moment to shake out my arms and legs. Crawling through the tunnel had given me cramped muscles and sore knees and elbows.

All right, up we go.

Being out of shape, it was difficult, and Vehrin's clinging power hung on me like a heavy blanket. My muscles burned and more often than not I had to leap from one landing to another. I landed short once, and had to windmill my arms and twist awkwardly to keep from tipping backward to my death on the rocks below. Kael would have had better luck traversing this terrain, especially with his sleek, jaguar muscles and reflexes.

I hope he's okay.

I cast my gaze upward as if I could see through the earth and to him. Lions were much bigger than jaguars, and he would likely be going against several.

After what seemed like hours of climbing, I pulled myself to the top, only to find the path sloped back down on this side. Why go all the way up, only to have to head back down?

I crossed my legs in front of me and took a moment to breathe. I twisted my torso and shook out my arms. I was utterly exhausted, which was likely the exact reason for the climb. The relic was probably down the path, and I had a feeling the horrible tunnel of snakes followed by the treacherous climb was to tire out whatever trespassers aimed to find the key.

I took a drink of water from the canteen in my bag. It was warm and tasted stale, but at least it would keep me from fainting before I got out of this place.

I closed my bag back up and slung it across my shoulders. I sucked in a deep breath, then pushed myself from the ledge and onto the steep path down. It was sort of like a slide, if slides were covered in grit and sharp rocks. I tried to keep away from the stones protruding from the surface like teeth, but as I neared the bottom, one sliced my palm. I hissed as my feet hit the floor and looked at my hand. Blood trickled down my wrist from the shallow gash. I shook it, blood splattering the floor. There was nothing I could do about it right now.

An arched doorway caught my eye. It was decorated with the same luminescent stones which had lined the path earlier. Magnetic energy pulsed in the air. The key was in there. My magic buzzed through me, ready to release at the first sign of danger, as I stepped through the doorway.

Thousands of the glowing stones flecked the low ceiling, which was split with a deep crack. Something about the dark line cutting through the ceiling seemed odd to me, but I couldn't put my finger on the reason.

I lowered my gaze in front of me. There were two altars. One held the ivory spear Bibi had given me. On the altar beside it was the key.

I took three steps forward, then noticed the guards. I had been so fixated on the ceiling and the relic, I hadn't noticed them standing the shadows. There were two of them, tall and lethal. They each held spears in their hands and looked as if they wanted to run me through with them. One of them yelled something, but I couldn't understand what he was saying.

"I don't want to hurt you." I held my hands up and took a slow step forward. They lowered their spears. "Please, I'm only trying to help."

I took another step forward and pulled on my magic. I didn't want to kill them. Instead, I would render them unconscious as I had done to the young man earlier. I took a steadying breath, but before I could release the energy coursing through me, the dark magic that had been trailing me swept around my body and toward the altar.

My heart leapt to my throat, certain Vehrin was snatching the relic. My brows furrowed as the magic wrapped around the spear instead. Confusion quickly evaporated, and understanding snapped into place.

"No!" I lurched forward.

Too late.

The ivory spear, in the grasp of dark magic, turned toward one of the guards and plunged into the man's throat. It yanked out, blood spraying the floor as the man gurgled and fell, then whipped around to the other. I reached the remaining guard just as the spear sank into his chest.

I dropped to my knees beside him. His gaze was wide and panicked as he struggled to breathe. I wrapped my hand around the bloodied spear. Though I couldn't save this man, I refused to let him die with a spear in his chest like some animal. I tightened my grip on the smooth, ivory shaft, and then the room groaned around me.

Bits of rock and dirt rained onto my hair and, suddenly, sunlight warmed my back. I blinked up to find the ceiling sliding away. The crack in the ceiling made sense now. It was a giant doorway. The room fell away as the floor rose beneath me. It only took a moment, and I was back above ground in the semi-circle of space in front of the village.

All eyes fell on me, with my hands around the blood-stained spear and two dead lion shifters beside me.

Behind the menacing glare of the chief, Vehrin stood with a small smile on his face.

CHAPTER 24

Murderer.

The crowd uttered condemnation around me.

Murderer.

Slowly, I unclenched my fingers from around the shaft of the spear as the shifter rattled his last breath. I ignored the accusing stares of his pride and pinned my gaze on Vehrin. A smile still touched his lips as he kept his eyes locked on mine. He didn't speak as the shifters continued their hushed words of blame and pleas for their chief to administer justice.

The shifter's blood stained my hands and painted me as some evil creature. I couldn't find my voice to deny their accusations. After all, I'd been the one to react too slowly to save them. Perhaps I did have a part in their deaths.

No. No, that isn't right. This wasn't my doing. My teeth ground together as I stared daggers at the dark mage. *It was his.*

There was a commotion in the crowd and suddenly, Kael burst through them. He hurried to my side with a trio of lions on his tail. They stopped when they reached the front of the crowd, though they continued to pace and growl.

Kael pressed his head against my hip in a show of relief. His sides heaved with each breath, and patches of blood stained his golden-brown fur. He hadn't been limping when he'd joined me, so he didn't appear to have anything broken. I hoped the wounds weren't too deep and would heal quickly.

More lions joined the small group which had been pursuing Kael, and I realized a good number of the shifters had changed into their lion forms. Kael moved to stand in front of me. He let out a vicious snarl, the vibrations of it tickling my legs. He was uneasy, and I laid my wounded palm on his blood-stained back in an attempt to calm him.

Something flared in my mind, and a strange sense of warmth and familiarity washed over me. It brought with it the scent of citrus-heavy air and rain-soaked jungle earth. I blinked in surprise, and the disconcerting part was the surprise wasn't entirely my own. A portion of it was *Kael's*. I could feel his surprise, could feel him deep in my bones.

What the hell?

Kael turned to look at me.

Livvie? A voice sounded in my head, and though I knew it was Kael's, there was something deeper, richer, more meaningful about it.

I'd always thought of him as a man who could turn into an animal, but for the first time, I realized perhaps he was an animal with the ability to turn into a man, and the tone that had caressed the sound of my name was his true voice.

My mouth parted. *Kael? Why can I hear you? What happened?*

A strong emotion sparked in him so fast I wasn't able to get a read on it before he swept it away. *We can't worry about it now. Stay focused.*

Right. At the moment, we had to deal with an evil mage and a pride of lion shifters bent on making me pay for a crime I didn't commit. Still, it was hard to shake off the disconcerting fact my partner was in my head. Could he only hear thoughts I projected, or could he read everything flashing in my head? Instead of words, I thought of Renathe wearing a bright pink fairy dress.

Kael let out a strange huffing sound which I could only assume was a laugh. *Well, perfect. This isn't going to be awkward.*

Livvie, focus.

I was never going to get over the way his feral-wrapped voice sounded saying my name. I wanted to hear the jaguar Kael speak more often.

I'll recite poetry to you later. Right now we need to worry about him. Kael had his attention on Vehrin, who was walking up to stand beside the chief.

I'm going to hold you to that.

Kael was right, though. I had to get my mind in the right place.

Vehrin spoke, and his words were loud enough for all in the vicinity to hear.

"Did I not warn you about her? Look what she has done. Not only has she tried to steal the key you have been charged with protecting, but she has killed two of your own to do so. She is a treacherous creature, who uses conniving words to twist the minds of those in her way. Just how do you think she obtained the relics around her neck in the first place? No doubt she has left a pile of bodies in her wake." Vehrin tipped his head down so only I could see the smirk on his face. "The blood of your brethren is likely still warm on her fingers."

The pieces had already been clicking into place for me, but his next words cemented what I'd already guessed.

The dark mage turned to the leader of the pride. "Entrust the key to me, and I will keep it safe from your enemies. She will not be the first to try and steal it. I know it has been under the protection of your pride for centuries, but how many more must die in order to keep it from falling into the wrong hands?" Vehrin swept his hands out toward the ring of shifters. "You are missing young ones, yes? Who knows what they befell at her hands?"

I despised Vehrin's accusations, and I knew denying his poisonous words would only fall on deaf ears, but to imply I had killed children enraged me more than I could have imagined.

"I would never hurt a child, you lying bastard!" Magic wreathed my fingers and my hands trembled with eagerness.

Vehrin merely leaned over to the chief and muttered something.

He said his own child was among the missing. Giving him the relic is his only chance to save his mate and the rest of his people, Kael said.

To my utter horror, the chief started to move toward us. He was going to give the key to the dark mage. Vehrin had twisted the man's thoughts so much, he would willingly entrust the key to him. I couldn't let him have it. The chief had told us the third key would override the power of the keys I already possessed. Would Vehrin be able to control the key bound to my soul?

I turned my full attention to the chief as he made his way forward, and the energy crackled at my fingertips. If I attacked him, it would only cement me as the villain. The others wouldn't believe otherwise. Still, I moved between him and the key.

"You can't," I said. "Vehrin is lying to you. He's poisoned your thoughts. You must know this."

Kael, shadowing me, crouched, ready to spring into action.

The chief's lips curled up in a menacing flash of teeth. His eyes were wide and wild, and I knew he was too far gone. Vehrin's influence had been strong and deep.

Do not hold back, Kael said.

My gaze swept over the crowd, picking out faces of women. There were still children among them. *I can't. They're innocent.*

So are millions of people around the world. Do you think Vehrin will spare them if he wins?

Eagerness pulsed through me, stemming from the magic

in my veins. *Bring me back, Kael. If I forget who I am, please, bring me back.*

Always.

Snarls ripped through the air, followed by angry roars as lions and lionesses charged toward us from every direction. For a split second, I wondered if Bibi's earring would keep me from harm, but as the first lioness took a swipe at me, I realized it wouldn't. These were not wild beasts, after all. They were innocent beings who, in their mind, were protecting their children and fighting for their chief. And I was the twisted young mage who had come to steal everything from them.

Magic swirled from me. I knocked out the lioness who had tried to swipe at my leg and another quickly filled her place. The energy left me slowly, the attacks that rendered them unconscious harder to conjure. Kael snarled, his sleek body twisting this way and that as he dodged claws and teeth, and traded attacks of his own.

The chief continued to maneuver toward the key. This wasn't going to work. The power inside of me purred in agreement.

A pair of young male lions, likely teenagers in their human forms, leaped at me, and I made a slashing motion with my arm. Energy whipped across them, and blood sprayed in the air. My breath caught, but before their bodies hit the ground, another lion charged.

I thrust a hand out, and the concentrated magic sinking into his chest reminded so much of the ivory spear in the shifter guard, I stumbled a step.

I can't do this.

Kael's iron voice hardened in my mind. *Fight, Livvie. You don't have a choice. It's that or die.* He lunged from my side to attack the guards shielding the chief.

Half a dozen shifters descended on me. Magic swirled around me like a maelstrom of death. Though I merely wounded some of the lions, I noticed many were dying, their blood soaking into the dry earth.

Tears stung my eyes. I wanted to roar at them to stop. I had to defend myself, but that didn't mean I wanted to harm them. Didn't they see what they were doing?

Something cracked inside of me with each innocent life I struck down, made worse by the almost joyful glow of the darker shade of magic inside of me at the sight of the bloodshed at my feet.

I didn't want this. I didn't want power and pain and sacrifice.

A sliver of agony sliced through my mind, and I found Kael pinned beneath a lion. I held my palm out as the lion snapped at his neck, but I hesitated.

Could I justify attacking him? It wasn't self-defense, but what if he killed my partner?

I couldn't lose Kael.

I pulled in a breath, preparing to attack, when every ounce of air whooshed from my lungs. I'd hit the ground. Hard. A snarling lioness had me pinned. Her claws dug into my back, and hot air warmed my cheek as she growled in my ear.

Pain ripped across my back, and I wondered if I would die from being crushed or having a vital organ punctured first.

"Please," I said. I could taste dirt on my lips as I gasped the word. "I didn't kill them." I tried to shift; the weight hurt so much, I couldn't stand it. I let out a cry as her claws sank deeper.

Kael was saying something in my mind, but I couldn't decipher them through the agony. Out of my peripheral, I stared at the lioness's eyes. Even in her animal form, I could see the pain and loss glistening in the deep, golden orbs. A thought suddenly occurred to me. Had one of her children been one of the ones the two women we'd met made off with?

"Bibi's. The children…they're at Bibi's."

The weight lifted slightly, and the lioness stopped snarling.

I was able to twist slightly, though she kept her claws in my back. A shadow floated toward her and wreathed her neck like a strangling serpent. Whatever doubt I'd placed in her was chased away as she roared with murder in her eyes. Before she could end me, I struck.

The attack was swift and lethal. She tilted off me, and as I sat up, she twitched once in a pool of blood before stilling. For a moment, everything went still. Then, a pained voice yelled out.

"Wife!"

I tore my eyes from the lioness to find the chief standing beside the altar. His gaze was wild, drinking in the sight of his dead mate.

I had just orphaned a child and tore away a man's lover.

Murderer.

What had I done?

Roars shook the air and rattled in my chest. The tawny bodies of lions ringed around me as I struggled to my feet. Agony lashed down my back, and made it painful to move my arms. There was a commotion on the other side of the lions, and as I raised my hand to attack those closing in, the chief's voice rang out once more.

"Stop!"

The lions parted, clearing the path so I could see unhindered. The chief held the key in one hand. In the other was the ivory spear, the point of it touching Kael's neck where he lay on the ground, teeth bared in a growl.

Vehrin walked into view. "You can only choose one, Olivia. The key, or your mate."

CHAPTER 25

My mate?

It would almost be amusing if we weren't both in peril at the moment. Why did everyone keep referring to Kael as my mate? I certainly wasn't a jaguar shifter.

Thank God for that. Kael's voice in my mind was strained, despite the light-heartedness of his words.

I stared at the spearpoint threatening to pierce his fur and flesh to rip through his jugular. *Are you okay?*

I'm fine.

Glad to hear it, mate. I laughed internally at my sarcastic comment, but Kael went suddenly stoic through our unusual bond. Perhaps he was in more pain than he was letting on. Blood stains melded into the golden-brown of his spotted fur.

I glanced up at the chief and swore I could hear a menacing growl rumbling through his heaving chest. The key was still clenched in his hand. Vehrin stood several feet away, hovering like a vulture. He was wanting me to choose between the key and Kael. If I chose the key, I could keep it out of his hands and he'd be less of a threat to the world, and I'd save thousands of innocent lives. My gaze dropped back down to my partner.

It was an impossible choice.

I'm going to get us out of this, I promised him.

Kael let out a low snarl, and his long tail flicked with agitation. *Don't be stupid. Take the key.*

And have you get killed? I don't think so. You owe me poetry and a date, remember?

I sliced a glare to Vehrin. "How do I know if I give up the key, you'll spare Kael's life?"

Vehrin smiled warmly, though no light of amusement or earnestness reached his unnerving violet eyes. He raised a hand and pressed his palm to the chest of his long tunic. The runes sewn into the fabric shimmered with the movement.

"On my honor as a mage, Olivia, he will not come to harm."

"Your honor? Do mages have any? From what I have seen, you are seriously lacking in that particular department of ethics."

He cocked his head. "You tell me. You are a mage, yourself. Do you not think of yourself as honorable?"

I could hear the soft padding of pacing lions around me, the air pierced occasionally by an impatient growl. They wanted blood. My blood, and Kael's. They wouldn't wait much longer.

"You and I are worlds apart," I said.

Vehrin's smile faded. "We did not used to be. We ruled together, you and I. You were magnificent, dark and fierce. We were unbreakable." Though the dark mage stood a distance from me, his voice crooned in my ear. "Do you not remember who you were?"

Memories flickered to life in my mind like a sputtering candle flame.

An incoming storm rumbled in the distance and already sent the canopy dancing below. Birds flew down, seeking sanctuary in the swaying branches. I held my arms toward the gray sky. The growing tempest sent a current of energy prickling over my bare arms. It vitalized me and sent my magic purring around me like a brilliant cloak. Beside me, Vehrin whispered in my ear.

"How beautiful you are," he said. "How strong."

A slow grin lifted my face. Thunder rumbled like the growls of my guardian at my back, and lightning pierced from the sky at my command. Rain fell, and I could taste the remnant of my own magic as the droplets rolled over my lips.

I blinked. The dark mage watched me with a knowing smile. "You could bring storms, and fierce winds. You could use your magic to bend people to do your will. You could hurt and maim, but also summon flowers to bloom and trees to bear fruit. Great things were done by your hands, things you cannot even dream of, trapped in this shadow of yourself." Vehrin held his hand out to me. "Come. Join me, and I will show you the full spectrum of your incredible capabilities. Join me, Olivia, and we will rule this world. We once were worshipped as gods, and with you by my side again, this earth will once again see great things."

I stared at his outstretched hand as if in thought, but not one ounce of me was tempted. There was no denying what I had once been—the magic in my veins and knowledge of forgotten text was proof of my ancient being. However, I was no longer some ruling sorceress with people worshipping me at my feet.

The air around us had gone still; the lions had stopped their pacing and snarling. Had Vehrin been so wrapped up in trying to convince me to join them, he hadn't really put thought to what he was saying?

I gave him a sly grin. "Pretty speech. You might want to be careful, though. You're losing your audience."

While the dark mage had been urging me to join him, telling me we'd rule together and be worshipped like gods, the shifters were also listening. More than a few of them curled their lips back to show teeth.

Vehrin was unbothered by the lions who began to turn

malevolent stares toward him. "It doesn't matter what they think. The chief knows you are the enemy, and since he is their alpha, they must obey his command."

The chief was still glaring daggers at me. Vehrin was right. It didn't matter if the other shifters doubted the validity of the mage's words. If the chief told them to tear me to pieces, they would. As long as their leader was under Vehrin's influence, we were outnumbered.

"Last chance, Olivia. I will not ask again." Vehrin still held his hand toward me. "Join me, or die."

Magic licked around my hand in preparation. "If I die, I'll just come back in three hundred years and make your life hell."

Vehrin's violet eyes flashed, and his nostrils flared. Magic cuffed his wrists like smoke-wreathed snakes. "So be it."

He turned toward the chief and raised his hand. The chief moved his hand to the key, ready to relinquish it to Vehrin.

I released an attack, but instead of striking the dark mage, my energy wrapped around the leader of the lion shifters. Magic swirled around his head, much like it had done when I'd knocked the youth unconscious, but instead of causing him to pass out, my attack hit sort of barrier. Vehrin's magic. And its touch was twisted and vile.

I pushed, sending more of my power ratcheting against the hold the dark mage had on him. My mind strained, and I gritted my teeth. The evil magic started to give, and then I felt a snap beneath the onslaught of my energy.

The relic flew from the chief's hand as he stumbled.

Kael, free from the threat of the spear, swiped at the key as it bounced across the ground. A terrible roar broke through the air, and the chief exploded into a massive lion. He shook his mane and roared again, the sound if it vibrating through my chest. He stalked toward Vehrin, and the remaining lions followed suit.

My partner was closing in on the key, but just as his paw reached for it, a burst of energy fanned out from Vehrin.

I grunted as the force of it sent me landing hard on the ground several feet back. Warm blood filled my mouth, and I sat up to spit it out. I'd bitten the inside of my cheek on impact. I wiped my hand across my mouth as my eyes locked on my enemy's glowing, violet gaze. His lips lifted in a cold, cruel smile.

The air went eerily silent. A tingle scattered over me as if a thousand spiders ran across my skin. Vehrin raised his arms, and brought forth chaos.

I had seen the soldiers he summoned and sculpted from shadow before, but not like this. The ones Kael and I had faced in the ruins in England had been dangerous, but Vehrin was stronger now than he'd been then. The soldiers dropping from thin air around us emanated only one powerful thing… the drive to wipe us all from the earth.

But there must be hope. Vehrin wouldn't have gone through all this trouble if his army was unbeatable. For all of his confidence and bluster, there had to be a weak point, a reason he hadn't taken this approach from the start.

The problem was, I didn't know what that was, and although the lion shifters had been attempting to kill us twenty minutes ago, I feared for their safety as Vehrin's ruthless soldiers rushed forward.

Kael, help the shifters. I'm going to get the key.

I caught a glimpse of him through the tangle of roaring lions and darting soldiers. He already had his jaws on the throat of a soldier thrashing in the throes of death, and a flash of fierce pride went through me at the sight. I tore my gaze from him and scanned the ground. The key was no longer where I'd seen it last; I hoped that was because it had been kicked away by the battling crowd, and not because it was in Vehrin's grasp.

My gaze darted up to seek him out, and I found him

standing safely outside of the melee. Coward. He would wait until the lions were dead before simply strolling in and plucking the relic from the dirt. My nostrils flared, and I curled my hands into fists.

Not if I got the key first.

I darted into the frenzy, eager magic burning across my skin. I gave into the urge and released it. Power swirled forth, and my wrists twisted, directing the magic toward the soldiers. A flicker of satisfaction bolstered me as each soldier fell. Lions ran past, and a few times only quick footwork kept me from losing my balance.

A lioness dashed by, and as she swept from my path, I spotted the key. My heart leapt. It was only a few feet away. I side-stepped around two young lions taking on a trio of soldiers. Magic crackled around my knuckles, ready to blast away anyone who hindered me. I was so close. I bent down, and just as my fingers brushed the dark key, a body slammed into me.

My magic fled as my head bounced against the packed dirt. Stars scattered across my vision, and a piercing ring stabbed my ears. A horrid smell of decay filled my nostrils. I blinked the flecks of light from my eyes and found one of Vehrin's soldiers pinning me to the ground.

He didn't say anything as he stared down at me with the eyes of a serpent. Instead, he grinned widely, and a forked tongue flicked against my cheek.

Ugh, *gross*.

As I shifted under his weight, I realized these weren't simply soldiers Vehrin had conjured from who-knew-where. They had to be demons. Which, if that were the case, they couldn't really do me harm.

I had Bibi's earring in my pocket. She'd said it would protect us against wild beasts…*and demons*. I wrestled it free with one hand right before the demon tried to strike. His curved claws stopped an inch from my throat, and his scant eyebrows pinched on his green-tinged face. I grinned and twisted my opposite wrist.

My bracelet turned into my sword, and the blade punched through the demon's gut. He flopped off me, a terrible squeal pouring from him. Within seconds, he was still.

I lurched up and tried to beckon my magic, but my vision blurred. I sighed sharply. My energy was too low. It would replenish, and I hoped it wouldn't take too long to do so.

Kael's snarl suddenly came from somewhere on my right. I scanned the still-battling crowd and found him standing alongside the chief as they advanced toward Vehrin. Though Kael was the largest jaguar I'd ever seen, the lion at his side was massive.

Demons came at me, but each of their reaching limbs and gnashing teeth seemed to glide around me like water. Kael's elephant tusk earring was lost somewhere with his shredded clothing. If an attack came up behind him, he would be vulnerable. I kept my eye out for the key as I ran to help him.

An icy laugh pierced the air.

There was a small smile on the dark mage's face as Kael and the chief stalked toward him. Cruel intentions burned in his gaze, and unease twisted in my gut.

Kael! Get out of there!

My partner paused and turned to look at me, but the chief dashed forward.

It was so quick, I couldn't tell what happened. One second, the chief was reaching toward Vehrin with tearing claws, and the next, he hit the ground several yards away in a lifeless heap.

My heart jolted. The lions stilled, heads swiveling toward their fallen leader. Kael ran with me toward the chief.

He couldn't be dead, could he?

Vehrin took advantage; more demons poured in. The lions jumped back into action, their attacks fierce, fueled by grief and anger.

The chief's lion form melded away to reveal a man lying on the ground. That meant he was alive, or it should have meant that, but I knelt down to check. With shaking fingers, I felt under his jaw. His pulse was weak, but it was there.

"He's alive," I said.

Kael made a noise that resembled a sigh. *Good. Now come on. We have to get that key.*

I stood, peering down at the unconscious shifter. If he was left unattended, a demon could easily come along and finish him off. I pulled out Bibi's earring and pressed it into his palm, then curled his fingers around it.

Kael stared at me, and even though he was in his jaguar form, I could still read the "that guy wanted you dead and here you are sacrificing your armor for him" look.

You'll be vulnerable, he argued.

I turned back toward the fighting. My magic was already beginning to warm back inside of me.

"I am anything but vulnerable."

I hefted my blade and strode back into battle once again.

CHAPTER 26

My skin prickled as the demons ran toward us. It was as if they somehow knew my shield had been cast aside and they couldn't wait to get their claws in my flesh.

Kael dashed from my side, muscles rippling as he ran sleek and deadly as the blade in my hand. He leaped with a snarl, and his jaws closed around the neck of one of Vehrin's demons. The demon quickly fell to the ground with a thud, and Kael swiped at the legs of another as it ran my way. A cracked scream fled him as the jaguar's sharp claws tore through the demon's tendon. He stumbled forward, and with a swift downward arc, my sword ended his life.

With each demon felled, more filled their place. I gritted my teeth. My energy had rejuvenated, but I was hesitant to use my magic. I still had a dark mage to contend with once we got through the onslaught of demons.

The lions hadn't stopped fighting. They darted in and snatched at demons with their powerful jaws. While Kael's strengths were speed and agility, the lion shifters were all muscle and power. They worked together in small groups, focusing on a few demons at a time. *Good strategy*. They were taking down a sizeable chunk of our enemies.

Livvie! Get to the key!

In the battle with the demons, I'd forgotten about the key. I scanned the ground through the churning bodies and puffs of dust. This was going to be impossible.

One of the lions backed into me by accident, and I stumbled into a demon. It screeched and whirled around, then knocked me to the ground.

This demon had a long-curved tail like some monstrous scorpion, and I had to roll as he jabbed at me with the venomous barb. When the demon's deadly appendage stabbed into the dirt beside my shoulder, I took the opportunity and swung my sword. My blade cut clean through the tail, and inky blood splattered across my chest. Thank goodness most of it landed on my shirt; the few flecks of blood peppered on my skin burned.

I lurched to my feet as the demon bellowed. Its eyes glittered like a beetle as it gathered itself and reached for me. A trickle of magic flowed from my fingers gripping the hilt of my sword and licked down my blade. I plunged it forward into the creature's chest. Its eyes widened in surprise.

After bracing a foot against the demon's body and yanking my sword free, I left the demon to gargle on the earth as I continued my search. The key had to be around here somewhere.

Focus. Instead of using my eyes, I tapped into the other sense of myself that could *feel* the key. A slight tug tingled at the edges of my mind, and I swiveled. *There!*

I looked toward a trio of lionesses snarling at a pair of demons. The relic had to be somewhere under their feet.

But I wasn't the only person watching them.

A sharp breath hissed in through my teeth. Vehrin also knew where the key was.

I surged forward, dodging around demons instead of confronting them. I had to get to the key before Vehrin had the chance, but it was still several yards away.

Vehrin laughed, and his voice rose as he spoke to me, somehow clear over the cries of battle. "Isn't this a fun little game we're playing, my friend? Who can get to the key first?"

My teeth ground so hard my jaw hurt. He would see this as a game, all this death and carnage. The grin spreading across his face dripped with wickedness.

A heart-broken wail pierced the din. Through the chaos, I saw a woman clutching a child to her chest. The little girl's eyes stared vacantly at the gray sky above.

Something inside of me snapped.

It wasn't the influence of twisted, ancient magic that had me tearing into the next demon with unmatched fervor. It was something fiercer, unhinged. A fury burned through me unlike anything I'd ever experienced. I was going to make every last one of Vehrin's minions beg for mercy as I sliced them apart.

Blood reddened my knuckles and flecked my face. I attacked with my blade and magic alike as I hacked through muscle and bone. Shrieks and wails followed in my wake as demon bodies twitched on the ground.

One after the other, they fell.

That's right, Olivia. Make them pay for the pain they caused. It wasn't Kael's voice that crooned in my mind, but Vehrin's.

A darkness like soft velvet caressed the edges of my mind. I wanted to resist, but with each strike of my sword and spark of my magic, the shadows became more welcoming.

Beads of blood continued to fly, and dark magic purred through my bones. I wanted to kill them all, wanted my boots to stamp on the blood-soaked earth. Screams and hisses filled my ears, and I danced to the pained song they created.

Cut them. Burn them. Bleed them.

Make them pay.

Livvie.

I ignored the soft, rich sound of my name.

Please, you have to stop. It's too much. You don't need to do this.

I shoved the intruding thought away. I *did* have to do this. I barely saw what I was doing as I moved from one demon to the next.

Olivia, remember who you are. Do not become the monster he wants you to be.

Those words gave me pause. *What?*

You are not this person, Livvie. You can be just, but this is not the way.

I was being swept away in a river of dark magic and malice. I clung to Kael's words like a lifeline and let them drag me from the clinging current. I blinked and peered around me.

Kael watched me warily, and behind him lay demon after demon. Many were moaning on the ground, clawing at the earth with the limbs they had left. Blood was everywhere, all over the dirt, all over my blade, all over *me.*

I swallowed hard. Defending myself and fighting in a righteous battle was one thing, but the slaughter I'd relished in moments before was another matter entirely.

Worse, in my vindictive attack, I'd lost sight of the key again.

I turned my attention back to Kael. "I…" Words escaped me. He stepped over to me and pressed his head against my hip.

It is okay to fight, Olivia, but do not lose yourself while doing so.

I nodded. *Good thing I have someone to remind me of who I am.* I tried to smile but my lips merely twitched.

Kael eased back, and his yellow-brown gaze watched me for a moment before giving me a nod and turning back to the melee.

Vehrin was still in the same spot, and a deep frown carved his face. Clearly, he wasn't pleased with the way this battle was going. Many of his demons had fallen, and it was only a matter of time before he was the only one left. He caught my eye, and this time, I was able to get a triumphant smile on my face.

"You forget who I am, little mage." His voice carried over the carnage toward me.

Then, he raised his hands. Shadow and fire snaked from his fingertips. The dark power wrapped around lions and tossed them easily away. He pulled the shadows back and as a few of the shifters recovered, more demons appeared.

How many could he summon? We were running out of energy. We couldn't keep fighting fresh demons over and over.

Kael lowered his head with a snarl beside me as I braced myself for the new onslaught. A lion came to stand by my side, then another, and another. Together, Kael and I ran forward with the pride. We crashed into the demons.

This time, I didn't lose myself in the violence. Instead, I cloaked myself with purpose. Every time I took a demon down, I searched for the key. My muscles burned with each stroke of my sword, and my magic prickled unpleasantly. I was losing energy. Lions fell beside me. I could hear Kael's heavy panting as he stayed by my side.

We were not going to win this battle.

A flash of dark magic pummeled over me, and I could almost feel Vehrin's satisfaction as I hit the dirt. My sword fell from my hand on impact. I rolled, then screamed as pain bloomed in my shoulder. A demon had sunk its teeth right through my clothes and into my muscle and was latched on like a hyena. I tried to shake it off, but it only bit harder.

A terrible roar shook through me, and a large, tan lioness crashed into the demon. I gasped when the painful hold fell away. My arms shook as I lifted myself up. Kael jumped off the chest of a demon he'd had his claws in and dashed over to me.

Livvie!

"I'm all right," I mumbled. Truthfully, I wasn't certain how much longer I was going to last. My shoulder was searing with agony and I really hoped it wasn't poisoned with demon venom. Aside from the fresh wound, I had nicks and bumps all over.

Hair rose on my arms. “Get back!”

Kael leaped to the side as another volley of Vehrin’s magic slammed into the ground. I skittered back, digging my heels into the dirt as another blast of dark energy nearly took out my legs. I glanced behind me to find a large boulder. It was worth a shot. I half-crawled over to it and shuffled behind it. Kael joined me.

I leaned my head against the rough stone and tried not to listen to the sound of pained roars and pitiful cries behind me. Vehrin was unleashing a barrage of magic into the pride, as if the demons weren’t enough. I wanted to help, wanted to get rid of him for good, but I needed a breath.

Kael watched me, and I saw the same fear in his gaze I knew was in mine. We couldn’t win this battle. There was a very slim chance the pair of us were going to make it out alive.

My heart constricted at the thought of losing Kael, and in that moment, my thoughts went back to the kiss he’d promised on the other side of the mountain.

I leaned over to him and let my fingers trace up the soft fur of his cheeks. I tilted his head down and pressed a kiss to the pattern of spots between his eyes.

“There is your kiss, my warrior.”

My warrior.

The words brought a vision, a memory, from the depths of my mind.

It was quiet, and the light from the flames caused shadows to dance among the ring of underbrush and tree trunks at the edges of our small clearing. The man at my side was tall, and dark-haired. He watched me with careful golden eyes. The hard edges of his face had been chiseled away to reveal an easy smile he reserved for me. It was a risk to be here with him, but it was well worth it.

He was, after all, the one I loved.

My warrior. My protector. My heart.

Like a snake slipping through the shadows, Vehrin stepped into the clearing.

"Traitor," he hissed.

I couldn't voice a protest before he sent forward magic like a spear. It pierced straight into the heart of the man by my side.

"NO!"

I crouched beside him. Blood bubbled up past his lips as he stared at me with wild eyes.

"I'll find you again," I promised him. "In this life, or the next, until the end of time, I'll find you."

A sharp intake of breath hissed in through my teeth as the memory faded. Vehrin had killed him, the man who had once been Kael. My warrior. My protector. My heart.

Kael watched me with a fierce intensity that made my body want to go rigid, yet melt into him at the same time.

My nostrils flared and my brows pinched together. "We will not die today."

Kael stood and rolled his shoulders as I got to my feet. Together, we dashed out from behind the rock and sprinted with renewed vigor toward Vehrin.

Magic swirled from my fingertips and Kael crashed into demon after demon. I could sense the key, and I knew the closer I got to it, the closer I would get to Vehrin. My feet pounded the ground as I dipped and swayed around demons and lions. My heart raced. I was so close.

My boot snagged on the leg of a fallen demon, and I skidded across the ground. I groaned, but as I looked up from where I lay, my gaze fell on the key. It was no more than a few feet from me. My body protested as I inched my way forward, and my shoulder screamed as I reached out for the key. A rattling breath chased me, and I glanced over my shoulder to see a demon closing in.

Just before the demon reached me, my fingers closed around the key. I rolled to my back and kicked the demon in the face with both feet, then quickly put the chain of the necklace around my neck.

Malevolent and dark magic crackled through the air. There was a fierce yell, and in the next moment, Vehrin was on top of me. He reached for the trio of necklaces I now wore. I grabbed onto his wrists, and both of our hands sparked with energy. With a powerful surge, he broke through my resistance, and his fingers grasped the keys.

My soul was in the dark mage's hands.

A glint of delight flashed in his gaze as he got to his feet, and urged me to follow. I did, against my will.

My pulse tapped in overdrive. He had me in his control.

Vehrin circled around to my back and kept one hand clasped around the keys as Kael stalked forward. He squeezed the keys, and as he did, air pushed from my lungs as a force pressed in on me.

"Kill him," Vehrin said in my ear.

I raised my arm as tears pricked my eyes. *Kael, run!* I screamed through our mental bond. *He has my soul. You need to run!*

Kael shook his head, and my heart shattered as magic buzzed at my fingertips. I couldn't even close my eyes as I released the attack that would end him.

Right before the swirls of magic plummeted into him, Kael dodged. He ran forward faster than I'd ever seen him go before. His jaws opened wide as he leaped, and for a second, I thought perhaps he was going to put me out of my misery.

Instead, he flew over my shoulder, and together Kael, Vehrin, and I slammed into the earth in a tangle of limbs.

I rolled to my back and, somehow, Vehrin straddled me. Kael's strong jaws were latched around his arm. The dark mage screamed in pain, and in the next moment, his arm was torn from his shoulder. Vehrin bellowed, but instead of reaching for the bleeding stump, he reached for the keys with his other hand.

With all the strength I had left, I lurched back. Something dug into my neck, but the pressure eased in a split second. I blinked, then Vehrin was gone. Silence fell. There was no more fighting. I was afraid to see if it was because everyone was dead.

Kael released his jaguar and shifted beside me. He grabbed my shoulders and gave them a light shake. "Are you all right?"

"Ow." I winced at the hold he had on my injured shoulder.

He quickly released it. "Sorry."

My mind whirred as I tried to catch up, and my thoughts latched on to the last moments with Vehrin.

"He had me. He had my soul." My voice cracked, the ghosts of the violation still pressing on me. I had never felt anything so terrifying.

Kael pulled me closer to him and held my face in his rough hands. "No one will ever have your soul but yourself." The promise burned in his gaze, and it warmed me, fluttered in me in a delightful way.

"I'd give it to you," I said.

A smile lifted the corner of his mouth. "I'd settle for your heart."

I laid a hand on his chest and leaned closer to him. "You already have it."

Kael's lips were soft and warm, but it sparked something inside of me that was fierce and binding.

He's mine, I told myself over and over as our lips moved together.

The taste and scent of him filled me, and I wanted to linger in it as long as I could, but all too soon, he was pulling away. He leaned his forehead against mine, and as we caught our breath, a thought occurred to me.

"Where's Vehrin?"

We pulled apart, and I peered around. There was no dark

mage, and no demons. Kael's gaze dropped to my chest, and I followed suit. My heart plummeted.

One of the necklaces was missing.

We had failed.

Vehrin had taken the third key.

CHAPTER 27

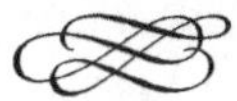

VEHRIN HAD THE THIRD KEY, the one capable of overriding the keys around my neck. I drew on my magic, and a breath of relief sighed through me as energy feathered across my skin. Perhaps he could only overpower the other keys if he was nearby? Of course, if that were the case, it would make any future confrontations with him nearly impossible to win.

Besides, the mage couldn't really do anything about my own magic, could he? It was mine, born again in me from an ancient past. Perhaps he could only hinder the darker magic within, the power tied to the first key bound to my soul. Not having the ability to access that magic was daunting. I wasn't exactly fond of the darker, more sinister side of the magic tied to me, but it did make me more powerful when I needed it. I just had to keep from being tempted and swept away by the shadowy power.

I tucked the keys under the dirt-and-blood encrusted collar of my shirt, then peered up at Kael. He was staring at my shoulder, worry etched in his forehead.

"Let me take a look." He pulled my shirt away. I didn't have to look to know there were teeth marks there. "Demon?"

I nodded. "I'm lucky that way, apparently."

Kael cursed under his breath. He probed his fingers around the wound. I winced slightly at the pain, but it wasn't too unbearable.

"Well, your skin isn't inflamed and the wound isn't oozing anything but blood, so as far as I can tell, it isn't poisoned."

Thank goodness. Bibi wasn't around to save my life this time.

"You need clothes," I said.

Kael quirked an eyebrow and his lips twitched. It wasn't as if I hadn't seen him naked before, but after our kiss, after everything we'd gone through, I found him extremely distracting.

"I'll see what I can find." Kael paused for a moment. "Stay here."

"There isn't exactly anywhere else I can go at the moment." I gestured around me at the carnage. There were dead demons and shifters alike scattered across the ground. Most of the living members of the pride had shifted and were tending to the wounded or mourning the loss of their family and friends.

As Kael walked away, I realized I couldn't hear his thoughts anymore. It was a bit of a relief to find I could only communicate to him mentally while he was in his jaguar form. The thought of him being able to read me at any time was terrifying.

Still, even though he had walked away and was no longer in sight, I could point right to his location. There was an undeniably powerful bond between us now, and I wasn't quite certain of the meaning of it.

Stares burned into me as I waited, but thankfully no one approached. I busied myself checking for bandages in my bag while I waited for Kael to return. Confronting the lion shifters wasn't something I was ready to do just yet, not with some of their blood staining my hands.

Thankfully, Kael made a quick return. I had to press my

hand to my mouth to stifle a giggle. It was inappropriate, given the circumstances, but mirth tickled at my throat nonetheless. I couldn't help it. Kael strode toward me looking a bit like Angus Young from AC/DC in the too short shorts he was wearing. Clearly, whoever he had borrowed them from had not been as tall, or as broad-chested judging by the shirt stretched across his shoulders.

"Don't." Kael's tone was sharp as he stepped up to me.

I lowered my hand. "Don't what?"

"Laugh."

"I wasn't going to." My lips twitched as he tugged at the collar of the tight shirt.

He caught the ghost of a smile and scowled. "I'm ready to leave this place and get back to civilization."

I had to agree. My gaze swept across the sorrow and broken bodies again. Then, I caught sight of a man holding a sword. I glanced down at my wrist to find my bracelet gone. It was *my* sword. It had fallen from my hand in battle.

Kael shadowed me as I walked over to the man and held out my hand. "Thank you for picking it up."

He held it closer to him and eyed me suspiciously.

"It's my sword," I said.

The man shook his head. "That decision will be up to the chief."

Was this guy serious? I stared at the weapon in his hands and concentrated, then smiled as it disappeared and the bracelet wrapped around my wrist. I left the man glancing around and wondering what happened.

"Maybe you shouldn't flaunt your magic," Kael murmured as we distanced ourselves from the shifters.

"I wasn't flaunting it. Besides, I'm not going to let anyone take my sword. I don't care what kind of authority they have."

Kael glanced over my shoulder. "Speaking of authority..."

I turned to follow his gaze and found the chief walking toward us. He was flanked by four guards, some of the few who hadn't been injured. He came to a stop before us, and I ducked my head.

"I'm so sorry for the losses your people have suffered at the hands of Vehrin."

For a moment, it was silent. The air around me felt heavy with the weight of the chief's judgmental stare. "Some of those losses were done by your own hand."

Guilt and anguish flashed through me as I lifted my eyes to his accusatory gaze. His eyes were rimmed red. He was mourning the loss of his mate, the lioness I had killed. I tried to find words to say an apology, to beg for forgiveness, *something*, but I couldn't, because he was right. I had killed her, and others.

Kael parted from my side and stepped closer to the chief. The guards flanking him shifted, ready to run my partner through with the spears in their hands.

"She only did so out of survival." Kael's tone was hard, rough. "We tried to tell you Vehrin was evil. We tried to warn you. What was she supposed to do, let your shifters kill her? What purpose does that serve?"

The chief's face grew dark as his brow furrowed in anger. I elbowed my way past Kael.

"I understand you were under dark influence…" I started.

"That does not excuse them from attacking the very people who had come to help them in the first place."

I laid a hand on Kael's arm. "It is not his fault. Vehrin is strong. I was about to attack you not long ago, if you recall." The thought still made my stomach clench. The dark mage had control of me, and I nearly struck Kael down.

Kael's features softened and he opened his mouth, but before he could say anything, the chief spoke.

"You are to be put on trial for the crime of murder."

The bottom fell out of my already shaky world. "What?"

"You can't put us on trial. We came here to save you." Kael tapped his chest. "I am an agent for PITO, and you have no right. We were sent here for a purpose. You cannot punish us for that."

The chief tilted his chin up. "PITO holds no sway here."

Without another word, he turned and left. Two of the guards went with him and the other two gestured for us to follow. We did so silently. Kael was likely too angry to speak. I was too stunned. We'd just survived a battle with demons and a confrontation with Vehrin. What would happen to us if they found us guilty?

We were led to a small home. It was empty, and as we were told to rest inside, I tried not to wonder if the inhabitants were laying in pieces outside with the other deceased. The beaded door in the entryway rattled, and then we were alone.

I sat down heavily on a bench against the right-hand wall and stared at a faded blue and yellow rug at my feet. *A trial.* It seemed an almost unbelievable thing to have to endure after what we'd just gone through. I wanted to be angry at the leader of the lion shifter pride, but I couldn't fault him for lashing out in his grief, especially when the cause was by my own hand.

Kael's shadow fell over me. "Livvie..."

The curtained doorway clicked again, and a small woman entered with a tray in her hands. There was a large bruise across her cheek and a cut across her brow, but she seemed otherwise unharmed. She didn't speak as she crossed the room to a table and set the tray down, but as she passed me, she gave me a small nod and the barest of smiles. Something in her glance told me she did not agree with this trial the chief insisted on.

Kael went to the tray as she left and lifted the lid to reveal fruit, cheese, and some sort of sliced meat. My stomach gurgled eagerly.

"You don't think it's poisoned, do you?" I asked.

Kael shook his head and rolled up a piece of the meat. "The chief is too honorable for that. If he's going to kill us, it will be after the trial in front of his people." He popped the meat into his mouth and moaned.

I plucked off a few fat, purple grapes. They were warm, but sweet. I went for some of the marbled cheese next.

"We can't linger here," Kael said. His voice softened to a murmur. "We need to sneak out."

I swallowed my bite. "We will do no such thing. We've already done too much damage here. Sneaking off will only make us look guiltier than we already seem."

"Vehrin could return at any moment. He'll still want the other two relics."

"Why, if the one he has overrides the two I have anyway?" I asked.

Kael thought for a minute while he chewed. "The keys in your possession are still powerful. If he had all three, Vehrin would be unstoppable. Besides, if he can take the opportunity to control you with the relic bound to your soul, he will." He reached for some cheese. "And who knows what limits the third key has? How close does he have to be to override your keys? Would it be temporary, or can he only fight the power of your relics for so long? He won't risk the chance. Trust me, he'll want the other two keys."

I nodded. "Still, he's likely recovering. I don't think he'll come after me again until he's at full strength. He's badly wounded, remember? *You bit off his arm.*"

Kael folded his arms across his chest, endangering the shirt taut across his muscles, and grinned. Smugness rolled off him. "That was rather satisfying."

"I'm glad you think so." I sampled some of the sliced meat. It was good, if a bit more gamey than I was accustomed to. As I chewed, I couldn't help but wonder what it would feel like to chew on someone's arm.

Kael's voice interrupted my morbid thoughts. "So, I take it we're not leaving?"

"Not without permission. This chief feels we owe him a

trial. We can at least give him that. If we're found guilty, well, then we can figure something out."

"It may be too late by then." Kael took hold of my elbow and pivoted me to face him. "I won't lose you, Livvie."

Kael's skin was warm and electric against my own. His touch felt like home. I pursed my lips and peered up at him. "Kael, what happened between us?"

There was something deeper, something more meaningful happening here that I couldn't quite put my finger on.

Kael reached up and touched my cheek. His soft gaze melted me where I stood. "Livvie, there's something we need to talk about, but not here, not now."

"Why not?"

As if in answer, one of the guards returned. The chief was awaiting us for our trial. Kael took my hand and gave it a squeeze as we followed the man back outside.

A circle had formed near the entrance of the chief's home. He was standing at the head, and Kael and I were led to the center. I couldn't help but notice the ground was still wet with patches of blood, even if the dead and wounded had been cleared away. The men who had moved aside to let us pass quickly closed the gap. If we were found guilty, fighting our way out would be nearly impossible.

I would endure the chief's questioning, if mostly out of guilt for the harm I'd done to his own people, but I would not let him make me or Kael out to be the villains in this mess.

The chief spoke, and his deep voice carried through the still air.

"You are being accused of murdering members of this pride, including the mate of their chief." His words were loud and strong, and his fists clenched tightly at his side.

"Murder is a strong word," Kael said.

Mouth pressing into a hard line, the chief's nostrils flared as he glared at Kael. "The accused will not speak until given permission to do so."

Kael's grip tightened on the hand clenched around mine, but he grew silent.

The lion shifter's gaze flicked to me. "Why did you come here?"

I thought carefully before answering. The last thing I wanted to do was word something in a way he would be able to twist into an admission of guilt. "We came to ask for the relic, to keep it out of the dark mage's hands. We knew he was seeking it, just as he tried to get his hands on the two I possess."

"You came to ask for the key, or to take it?"

I shifted. I hated the weight of the judgmental stare the man pressed upon me. Thankfully, he seemed to be one of the few who felt as if we were a guilty party. Most everyone else in the circle seemed…numb. I suddenly felt bad they had to be here, instead of with their families.

"As I said when we first arrived, we came to trade the spear for the relic, as we were instructed to do."

The chief crossed his arms. "And did you intend to harm my people?"

"Of course not." I stepped forward, breaking my grip from Kael's. "I would never harm an innocent person."

"And yet, I saw you slay my mate," the chief said.

I heard my partner's angry grunt and held out a hand to stop him from coming to my aid. I could handle this.

"I did." The silence was so deafening, I could hear my blood pumping in my ears. "I killed her, and you will never know how truly sorry I am, not only for her death, but the others, as well. I didn't *want* to kill her. I wanted to help. We were trying to stop Vehrin, but she was attacking me and I had to protect myself. I cannot fathom the depth of your loss, just as you cannot fathom the need for me to stop that dark mage before he destroys hundreds of people, humans, shifters, and fae alike."

The chief regarded me for a long, calculating moment. "You possess magic?"

"I do."

"The same magic the mage is capable of unleashing?"

I shook my head. "I don't think so. My magic is my own. It is ancient, tied to me in a way even I cannot understand."

The planes of the chief's face were hard. Instead of being creased with age, adversity had chiseled strength into his features. They didn't soften, no matter what I told him, and with his next words, I knew this was a losing battle.

"How do I know you are not working with Vehrin? He said not to trust you, you said not to trust him. What choice did I have but to give one of you the relic?"

There were no words I could say that would sway him. He was beyond all logic, it seemed. We should have left when Kael suggested it, but I wanted to try and make things right.

I had killed innocents, and no matter the reason for it, the guilty part of myself felt deserving of punishment.

Kael was silent behind me. He was likely in the midst of making a plan to get us out of here.

The chief gestured to the circle of onlookers. "Does anyone have anything to add, or should we proceed?"

"I have something I would like to say."

A collective gasp whispered around me, and my heart jumped. I knew that voice. I turned to find a woman walking into the circle, with white dots painted down her forehead and to the tip of her nose.

Bibi.

Children accompanied her, the ones who had managed to flee before we arrived back at the pride. They ran toward their family now, though I knew by the crying of some they would not be reunited with loved ones.

A little boy ran straight to the chief and wrapped his arms around him. He was asking a question and peering around. I didn't understand his words, but I knew who he was seeking.

His mother. I wanted to wipe at her phantom blood staining my hand.

The chief didn't speak to his son. Instead, he inclined his head as Bibi came to stand beside me. The rest of the crowd did the same, and I wondered at the reverence they held for the woman. Respectfully, Kael and I did the same.

"Forgive me, Bibi, but you must leave the circle. It is only for the accused," the chief said.

Bibi gestured down at herself. "Then you must accuse me, for I am the one who sent this woman and her companion here in good faith, and you threw dirt in their faces and spat on their wounds. Did she not present the spear to you?"

The chief's mouth opened and closed a couple times. "She did. And then she killed members of my pride."

"No. You did, by letting Vehrin take a hold of your mind."

A deep line furrowed his brow. "I was not myself. The dark mage held me under his influence."

"An influence which would have been harder won if you were not such a proud and suspicious man. You made it all the more easier for him to slip his dark tendrils inside to take root. I know this woman would never intend harm on another. She is the one chosen to bring down the dark mage, and she cannot afford to take any chances. If she dies, we all will perish."

"No pressure," I muttered.

Bibi glared at me and I fell silent.

"You will release her, and give her and her companion enough food and supplies to make it back to civilization."

Whatever sway Bibi held over these people, it seemed he could not argue. He nodded, though reluctantly.

"If you have faith in them, then I must, as well." His mouth twisted as if the words were bitter. He started to walk away.

"You owe her your life," Kael said. The chief glanced back. "She gave you an earring bestowed by Bibi, and in doing so, kept the demons from finishing you off. If she had not, your people would be without a leader right now."

The chief stared at me, then gave me the barest of nods before picking up his child.

"A gift he was not worthy of," Bibi grumbled. "His father was a great leader. Despite his years, he still has much to learn."

I smiled at her. "Thank you for saving us…again."

She waved a hand. "I didn't do it for you. I meant what I said. If you die, we are all doomed."

"I'll do my best to stay in one piece, then."

A rich laugh bubbled up her throat. "Yes, do so."

Silence fell between us before she gave a small smile and strode off to see to the wounded. Half an hour later, Kael and I were laden with packs of supplies. There was no doubt in my mind the chief was eager to see us go, so when he walked toward us, I was surprised.

"As a thank you for saving my life, and not leaving my son an orphan, I will give you something."

I looked toward his hands, but they were empty. I glanced at his face with a raised brow.

"A bit of knowledge," he said. He lowered his voice. "It's a rumor I have heard my whole life, but given the circumstances, I feel it has worth."

He paused, and I wondered if he were considering keeping the information to himself after all. Finally, he spoke.

"There is a fourth key."

CHAPTER 28

Kael grunted as I bounced hard off his back. Too caught up in my thoughts, I hadn't noticed him pause. He turned and looked at me with a smile on his lips.

"You know, it's a wonder you haven't stepped on a cobra or something."

I shuddered, recalling the den of snakes I'd had to crawl through. "Don't say that." I glanced around, hoping for a hint of civilization but seeing nothing except the same grasses and dotting of trees. "Why are we stopping?"

"It's going to be dark soon. We need to make camp. We should reach Nairobi tomorrow."

The last thing I wanted to do was spend another night in this place, but I also didn't want to end up hyena chow by trekking through the dark. Besides, I was exhausted. Even though my shoulder hadn't been poisoned by the demon, the wound still hurt, as did the cut on my hand from traversing the underground pathway to the hidden altar.

"Sit down, Livvie." Kael's voice wasn't demanding, but soft and quiet, almost as if he were pleading. His eyes were wide as he watched me. I couldn't argue with that face.

I folded myself to the ground as he went to a nearby acacia tree to scrounge up fallen wood. I hoped demons wouldn't crash our party this time around. I could use a night of uninterrupted sleep, even if it was in the open air and on the hard ground. After Kael returned with an armful of fallen branches, I stretched my legs out in front of me and watched him.

He seemed different, somehow. Not in appearance, though he had managed to find clothes which actually fit him before we left the lion shifter pride. It was more like my perception of him had changed.

I tilted my head as he carefully piled kindling in a patch of earth he'd cleared of grass and debris. It was the strange bond I now felt with him, but something told me it had nothing to do with the fact we had been bound not only as a sorceress and her guard, or that we had been former lovers in that past life. It was something else…

"You going to tell me why you're staring at me?" Kael said suddenly.

I didn't bother denying. "How did you know I was staring at you?"

He chuckled. "I could feel it."

"Is that a shifter thing, or because we seem to be, uh, more connected?"

Kael glanced up at me for a brief moment, then turned his attention back to the sticks. "Don't most people know when they are being watched?"

"I suppose so."

My partner brought forth a spark, then a flame using only a flint from the packs with all the expertise of a survivalist. He placed more firewood amongst the flames and waited until he was certain it wouldn't go out before standing.

"I'm not sure what's in those packs to eat, but it likely isn't fresh. I'm going to hunt something down."

I wrinkled my nose. "I don't see how you can kill something like that."

"It's in my nature. Don't worry, I won't eat it raw in front of you."

Gross. "Please, don't. I enjoy my antelope steaks medium-rare."

"You're kind of odd, you know that?"

I climbed to my feet and jabbed him in the chest with a finger. "Hey, I'm not the one plucking something from the menu with my teeth."

Kael grabbed my hand and held it to his chest. His gaze captured mine, gripped it as strongly as his fingers wrapped around my own. "You are a fascinating woman."

I laughed softly. "You just said I was odd."

"Odd is fascinating."

His warm breath brushed against me. I'd closed the distance between us without even realizing it. "Calling me odd is not a good way to get me to kiss you, you know."

Kael's lips were so close to mine, I could almost feel his smile. "And who says I want to kiss you?"

I pressed my lips to his. Energy wanted to explode from me at the taste of him, the strength of his grip, and heat of his mouth on mine. Kissing Kael sent tremors through me, and left me feeling unsteady.

Damn, even the earth seemed to be moving beneath my feet.

Kael broke apart from me with a startled expression and gripped my shoulders before I could be knocked backward. I glanced around frantically as a loud groan filled the air.

The earth *was* moving.

The ground lurched and jumped beneath us as an earthquake growled beneath the dirt. My feet shuffled in an attempt to keep my footing, but my bones seemed to rattle and I collapsed to the ground. A grunt whooshed from my lungs as Kael landed on top of me. He rolled off but kept one hand on me as his gaze danced frantically around us.

The cries of birds and beasts echoed through the air. Sparks from our small fire rose into the air like fleeing fireflies. I rolled to my stomach and gritted my teeth against the jostling. As I peered out into the shadow-swathed landscape, a sensation of trepidation rippled through me.

This was no mere act of nature. I could sense the dark power tainting the atmosphere.

"Vehrin is doing this," I said. I was barely able to get the words out. Kael jerked a nod beside me.

The dark mage wasn't nearby, but I knew without a doubt this was his doing. The third key must have been more powerful than we assumed.

A horrible sound, like rocks scraping together, deafened me. Kael shouted something, but I couldn't make out his words. He tugged hard on my shoulder, and pain lanced through me. I attempted to bat him away, but his fingers dug in, and in the next moment, he was pulling me against him.

We rolled a few feet before coming to a stop. I picked my head up from his chest and peered over to where we were laying just a moment before.

A giant crack had ripped its way through the earth, and we'd nearly fallen into it.

The ground continued to shake violently. Why was the earthquake lasting so long? We had to get somewhere safe, but where? There was nowhere we could go. Being out in the open had to be the safest place, right? There were no trees, rocks, or buildings to fall on us.

My heart leaped to my throat as the ground shifted beneath us. We started sloping downward as the earth gave way, tipping us so we fell into the massive crack.

"Kael!"

With one arm still around me, he pawed at the ground with the other. His fingers grabbed fistfuls of grass, but it was no use. I cried out as the earth opened out from under our legs.

I risked a glance down, and fear tightened my throat. There would be no surviving a fall from this height. I'd never been so afraid of descending into the waiting arms beneath the ground.

"Hang on," Kael said through gritted teeth. His grip tightened on me, his fingers digging into my ribcage. My own were clenched into his shirt.

Another terrible growl sang through the air, and no matter how tightly we tried to hold to each other, the tremendous jostling loosened our grips. I slid farther down and just managed to dig my fingers into the ground enough to keep from falling to my death as the rest of my body dropped over the crumbling edge.

Kael's broken voice hollered my name as I lost my grip. I dangled over the endless pit, both my feet swaying in the split open land.

The pads of my fingers ripped against the shivering rock and grit of the earth as I fought for purchase. Dirt rained onto my face. Kael reached for me. His arms jumped wildly with the swaying ground. I was afraid to let go long enough to reach for him.

"Livvie, give me your hand." He grimaced as he strained to reach farther.

I shook my head. He was going to fall, too. The muscles in my arms strained as the unnatural earthquake tried to shake me into the bowels of the earth. I kicked my feet, but the toes of my boots found nothing to use as leverage.

"I'll get you," he said.

I took a chance and reached for him with one of my hands.

I wanted to cling to Kael's promise, but as I reached for him, I knew it was no use. Fear writhed in me, and somehow I knew it wasn't entirely my own. I stared up at the man who was absolutely terrified at the thought of losing me.

"I'm sorry," I said. I tried again to reach him, but I only fell farther. I was going to fall to my death.

I'd never seen Kael's eyes so wide. "No!"

He surged forward, and just as his hands clasped around mine, we both plummeted.

CHAPTER 29

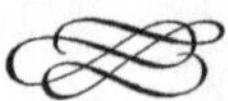

Kael.

His name was the only thought racing through my panicked mind. Where was he? His hands had been on mine, but now he was gone. All I had left was darkness, and cool air whipping my hair around my face as I descended into the black pit rent open by the earthquake.

Kael and I were going to be entombed in the earth, like so many artifacts and long-dead corpses I had discovered.

I gasped as something wrapped around my middle and squeezed.

"What?" The frantic word was all I managed as I was suddenly moving upward.

There was an odd whooshing sound, and I realized the pressure hugging my ribcage was a pair of arms. I tilted my head back but could make out nothing but a vague outline of what seemed to be a person.

Below my feet, the ground fell away as we lifted into the night sky. "Wait! Where's Kael?"

There was no reply as shadow-swathed landscape and dark sky blanketed my vision in an inky darkness.

My heart hammered as I fought against the arms gripping

me. Whoever held me made a slightly impatient noise and squeezed me tighter, almost to the point it was difficult to breathe.

A fearsome thought spiked in my brain. *A demon.* If I was right, I'd have been better off plummeting to my death than being tortured and who knows what else. I wriggled to get free, to take my chances on the fall, but it was no use.

Voices broke through the dark, soft and crooning and melding together into a song of peace and contentment, lyrics of soft meadows, cool waters, and lilac-heavy breezes.

Unbidden, my eyelids grew heavy. Then, they closed. Right before I was swept into sleep, one final thought swept through my mind.

Kael.

~

A COOL BREEZE brushed against my cheek, and fresh air filled my lungs as I pulled in a deep breath. There was the scent of damp earth and something sweet and smoky. Slowly, I opened my eyes.

The sky filled my vision, and though it was a dreary gray, I had a sense it was late morning. Morning? Hadn't Kael been making a fire for the night?

I sat up, fear gripping me. The earthquake. Kael and I had been falling to our deaths.

"He's all right, for the most part," an unfamiliar voice spoke from behind me.

I turned. There were roughly a dozen *beings*, though only one was near enough to have spoken.

The woman had the same dark complexion as Bibi, but a contrasting spray of blonde hair crowned her head, reminding me of the stiff bristles of a paintbrush. She had large, curious eyes, and she tilted her head as she gazed at me. My own stare drifted to the wings on her back.

Wings.

They were mostly black, with a few white feathers dispersed throughout. The woman had them half-folded, tucked behind her back, but I had a feeling if she were to completely open them, they would be huge.

As I stared at the stranger, I was suddenly reminded of a flock of crowned cranes I had seen on our travel through the African wilderness. Could she be some sort of crane shifter?

"Who are you?" I asked. I cast a quick glance behind her, but her brethren didn't seemed interested in our conversation.

The woman grinned. "Have you forgotten your worries already?"

It took me a second to realize what she was referring to. "Kael?" I looked around and found him lying several feet away. I crawled over to him.

Kael was asleep, his breathing slow and even. A large knot protruded above the corner of his left eyebrow and was accompanied by purple and blue bruises. I lightly touched it, and he shifted a little.

"I believe he hit his head on the way down."

I hadn't realized the woman had followed me. She squatted down at my shoulder and studied Kael.

My eyes swept to her wings, then to her face. "You caught us?"

"I caught *you.*" She smiled. "It took two of my brothers to carry *him.*"

Carry us where, though?

We were no longer in the doomed campsite Kael and I had chosen for the night. We were higher up, on some sort of steep rise, or small mountain. I got to my feet, thankful to find myself steady and uninjured, and looked out at the landscape.

My heart nearly stopped.

Deep cracks ran through the ground for such a distance, I couldn't see where they ended. For miles, the earth was broken, like cracked glass. The atmosphere was unnervingly still, and my gut twisted as I wondered if the lion pride and Bibi had survived the earthquake unscathed.

A low moan broke the silence. I looked down to find Kael trying to sit up.

"Easy," I said. I got on my knees beside him and pressed a hand to his shoulder.

When Kael's eyes focused on me, he pulled in a shuddering breath. He wrapped an arm around me and drew me close.

"Livvie, you're okay. We're okay."

"Well, mostly." I laid a finger on the wound on his head. "You have a bump."

He groaned as he sat up against my wishes. "I'll live." He studied our surroundings, then narrowed his eyes as he found the group of winged people.

"They saved us," I said, though I still wasn't certain exactly who "they" were.

The woman who had caught me sank to the ground beside us, the tips of her wings rustling against the dirt.

"Renathe sent us to look after you. He wanted us to keep you safe." The woman tilted her head again, making her seem more birdlike. "But we were to only interfere if your life was in danger."

Yeah. That sounded like Renathe. Only interfere if *my* life was in danger. Kael was only saved as an afterthought. Still, I was grateful.

"You've been following us?" I asked. "For how long?"

"Since you left Nairobi."

I thought back to the demon attack, which had nearly killed me with poison. Then there was the attack after the pride chief had turned us away. Our battle with Vehrin and his minions had nearly ended in my death, as well. I mentioned all of this to the strange woman.

"As you can see," I added when I'd finished, "our lives

have been in danger a few times since then. Why didn't you help sooner?"

The woman, who I now knew must be some sort of fae like Ren, shrugged a delicate shoulder. "You were entertaining to behold."

So, they had just watched because it was interesting? How far would they have let it go? Vehrin had me under his control, and they still had not rescued me. It reminded me a little of Ren, with his morbid curiosity, and I wondered if all fae were the same. Judging by Kael's annoyed growl, they were.

I peered back out at the ruined plains, again finding myself hoping the pride and Bibi were safe.

"An unnatural earthquake, wasn't it?" the fae said.

I knew she wasn't really asking me, more stating a fact. "It was Vehrin," I said. "He's getting stronger, growing more powerful."

He'd caused the earthquake, whether out of anger or some sort of attempt at revenge, I wasn't sure.

She was staring out at the open with worry dulling her gaze. "A dark mage powerful enough to manipulate the weather is a daunting thought, indeed."

I thought of what I knew of the fae. They helped control the elements. They could conjure snow, or rain, or bring out sunlight.

"Did you stop the earthquake?"

She nodded. "Yes, though it took all our effort." She gestured to the group behind her. A few glanced our way, but most still didn't seem to care about us one way or another. With Vehrin influencing the weather, perhaps they had more pressing things to worry about.

I shuddered to think what other disasters he would be capable of causing. I glanced up as if expecting a tornado to descend upon us. The sky was still gray, though not heavy with unspent rain. It seemed more as if someone had simply shaded out the sun. There was an unnerving permanence to the dreary sky. When was the last time I felt sunlight on my face? Could Vehrin's influence on the world already be taking such a hold?

My gut clenched as I realized, without the sun, crops couldn't be grown. Animals would run out of grass and foliage. Food would grow scarce. People would riot, steal, and murder.

Could this be Vehrin's plan? End the world with starvation and chaos? And for what? What could he possibly have to gain from that?

I peered at Kael and saw the same question burning in his eyes. How could we stop something like that?

The fae woman looked back at the other group. "We must go." She pointed to the distance. "Nairobi is that way. You'll be there by midday if you start now. I will get word to Renathe that you are accounted for."

I wanted to tell the woman to tell him I didn't need a babysitter, but then remembered her and her fellow fae *had* saved us.

"Thank you," I said. "For everything."

She stood and studied me for a moment. "Your fate is tied with the dark mage's. I think by saving you, we may have saved the world…or we may have doomed it. Only time will tell."

She grinned, as if eager to see how it would turn out. I supposed that was fair enough. If my world were destroyed, she probably would still have another world to return to.

The fae's wings spread wide, and in a flurry of dust and feathers, she quickly left with the others. I watched them until they disappeared.

"I didn't know fae could have wings," I said. "They look like angels."

"They most certainly are not anything like angels," Kael said. He rolled his shoulders and stretched his legs out, loosening his muscles. "Most high fae have wings, either leathery or feathered."

"Ren doesn't have wings."

"He does. He just keeps a glamor on."

I stood and searched the area for my bag. I found it propped against a stone a few feet away. "I wonder why he hides them? It's understandable if he's around humans, but I've never seen them."

Kael got to his feet and joined me, smirking. "Maybe he has tiny wings, or they're pink, like a flamingo."

He seemed absolutely delighted by the thought, and I couldn't help but laugh. Poor Ren. I was going to insist on seeing them next time we met, right after I scolded him for his poor choice in bodyguards on my behalf.

"Now what?" I asked, shouldering my bag.

My partner studied the direction the fae had pointed. "Time to get back to civilization."

I nodded. "This is the worst camping trip I've ever been on."

Kael smiled and touched my cheek. "It had its moments."

Yes, it certainly had. I took Kael's hand, eager to leave this place far behind.

I SHIFTED IN THE SMALL, metal chair. It creaked in protest, a crack in the plastic biting at my thigh. Kael was motionless beside me as we waited for our flight to whisk us away from Africa. He'd had a dark glower fixed to his face from the moment he'd ended the call to his boss back in the States.

Kael was in trouble, it seemed. When he'd gotten off the phone, he said we needed to head home immediately. We had no time to take a day or two in a hotel and rest. I yearned for a long, hot shower and a soft bed. I'd had to make do with cold water in the bathroom in an attempt to freshen up and a poor nap on the horrid little chair I still sat on.

I glanced down at my phone, the charger plugged into an outlet behind me. I'd been scrolling through breaking news articles, and with each one I read, I felt sicker. The earthquake had been the most massive in Africa's history. Destruction spanned at least three countries, and I tried not to dwell on the number of people who had been killed. I especially tried not to think about Bibi and the lion shifters. They just *had* to be okay. I couldn't emotionally handle any other thought.

I set my phone down with a sigh. I needed a break from the terrible stories of ruin and death. Leaning on Kael's shoulder, I said, "Are you in trouble?"

"I withheld information about Vehrin and our knowledge of the third key."

"What we're doing is more important than following the rules."

Kael studied his hands in his lap. "I know it is, but I'm not certain my superiors and fellow agents will agree. We have rules, regulations, and structure for a reason."

I wiggled my arm beneath his and twined my fingers through his to stop his fidgeting. "Will you be fired?"

He shook his head. "I know too much." His tone suggested he wasn't entirely convinced.

I sat up and jabbed him lightly with an elbow in the ribs. "Hey, if you get sacked, you can come work with me. I could use someone to do the heavy lifting."

Kael gave me a small smile that didn't reach his eyes. "My boss would have an easier time firing me than letting you get back to your life so easily."

I froze, then slowly turned to Kael. "Wait, what?"

"Livvie, you know too much as well."

The crackling voice through a speaker above our heads announced it was time to board our flight. As we walked across the yellowed tiles of the small airport, I realized I hadn't considered what would be waiting for us back home.

We had an enemy with Vehrin, that much was certain, but what would PITO do when they realized Kael and I hadn't been, and certainly wouldn't begin, playing by their rules?

Was my life as I knew it really over?

CHAPTER 30

"I FEEL like I'm in the principal's office," I muttered.

Kael huffed a quiet laugh beside me. "How do you know what it's like to be in the principal's office?"

I gave him a sly grin. "In junior high, there may have been an incident involving mice and Mrs. Tillman's music room. Kids were finding mice for weeks. Imagine picking up a trumpet and a mouse dashes out."

"Why am I not surprised?" Kael shook his head with another chuckle before settling against the back of his chair.

Exhausted, I mirrored him and let out a deep sigh. The flight back to Charleston, South Carolina had been long. We hadn't had the time to freshen up after arriving, either. Kael's boss had wanted the pair of us to come straight to the PITO headquarters for an immediate report. On the way from the airport, Kael had tried to persuade his boss, Mason Anderson, to let me be dropped off at a hotel. It had been a flat no, though my partner had managed to swing by a fast food joint on the way. Never had a cheap, greasy cheeseburger tasted so much like heaven. If I could only have a steaming bubble bath next, I'd be set.

"Sorry, Livvie," Kael said quietly, as if he could read my thoughts. "This shouldn't take too long."

I gave him a smile to let him know I was fine, then the door to his boss's office opened. A woman—Mr. Anderson's secretary, no doubt—bustled out. On the way she informed Kael he could go in.

Kael made a vain attempt to fix his hair by combing his fingers through it before he went to the office, but it was no use. It stuck out in odd directions, and there was no way he was able to look presentable after spending days in the African wilderness fighting demons and confronting hostile lion shifters. The door shut behind him, and I was left alone in the silence.

I glanced out the window at my shoulder. It was late evening, so there wasn't much to see except the lights of the city. It was strange being in such a populated area again. I found myself missing home. I wanted my study, my books, my bed. When would I be able to return?

An opening door on the left side of the room drew my attention, and I looked over, then smiled.

"Aidan." I gave a little wave.

The burly bear shifter grinned back and walked over. "Hey, there. Been a little while. Have fun on your adventures?"

"I wouldn't exactly call it fun, but it was definitely interesting."

The bear shifter sank into a chair across from me. His hair was damp with sweat and his cheeks were a bit flushed.

"Been at the gym?" I asked.

"Aren't I always?" For such a scary looking guy, he sure was jovial. I hardly ever saw him without a smile. We fell silent for a moment, and Aidan watched me. Then, his gaze narrowed slightly. "You seem different."

"Different? How?"

He leaned forward, and I wanted to shrink back from his scrutiny. "What happened while you were away?"

"I don't really think I should say anything until I speak to your boss, or at least get permission."

Aidan waved a hand. "Not about your assignment. What happened between you and Kael?"

Between me and Kael?

How could Aidan possibly know there had been a shift in mine and Kael's relationship just by looking at me?

"That isn't your business." I hadn't meant to snap, but I was on edge, and tired.

He held his hands up in surrender. "No need to be so tense." He laughed, but the corners of his eyes were crinkled, and something about his expression seemed concerned. My stomach tightened in response.

Why would he care about the kind of relationship I had with Kael? Before I could ask him, the door across from me opened, and Kael poked out his head.

"Olivia, could you come in here, please?"

I got to my feet and adjusted my bag. "See you later, Aidan."

The bear shifter winked at me. "Good luck."

The office was spacious, thought it felt a bit smaller with the blinds shut, blocking the view of the cityscape below. Kael stood in front of a desk on the right, so I started to move toward him. I faltered when he waved me away with a finger and a slight shake of his head. I frowned but kept my distance, opting instead to hover farther on the left.

Mr. Anderson was bent over a paper, but even his stooped position didn't hide his physique. His black slacks and gray, buttoned shirt covered lean muscle. He wasn't tall, but when he looked up, his pale gaze made no secret he was a man to be obeyed.

He gave me a polite smile. "Olivia, nice to see you again." I had only met the alpha wolf once before, after my first encounter with Vehrin. He was handsome with his salt-and-pepper hair and nice build, if a bit reserved and rigid for my taste.

"Nice to you again, too, Mr. Anderson."

He waved a hand. "You can call me Mason."

Kael let out an indignant sound. "Even I don't get to call you Mason, and I've known you for years."

Mason cut a sharp gaze at Kael. "You work for me, she does not."

My partner fell silent. Mason was obviously not in the mood for light-hearted conversation.

The head of the agency returned his attention to me. "I already have Kael's report on the events, but I would like to hear your side of the story as well."

I didn't glance at Kael as I recounted our ventures. I stuck mostly to the truth, though I did leave out the part where I had killed members of the shifter pride. Kael and Bibi may have been understanding, but Mason was a shifter as well, and I wasn't entirely sure how he would react to the news. Besides, speaking of it out loud would only bring back guilt to churn in my stomach like acid. I was never going to get over the feeling of being a murderer.

When I was finished, Mason nodded. "Same story as Kael."

Something had been bugging me since right before our departure from Africa. Kael had said Mason and PITO would not let me go so easily. I'd felt shackled since the moment we had entered the building.

"May I leave?" I asked.

Mason leaned back in his leather chair. "Where to?"

"I'd like to go home."

Kael suddenly went very still across from me, and a quick glance his way showed his Adam's apple bob in a sudden swallow.

The room was silent for a stretch before Mason spoke. "I'm afraid we will need you to stay a while longer."

I crossed my arms. "I can't just stay here. I have a job to get back to." It was a lie. Both Kael and I knew I couldn't return to the university for some time, not until Vehrin was stopped.

"You are safer here, within the proximity of PITO and our protection."

Kael had been right. They weren't going to just let me go. I hadn't exactly been planning on leaving anyway, but knowing I couldn't, even if I wanted to, unsettled me.

"I can't stay here forever. I don't have the money to afford a hotel room indefinitely."

Mason stood and rounded the desk. "Of course not. A hotel room wouldn't be appropriate now. We have arranged for you to have a house for the duration of your stay."

Somehow that seemed *worse*.

He held out a piece of paper with a picture of a little Cape Cod with blue shutters. I squinted at the address. It was only a few blocks away.

"You...you bought me a house?"

"Rented," Mason corrected. "This way you'll be safe nearby, but more comfortable than in the hotel."

More comfortable? Or easier to keep track of?

I supposed I should have thanked him, but I was furious. This was a whole new level of control. "Is this really for my safety, or for yours?" After all, I was the reincarnation of a sorceress, someone who had once been a powerful equal to the dark mage himself. Maybe they wanted me close to make sure I didn't cause problems.

Mason narrowed his gaze a fraction. "For yours, of course." He turned to Kael. "You've both had a long trip. Go get some rest."

Kael and I turned at the dismissal. Mason didn't say

anything else to me as I left the office, but I could feel his gaze on my back.

I'd spent weeks being hunted, only to end up trapped after all.

~

A FEW NIGHTS LATER, I was still grumbling about the situation as I pulled out a tub of chocolate ice cream from the freezer. It was a nice house, if a bit plain and void of the character my own house held.

I skipped a bowl and instead just grabbed a spoon before heading to the living room. I settled on the couch, then turned on the T.V. to find something to watch while I waited for Kael. He'd been at PITO headquarters all day but had promised to spend some time with me.

I hadn't forgotten the odd connection I now held with him, and he told me tonight we could finally have the talk he'd been saying we'd have. I'd asked him why he'd wanted me to keep my distance in Mason's office, but he never did give me a straight answer. He'd merely mumbled something about Mason being an alpha.

What did that have to do with anything?

Kael was acting weird. I'd decided to go to the gym yesterday, much to Aidan's delight, and a guy had accidentally bumped into me. Kael had jumped all over him until Aidan told him to back off. The bear shifter had looked between us with a knowing, and disapproving, glance.

I huffed out a sigh and dug into my ice cream. *Men.* Why did they have to be so complicated?

I peered out the window across the room. It was already dark, and a sensation prickled across me that I was being watched. It always did when I was in this house, and often times while I was out of it. No doubt Mason had agents trailing me "for my protection."

A sudden knock at the door made me jump. I shook my head with a laugh. I was ridiculous. I opened the door, expecting Kael, though he never knocked, and instead I stopped short.

"Ren?"

The fae man was standing in my doorway in a blue suit that brought out his teal eyes. His lips lifted in a charming smile as he held a bouquet of red roses toward me.

"Olivia, as beautiful as ever."

I very much doubted that. I glanced down at my yoga pants and T-shirt outfit. "Right," I said. "What are you doing here?"

Ren swept past me before I could offer to let him inside. "Is that how you always treat your dates?"

I shut the door with a snap. "Excuse me? *Date?*"

The fae set down the roses. "You owe me a date, remember?"

"Yeah, but *now*?" I gestured around as if to prove this wasn't the best time.

"When you get to be my age, darling, you realize there is no time like the present."

There would be no getting him out of the house, so I decided I may as well sit down and enjoy my ice cream. "I'm already eating."

Ren sat beside me on the couch, much closer than I would have liked. "It's all right. I haven't had my dessert, yet." His voice brushed against my ear, but I just rolled my eyes.

There were more dangerous things about Renathe than his flirting. Like his poor choice in allies, for example. "You know, those fae you had tailing me in Africa nearly let me die on more than one occasion. Apparently, I was quite the entertainment for them."

When Ren didn't respond, I turned to look at him. He was staring at me strangely, his gaze narrowed like he was trying to solve a puzzle.

"What?" I asked.

Renathe pressed a finger to my lips. Then, his eyes widened. A large grin spread across his face. "Well, well. Looks like you had more fun in Africa than I first thought."

"What do you mean?"

Before he could answer, the door opened and Kael walked in. He stopped when he saw Ren beside me on the couch. A deep growl rumbled through his chest.

Ren stood and distanced himself a few feet away. "Apologies, Kael. I assure you I was not touching your mate."

I'd had about enough of people saying that! I bolted to my feet. "Why does everyone keep saying that?"

No one said anything, but Ren looked between Kael and myself several times. Then, a devilish smirk touched his lips.

"She doesn't know?"

Kael took a step toward Ren with his fists curled. "Get out."

Ren put his hands in his pockets and rocked on his heels. "Oh, no, I certainly cannot accommodate that request. This is too much fun."

I finally abandoned my ice cream, setting it on the coffee table. "What's going on?"

My partner was doing nothing but glowering at the fae, so I raised an eyebrow at Ren.

He put a hand on his heart and bowed. "Why, my dear Olivia, congratulations are in order."

"For what?"

Ren's eyes practically glittered with mischief as he straightened. "For your mating, of course."

I scoffed, then looked at Kael for my long overdue explanation We hadn't slept together. We weren't even dating, exactly. I waited one heartbeat, two, three. When he didn't deny Ren's words, I knew it was true. Of course, it was true. The strange bond between us, how I seemed to know where he was and could sometimes even sense how he felt. But it still didn't make sense.

I forgot about Renathe and stalked toward Kael. "When? How?"

Kael looked contrite as he stared at his boots. "The battle. You had blood on your hand, and you touched an open wound on me."

"You mean all someone has to do is *exchange blood* and they're mated? Isn't that something you should have warned me about?"

His head snapped up. "No, blood exchange *isn't* all it takes. There has to be a mutual feeling of…of affection."

Had this been the reason Aidan had been watching us strangely, why Kael hadn't wanted me too close in Mason's office? He didn't want them to know?

Didn't want *me* to know?

"Why didn't you tell me?"

Kael took a step closer and lifted his hand like he wanted to touch me, but he dropped it back down. "I came to tell you tonight. I've been wanting to tell you, Livvie, but I wasn't sure how you would react."

"I think what he means," Renathe said, "is he didn't want you to deny the bond."

We both turned our attention to the fae, who still looked like his favorite soap opera had come on. "If you deny the bond, it won't stick, and you can go on your merry way without being leashed to a cat for the rest of your life."

Fury rolled off Kael as he pushed past me to get to Ren. "Get the hell out!"

"Not without my date," he said.

I groaned inwardly. Why would he say that? Now of all times?

Kael swore and took a hold of Ren by the shoulders, looking ready to toss him through the window. Renathe began making threats I was certain he'd follow through on if Kael didn't release him, and I just wanted both of them out of my house.

Then, a name caught my attention on the news.

"Shut up!" I shouted. Surprisingly, they both did, and turned toward the breaking newscast.

"...team of archaeologists were found brutally murdered in their hotel room last night. There has yet to be an official statement regarding motive, but it has been released that the relic they had unearthed and were transporting back to the U.S. has been reported missing."

The rest of the anchor's words was chased away by a buzzing in my ears as I stared at photos of the murder victims. I knew every single one of them, but my eyes stuck on a picture of Sarah, my friend and colleague.

She was dead.

I shook my head. *No*. Stepped back. Couldn't stop trembling. This was wrong. This wasn't right. But I couldn't pull my gaze off the unmistakable images on the television.

"Livvie."

The heartbreakingly soft sound of my name broke through my shock. Kael stepped over and laid his hands on the side of my neck. He didn't say anything, but the sadness in his eyes let me know he understood what had happened and the loss I felt.

"Vehrin killed her. Whatever that relic was they found, he killed her for it."

Kael laid his forehead against mine. "I'm sorry."

"She didn't deserve to die."

"No one deserves to die," Ren said. "Not by his hand."

All delight and joking had left his face, leaving his expression cold and serious.

I drew back slightly from Kael, and we shared a brief glance. I wasn't sure how to take the news that I was mated to him, but it wasn't something I could think about at the moment. My thoughts were consumed with Vehrin.

A trickle of magic licked my fingers as I balled my hands into fists. I looked between Kael and Renathe. "We are going to find out why Vehrin wants that artifact."

Kael and Ren both nodded, for once agreeing on something.

"We're going to find the fourth key before he gets his hands on it."

My next words seemed to ring with ancient approval, and I spoke with a voice which didn't feel entirely my own, but were uttered by someone deep inside myself.

"And then that dark mage is going to wish I'd never been reborn."

ABOUT THE AUTHORS

ABOUT MIRANDA BROCK

Get a FREE Book from Miranda Brock!

From an early age Miranda Brock has always loved fantasy and adventure everything. Since she doesn't live in a world of enchanting powers, mythical beasts, and things unbelievable she has decided to write about them. (Although, if you happen to see a dragon flying around, do tell her.) Born in southern Illinois, where she still resides with her husband and two children, she grew up running through the woods, playing in creeks, and riding horses.

ABOUT REBECCA HAMILTON

Get a FREE Book from Rebecca Hamilton

New York Times bestselling author Rebecca Hamilton writes urban fantasy and paranormal romance for Harlequin, Baste Lübbe, and Evershade. A book addict, registered bone marrow donor, and indian food enthusiast, she often takes to fictional worlds to see what perilous situations her characters will find themselves in next. Represented by Rossano Trentin of TZLA, Rebecca has been published internationally, in three languages: English, German, and Hungarian.